Azyl Academy

Elemental Gatherers
Book 1

D1525656

ACKNOWLEDGEMENTS

First off, I need to thank my wife Joy, not only for being the example in publishing a book first, but also for encouraging me every step of the process of writing this. She doesn't normally like fantasy, but she continually said she loved my book. Without her, I would not have finished this, nor would it be as good of a product as it is. I followed Robert Jordan's model and had her be my editor as well, leading to her catching the many, many mistakes and inconsistencies in the novel.

I would also like to thank Chris L. and Laura A. for beta-reading the novel and giving me great feedback on how to make the novel and characters better. If you love this novel, thank them. If you hate it, let me know so I can do better next time.

Lastly, I'd like to thank Lesia from germancreative on Fiverr for producing the amazing cover. I'm definitely going back to her for the next book.

PROLOGUE

"Schofield's quote, go!" I shouted from the front-leaning rest position. The freshmen and their sophomore mentors mirrored my position, arms locked straight and ready to do push-ups.

Their voices chorused back, "'The discipline which makes the soldiers of a free country reliable in battle is not to be gained by harsh or tyrannical treatment. ...'"

This was a normal morning ritual that I presided over as my squadron's training officer during my senior year at the Air Force Academy. We never required more from those under our command than we were willing to do ourselves. I shouted with them as we did our push-ups. "'... He who feels the respect which is due to others cannot fail to inspire in them respect for himself; while he who feels, and hence manifests, disrespect towards others, especially his subordinates, cannot fail to inspire hatred against himself!'" I loved this quote. "All right y'all, up and at 'em. You've got fifteen minutes until breakfast. Get your stuff ready and have a great day! It's Friday with a three-day weekend coming up. If I don't see you before you leave, have a great weekend. Remember to study for your knowledge test on Monday night when you get back. Failure leaves you stuck here next weekend. No one wants that. See y'all at breakfast, dismissed!"

The gathered freshmen yelled back, "Valhalla." That was the chant of my cadet squadron, Squadron Nine, the Vikings. They all filed towards their rooms, walking on the sides of the hall to leave a path open in the middle for the upperclassmen.

It was a typical day. Breakfast was followed by my classes in chemistry and math. After lunch were more classes, including Military Strategic Studies. Then it was time for the weekly Chemistry 110 homework study session I conducted to help the freshmen in the squdron. "All right y'all, good luck on the test Tuesday. I'll be back Monday evening, so let me know then if you've got any last questions. Have a great three-day weekend!" I turned and headed toward my room.

"Cadet Helm, sir, I was wondering if you'd lent your car out yet?" a sophomore asked me as I walked past the squadron desk.

"Not yet, no one's asked. Here!" I said as I tossed him my keys. "Just bring it back with a full tank." It was tradition at the Academy for upperclassmen to loan their vehicles out to the lower two classes, who weren't allowed to have a car there yet.

After hitting my room to change into civilian clothes and grab my bags, I met my fiancée in the senior's parking lot. "Hey Jasmine, ready for a long weekend of skiing?" I asked as I admired her, her green eyes twinkling as she approached.

2

"Of course, Caleb. Fresh snow starting at midnight is going to be epic!" she exclaimed as she threw her arms around my neck. One spinning hug and kiss later, we were packing Jasmine's car. Throwing on some rock music, we headed out on the two-and-a-half-hour drive to Breckenridge. "I love the mountains of Colorado! Do you want Bermuda, Jamaica or Cancún for the first part of the honeymoon?" I asked as we hit I-25 North. "Any of them are fine; surprise me!" Jasmine said. "Although I like the thought of an all-inclusive resort, that way we don't have to worry about anything but each other while we're there."

"Okay, I'll look through our options tomorrow and narrow it down. Have you found a DJ yet?" Our conversation for most of the drive consisted of wedding planning, as it had for the majority of drives we'd taken since I proposed over Thanksgiving break.

It was fairly late in the evening by the time we made it to Breckenridge and found the condo where we were staying. After parking in the underground lot, we headed up to the office and got our keys. "Ms. Dempsey, you are in room 131, and Mr. Helm, you are in 132," the receptionist said as she handed us the keys with a questioning look on her face.

"Thank you!" Jasmine replied as she grabbed both keys. My hands were full of our bags and ski equipment. We were used to getting looks, since we were obviously together, but always got separate rooms. I believed in saving myself for marriage, and Jasmine had agreed to not press the issue. Thankfully, it hadn't been a problem when we first talked about it, although it was becoming harder to maintain my convictions as we got closer to the wedding.

Jasmine opened her door, and I followed her inside, laying her bags down on the bed. "See you in fifteen to head out for food?" I asked as I took my bags to my room.

"Yup!" came the shouted reply before the door closed behind me. I quickly changed into some warmer clothes and got stuff ready for tomorrow. I knocked on her door exactly fifteen minutes later. Jasmine opened it to reveal a stunning mid-calf-length, strapless black dress that complemented her caramel skin perfectly.

"You look amazing," I said after I gathered my wits, "but I thought we were going to walk to that new Thai place?"

"Yeah, I brought this to show off, and I have a jacket for the walk over," she said as she pulled out a large, elegant trench coat and handed it to me. She turned around, showing that the dress dipped fairly far and highlighted her flawless figure, partially obscured by her long, brown hair. I helped her get into the coat and offered my arm.

"Shall we, my lady?" I asked, gesturing to the hallway.

"Of course, good sir," she replied in a bad English accent. We headed out into the cold, enjoying the brisk snowy air and each other's company. "So, are you going to come with me to Peak 8 tomorrow? I think you've gotten to the point where you could handle the Imperial Bowl if you wanted to."

"Nah, I'm not as much of an adrenaline junkie as you are. I'm perfectly fine staying on the groomed trails. But don't let me stop you, as long as you meet me for lunch."

"You know I'm not going to let you ski alone. It's more fun to ski with you."

As we walked down the street, I noticed a group of kids sledding on the hill next to the road. They looked like they were having a lot of fun. "You think we'll come back here someday with our kids?" Jasmine asked suddenly.

"Probably," I replied, watching as a young girl started sliding down the hill. As she started sliding, I noticed that her path changed from the others. She had missed the track and hit a rock, sending her down the wrong side of the hill. "She's going to go into the road!" I yelled and dropped Jasmine's arm. I took off at a sprint as the girl started screaming. The fifty-yard distance disappeared as I put everything I had into the run. Just before she slid off the sidewalk, I reached her and knocked her into a snowbank with a push. My next step landed on her sled, which promptly threw me off my feet as it skidded sideways. I rolled partially off the sidewalk into the road. Bright lights shone into my eyes as a truck's bumper approached. A flash of light, pain, and then pressure were followed by blackness as I was crushed by the Ford truck.

An indeterminate amount of time later, I awoke in a void. There was nothing. No one. There was no light, no heat, no air, no ground, but I was comfortable. I didn't have a body. "Where am I?" I wondered, somehow speaking into the darkness.

"This is the place between worlds," a male voice thundered through my existence. "You have been brought here as your path is not decided yet. Your act of heroism and your spirit's potential have garnered an offer." As he spoke, the darkness surrounding me resolved into a small sitting room, with two chairs. A figure draped in black clothing sat in one of the seats. His face was covered by a hood, with a darkness underneath it that discouraged you from looking into it. "Please sit, we have much to talk about. The offer is that you may continue on, to see what is beyond this life, or you may choose to enter another world. A world where your presence may be the difference between salvation and destruction. A young man with a compatible body has just passed away, and you would take his place. Which do you choose?"

4

I was dumbstruck, still not sure what was going on. "What happened? Beyond this life?"

"You died saving that girl. Saving her, sacrificing your life for hers, inspired not just her, but the entire youth group she was with. A third of them went on to become doctors, nurses, firefighters or workers in other professions with the goal of saving lives. As I said, your act of heroism is mostly what earned you this opportunity."

"Um, will I be a good influence? The way you phrased that I could be the one to cause the destruction. I joined the Air Force because I wanted to be the shield between my loved ones and the world. I am willing to do that again for a different world, if I can, I guess." As I said that, I realized that my emotions were muted, as I barely felt any grief or pain.

"You have chosen and been chosen. Thank you. My world will soon face a storm, and I am betting on you being a key factor in civilization weathering it. You have some time, but not a lot. I would tell you more, but you won't be able to remember any more of this conversation after you arrive anyway. Now, it is time. Grow stronger and save my world."

"Wait! Who are you?" I asked as the light faded again, leaving me in a void.

"I am Darkness, one end of the cycle of Light and Dark. I am shadows, night, and the rest that is necessary for life in the Light. I am one of the last two gods left in my world after my children sacrificed themselves to save it. I am the one who chose you to save my world! Now you must GO!" As his voice echoed around me, light flared from everywhere and nowhere. A pulling force sucked my being into another plane, and my consciousness dissipated.

CHAPTER ONE

The next thing I knew was darkness, but this was the darkness of closed eyelids. My body felt weird, disproportionate. I opened my eyes to see a simple wood-plank ceiling over handmade, but well-formed and sturdy wood furniture. The bed was comfortable enough, but less smooth than I was used to. With some difficulty, I threw the blanket off and nearly yelped in surprise. I was not me.

My legs were much smaller than they should have been, thin as if I was malnourished or had been in bed for a long time. They were also shorter, and my body was that of a teen, not the twenty-two-year-old adult I'd been. My skin looked as if I used to have a decent tan and could get one back, just like I'd always wanted. That was a big contrast to before. Being half Irish and half English, my skin was always in one of two states: blinding white or lobster. My new arms were emaciated as well, though my hands looked like they had been strong. They were covered in calluses that were common for someone who worked with their hands.

I swung my legs out of the bed and tried to push myself up with my arms, as I always did. Thankfully, no one was around to see me flop like a dying fish. "Well, that could have gone better," I muttered to myself, though it came out wrong. "I'm not speaking English, but my brain is receiving it as such," I said out loud, to hear the difference. "Um, apparently I'm the protagonist of a Japanese light novel. Wait, they usually get memories!" I exclaimed, trying to remember anything from this body.

After a couple minutes of sitting with my face scrunched I gave up. All I could remember was my life on Earth, and then a strong sense that I needed to grow stronger to stop something evil. I then remembered my conversation after death.

"Dang it, Darkness, not remembering anything is gonna make things difficult. Wait, why am I talking to myself? Maybe the truck only knocked my senses away and I'm in a loony bin. Maybe. I'll proceed on the possibility this is real, though, else I could die again while ignoring this world. Now, to stand!" I said as I pushed myself up, one arm held aloft with a finger pointing straight up. Thus I ended up face down, on the floor, with my hand pointed at the door. *Ow, my nose.*

I spent the next couple of minutes wiggling my hands and feet, getting feeling back into them. *I wonder how long this body spent dead. It can't have been that long or they would have buried it. Should I pretend to be the person the body was, just with amnesia?* I thought. After a minute spent thinking I decided. *No, I can't deceive this poor kid's family like that. That would be wrong. I'll have to hope they won't attack me or call me demon possessed or something. Hopefully, they'll simply let me leave and I'll make my own way in this world. I can play it off as being a close cousin or something, here to say goodbye. Though pretending to the rest of the world to be him would be easier, if the parents or family would support me. Faking amnesia with help would be the best way to start life here.*

Getting to my hands and knees was easier than standing. I practiced crawling for a little bit. "Look at me, going through the ages super-fast. Why soon I'll be feeding myself and – *gasp!* – potty trained!" I exclaimed softly, still not ready for anyone to find me. I wanted to at least be on my feet before that happened. A few more minutes let me accomplish that goal, and I staggered to the plain wooden door, leaning against it to catch my breath. *What is the technology level of the people? It can't be too low, this wood is well made, but everything looks handmade. I remember I was told to grow stronger by Darkness, who said he was a deity. What does that mean? Maybe he wants me to introduce new technology and gain power that way. Maybe they will be invaded by extra-dimensional beings and the only solution is a forceful jump from the Iron Age to the Industrial Age? I hope not, because I can do some of that but not enough.*

Wait, maybe he meant personal power. Can I be a superhero? Maybe they have magic and I need to combine technology with it and become amazing! A steampunk world would be awesome! Or maybe this really is a Japanese light novel and there are super martial arts, like Crouching Tiger, Hidden Dragon! I was daydreaming as I leaned against the door. I shook myself and stopped dreaming. *Okay, enough dithering. Time to meet the family.*

I slowly opened the door. Without it in the way, I could hear crying from down the hallway. To my right was a hallway extending into a room at the end. Across from me was another door, and down the hallway to the left were doors on both sides. Stairs down were visible at the end to the left. I heard a woman's voice, streaked with pain, from the room to the right. "What are we going to do, Jordan?" Again, it was the same foreign language translated for me. "We barely have anything left, and it didn't work. We still lost Aiden. We might lose everything else too," she sobbed. The ending words were muffled, as if she was speaking into a pillow.

"We'll make do. We always have. We pulled ourselves out of poverty once before, Elena, and by Darkness we can do it again. We'll have other children, or we can adopt once we recover. There are always orphans who need homes. You have too much love to not give it to others. We'll make do." A man's voice, with a barely concealed pain in it, comforted the woman, Elena. I was surprised by the names, but I guess the auto-translate was changing them as well. Hopefully it worked fully the other way.

I stood and listened to them for a minute, gathering my courage. I didn't want to hurt the grieving family, but I knew if I snuck off it would be worse for them. Having their son's body just vanish would be horrifying. Of course, so would someone else stealing it. *Crap.* After psyching myself up, I stumbled down the hallway.

As I started walking, the man's voice called out, "Who's there? I'm sorry but the store is closed until the official mourning period is over, so please return in three days…" His voice ground to a stop as I came into the light from the room. The man's eyes were huge, disbelief written all over his face. The woman looked up from his shoulder.

Her eyes expanded, and she screamed "Aiden!" while throwing herself at me. She picked up my withered body and spun me around. She was much stronger than she looked. She was five nothing and a buck oh five soaking wet if anything, so I wasn't expecting her to be able to pick me up.

"I'm not Aiden," I said gently as she set me down. "My name is Caleb."

She leaned back, still not letting me go, and asked, "What do you mean?"

I thought about faking amnesia again just then, but then said aloud, "I am so sorry, but I am not Aiden. I'm not going to lie and pretend to be your son. I believe he has passed on. When I died on my world, somehow my spirit moved here. I remember a vast voice, offering me a chance to help people again. When I said yes, I woke up here," I said, leaning against Elena as my legs had given out. "I'm sorry," I said again, tearing up at the pain I saw in her face, the denial forming all over again.

For a moment, when she had been holding me, I was experiencing everything I had dreamed of as a child. My mother had abandoned me and I grew up in an uncaring system. I felt the love of this woman for her son, and then I took it away again. I looked over at the father, and the look on his face told me I was right in what I had done.

"Welcome, Cal-led? Is that your name?"

"Cay-leb." I enunciated it slowly.

"Caleb. Thank you. I'm sure we would have figured it out soon enough. The hurt that would have caused would have been greater than we could deal with. What are your plans now?"

"I haven't thought much. I only woke up about ten minutes ago. If my presence is too much, I can leave. I'll make my way somehow, I've been an orphan before and can do it again. I'd like to stay here. Learn about your world and how I can fit in here. I know nothing about where I am," I said, looking down and then at Elena, before looking at my feet again.

"You've been an orphan?" Elena asked, her tone fluctuating from hurt to questioning.

"My family left me when I was young. My father probably didn't even know he had a son, and I grew up in an orphanage as my birth mom was unable to care for me. To change my lot, I worked hard and was accepted into a military academy, where I was engaged to an amazing

8

woman. I died saving a girl from a car, a runaway carriage … I died," I whispered, sinking to my knees as the enormity of what happened hit me. *I'll never see my friends again. I'm never going to hold Jasmine again. I died! At least I don't remember the pain,* I thought as I broke down, sobbing into my hands. As I cried, I felt arms encircle me and a hand pat my shoulder. I glanced up, seeing Jordan looking at me with sympathy as Elena hugged me to her.

Jordan looked at me and asked, "How old were you? Aiden was only fourteen years old."

"I was twenty-two," I whispered, still crying, finally breaking down from the trauma I'd just experienced. The comfort they were giving me, even while I stole their dead son's body, exclaimed louder than words that these were good people.

"Of course you will stay here," Elena declared. "We can't have someone looking like our Aiden wandering the city lost and confused. We'd become a laughingstock, and you'd be drug back here anyway."

Jordan asked, with hope in his eyes, "Do you remember anything from Aiden?"

"No, unfortunately not, though I can somehow speak your language. I can tell it is different from what I used to speak, but it is translating itself as I speak. If you'd allow it, I can be a cousin, or I can be Aiden to everyone else. I would just tell others I lost my memory due to Aiden's, I mean my … sickness?" I ended my statement with a question.

"Yes, Aiden got very sick. The best Healers and concoctions we could afford were unable to help him. We tried everything, sold everything from the store at discount prices to pay for it, and nothing worked. Except it somehow brought you here. What did you say about speaking with a god?"

"When I died, I awoke in a void. A being who said their name was Darkness asked me if I was willing to go to a world where I would be the difference between salvation and destruction. I have no idea what that means, but I wanted to help people. Hopefully, I can figure out how to be that pivot point," I replied, still not sure that I wasn't crazy.

"Well, I have no idea either, but we would be remiss in not helping Darkness's chosen. What do you think, Elena, can you handle letting Caleb here stand in for Aiden?" Jordan asked Elena gently.

She looked at him with fire in her eyes. "I'm not porcelain, Jordan. I am the stronger of us two physically, and I can be strong enough for this. You will stay with us, Cay-led, and outside this place or around others you will be Aiden. We will explain that you lost your memories due to all the treatments and teach you how to live here. You'll work in the store and get your affinity tested in six months like Aiden would have. Hopefully that is enough time to teach you how to mostly blend in. You can tell us more about your world at the same time." She finished her declaration by drawing me to my feet.

I looked her in the eyes and simply said, "Thank you."

CHAPTER TWO

Elena moved me over to the couch, which was surprisingly comfortable for something that appeared to be stuffed with straw. She put on tea while Jordan made me a bowl of the soup they had been eating. They flinched a little every time they looked at me again, though it was slowly getting better. I devoured the soup, and two more bowls after that. We spent the next hour talking about Earth and my life there. They were amazed at my descriptions of cars, plastic, and television. They weren't amazed by running water, which made me very happy. *I don't think I could take long-term usage of chamber pots*, I laughed to myself.

They started telling me about their world, Zemia. We were in a city named Azyl in the Kingdom of Craesti. Azyl was the third-largest city in the Kingdom. Craesti was surrounded on three sides by water and cut off from the neighboring country Toprak by a mountain range that spanned from sea to sea.

They pulled out a small map, which surprised me. I hadn't expected them to have a map. It only showed Craesti, which was a full two hundred miles wide from sea to sea and almost seven hundred from sea to mountains. This was significantly larger than I expected from Jordan and Elena's description. The map showed the city we were in to be southeast from the capital of Craesti, cunningly named Craesti too, along a river. Craesti City was on the coast of the Dividing Sea, which I likened to the Mediterranean from Earth. Though apparently the center wasn't explored much and was marked with a line that said, "Beyond here are Beasts."

"What does that mean, beyond there are Beasts?" I asked Jordan, who was pointing out cities and major features on the map. It wasn't too detailed, but it did show roads between many cities.

"The water there gets deep enough that Kraken, Tizheruk, and Leviathans can attack ships, thus preventing most commerce from going across the Sea. The Water and Wood Gatherers of the Trade Union have been working on ways to prevent attacks, but so far no method has worked on all three major threats. Each trip is a significant risk, but we do have some trade across the Sea."

"Kraken, Leviathan, and Tizheruk? You have actual giant monsters in your oceans?"

"Of course, many Water Elemental Beasts can grow to enormous sizes, feeding mostly on Aether and other Beasts. Did you not have any in your world?"

"Well, we have whales and sharks, but they don't attack ships. They can be big, but never really had much impact on ships unless people fell off them. Um, what do you mean by Aether?"

"What about Aether?"

"What is it? Our world used to think there was something called ether that let light propagate, but we disproved its existence over a hundred years before… uh, my time. It sounded like you meant something different though. What do you mean by Elemental Beasts?"

"You don't know what Aether is? Aether is… um… an energy that exists all around us. Every person is able to gather this energy into themselves, slowly increasing their capabilities. Aether has ten elements, though people can only gather eight of them. Hold on," Jordan said while he walked down the hallway. He entered the room next to the one I left and came back out with a small book. He opened it and walked over.

"Here is the basic diagram explaining the elements." He pointed to what looked like a compass rose. North was labeled Air, northeast was Lightning, east was Fire, southeast was Metal, south was Earth, southwest was Wood, west was Water, and northwest was Ice. The center was labeled Light, and a circle labeled Darkness enclosed the whole thing. "Gathering is the process of absorbing Aether from the world around us, flowing it through your meridians and gathering it into your center. From there it will circulate throughout your body, slowly strengthening it and letting you perform magical feats. Everyone is capable of it to some extent, though most have a talent level of only one or two of five, often said as so they won't ever be able to condense a Core. Everyone also has an element they are linked with, allowing them to more easily gather and channel that element. I am an Earth Gatherer, and Elena is Metal linked."

I knew it, Japanese light novel protagonist. "Wow. That's amazing. We had nothing like that on Earth. How do you know what your talent level and element is?"

"There is a testing ceremony held every three years at the Azyl Academy that everyone from fourteen to sixteen years old may attend. They will evaluate your talent and elemental affinity and determine the fee to be trained there if you desire. The higher the talent and the more elements you have a high affinity with, the lower the fee since their renown grows through the accomplishments of their students. They want talented people and will pay for them. Talented people will be able to accomplish more and earn more for the Academy. The next testing will be in six months, as Elena mentioned earlier."

"Is there a way to start… gathering, is it?… before being tested?" I asked.

"Yes, it is recommended that you start gathering before being tested. The test is more accurate if you have done so. Your center develops to being able to gather Aether usually some time between your thirteenth and fourteenth year, hence the age limit on the test. The Academy and the City Lord publishes this book"—he waved the book with the elemental drawing—"that is free to every family with a child to start teaching them. Without knowing your element, though, it is impossible to condense Aether into a liquid, which is the first step to forming a Core. A healthy body is required to start, so Aiden had not been able to start yet. You probably shouldn't start until you regain your health either."

"Yeah, that makes sense," I said, my head drooping in exhaustion. "If just talking is taking this much out of me, I shouldn't do much else." I looked out the window in the room, and saw a sunset, or sunrise, out of it. "Is it late or early?" I asked.

"The sun is just setting. Why don't you go rest? Elena and I will tidy up the area and reopen the store. With three of us again, we'll have to recover." Jordan helped me up and to the room I woke up in. I collapsed into bed, asleep as I hit the pillow.

I woke early the next morning, consumed with a burning desire to pee. I got up and hobbled to the door, then stopped. "Um, where is *un baño?*" I shrugged and walked to the room to my left, trying the door. It opened onto a small room with a bathtub, a toilet, and a sink. *They do have plumbing! Hooray!* The toilet was only a circular pedestal that was just over knee height. The seat was attached, and it was directly next to the wall. Looking inside, I saw that it was empty of water, but a lever was connected to a pipe into the side. I pulled the lever, and a valve opened, allowing water to flow.

I relieved myself and looked at the sink. A bar of harsh castile-type soap was next to another pipe with a lever attached. After washing my hands, I dried them on my clothes. *That probably wasn't sanitary. I'm still wearing the clothes I died in. Well that's a weird thought.* I stumbled back to the bedroom and found some clothes in a closet. I chose a long tunic and some loose pants and changed before collapsing into bed again. When I next woke up, the room had grown fairly stuffy. I walked over to the window shutters and opened them, gazing out through an opening at the city.

It looked like it was midmorning, and there were people walking down the alley the window looked upon. I could see a couple of people dressed similarly to me, though in brown instead of green. They were leading a wagon pulled by an ox with strange horns. The ox almost looked like it was made of wood. Two of the people were armed, one with a bow and another with a spear. *So weapons are old school, pre-firearm. But they have a type of magic, though that seems more like the Chinese concept of Qi than normal fantasy magic.*

The building across the alley was built of stone, as was nearly every building I could see. The roofs were magenta slate tiles. Looking to the right, it seemed like the alley intersected a major street a couple of shops or houses from where I was. A stream of people and animals moved up and down the road. I saw a person on a tiger leap down the road. *Wow! That tiger was as big as a horse!*

My stomach rumbled. "Yes, master," I said to it in a fake evil-minion voice. I staggered to the door and down the hall to the living area, leaning against the wall the entire time I walked.

"May Light guide your way today," Elena said to me as I walked in.

"Um, you too," I said, confused.

"Oh, you never did get an explanation for why we called you Darkness's chosen yesterday, did you? You appeared on Darkness Day, the last day of the month, and said you had spoken to Him. Today is Light Day since Light always follows the Darkness and is the first day of the new month. This is the third month of the ten-month year."

"How many days in a month? Um, also, who is Darkness?"

"There are forty-two days in a month, divided into five weeks of eight days each plus Light and Darkness on either end. As for Darkness himself, there were originally ten gods of this world. Legends say some time in the distant past, at least a thousand years, eight of the ten gods sacrificed themselves to save this world from a terrible catastrophe, leaving only Light and Darkness, who were both weakened considerably. In a couple months will be the annual festival to celebrate this sacrifice, on the Day of Light. It is thought that Light and Darkness now don't interact much with people anymore, leaving most acknowledgement of them to only four events every year and the first and last day of the months. Light is celebrated on the longest day of the year in midsummer, and Darkness on the longest night. Darkness and Light are celebrated together on the days of equal night and day during fall and spring."

"Is Darkness a good god? In the mythologies of my world, most deities whose domains included darkness were usually evil," I asked.

"No, none of our gods were evil. Darkness does rule over death, but all life has death, so why would that be evil? There is the occasional rumor of death cults or demon worshipers, but they usually do not espouse Darkness."

"That's interesting, and good. I'm glad he isn't evil. So your year has four hundred and twenty days? The year on my old planet was only three hundred and sixty-five days. Is the worship of Light and Darkness the only religion?"

"Four hundred and twenty-two days. The Day of Light and the Night of Darkness are separate even from the months. Uh, if your year was shorter, that would mean you would only be nineteen or so in our years. In the Kingdom there is no other religion that is followed openly. The Topraks worship something else, though I don't know what. There are some other beliefs from other countries, though they also worship Light and Darkness, I think," she said as she stood up. "Now, let's get you some food." She started preparing something for dinner as we were talking.

"Great, I am super hungry right now. I'm probably going to need more food than I would normally to recover," I said.

"That's probably right," she said as she cooked. After a couple minutes, she set down what looked like a meat crepe. It was delicious – flavorful meat combined with an almost sweet bread. She also handed me a steaming glass of tea. After downing the food and several cups of tea, I was drooping again.

"Thank you for breakfast. It was delicious. I'm going to go to sleep again. I am still terribly weak."

She helped me up and to bed. "Rest well. We'll talk more of your world and ours tomorrow. Do not push yourself too hard, you don't want to hurt yourself more," she admonished me. I agreed as I collapsed, quickly falling asleep again.

CHAPTER THREE

I woke up a couple hours later, feeling slightly better. My stomach growled in anger at being empty again as I sat up. *I'd guess I'm healing and growing towards normal faster than I would on Earth. Not sure how much faster though.* I got out of bed and decided to do a squat to see how fast I was healing. I slowly bent my knees, working to maintain good form, before collapsing onto my bottom. *Ow!* "Well, I guess no working out yet. I'll go see if I can make lunch, help out with chores or something at least."

I stumbled to the door and out into the hallway. Jordan was walking right there holding a couple books as I left my room. "Whoa there!" Jordan exclaimed as I nearly ran into him. "Still stumbling around. Would a cane help?" He balanced the books on one arm and helped steady me with the other.

"Probably not. My arms are as weak as my legs. Hopefully this will get better soon. Can I help with anything?" I asked.

"Not yet, once you're steadier we can have you help out in the store a bit." He assisted me in walking over to the table in the living area, where I sat gratefully. *I hate being weak!* He set the books down and walked over to the pantry. I noticed a moderately sized box in the pantry when he opened the door.

"What's that box?" I asked.

"That's our cold box; it keeps the meat and vegetables fresher if we store them cold. It has an Ice inscription on it that maintains the low temperature, though one of us has to add Aether every couple of days." *Wow, it's a fridge!* He pulled out some bread and cheese from the pantry, then handed me a hunk of both. The bread was thick, filling, and one of the best things I'd ever eaten. *This is real bread, the kind people could almost subsist on alone.* After finishing the food, I made puppy eyes at Jordan until he gave me part of his meal, which I also scarfed down.

"It's been long enough that I forgot how much growing boys eat. Thankfully we should be getting a new shipment in tomorrow, so we will be solvent at least," Jordan remarked as I ate.

"Shipment of what? I was wondering what y'all sold," I asked.

"Y'all? Um, we mostly sell books, writing supplies, and transcription or binding services. That's what I've got here. We were given a request to copy a book for a client."

"Y'all is short for you all. A common term where I am originally from. I guess I'll have to stop using that. Are there a lot of people who are literate? You mentioned that gathering book was free for everyone with a child."

"Maybe half the people in the city are literate. There is a school that children can attend from the ages of seven to thirteen. Usually afterwards you would become an apprentice to either your parents or a family friend. Unless you had enough talent to be accepted into the Academy, or decided to join the army. The Academy trains nearly every potentially powerful gatherer. The graduates of the Academy form the backbone of the Kingdom's protection from high-level Beasts and are almost always elevated to the lower nobility."

I nodded as I listened to Jordan. He went on to describe the lower nobility as essentially knights, who had some extra privileges and responsibilities. There were four noble clans in the city, the Kowalski clan, the Lo clan, the Haodha clan, and the Volkov clan. The City Lord's clan, the Kowalskis, ruled the city and the City Lord himself was accountable to the King for keeping the peace, delivering taxes, and maintaining a military and Beast subjugation force. The Haodha clan was mostly in charge of farms that grew gathering herbs for alchemy, the Volkov ran a significant portion of the inscription trade in the city, and the Lo were renowned Beast hunters.

He then talked about the Merchants' Association, the Laborers Union and several other groups of merchants and commoners who held power nearly on par with the nobles, though without the near immunity to prosecution the nobles enjoyed. I started drifting by this point, my body losing steam like a leaky boiler. Jordan noticed and stopped his discussion before he helped me back to bed.

The rest of the first two weeks of my new life followed this pattern. I would wake up, eat, talk for a bit, and then collapse for several hours. I slowly got stronger, finally able to walk without leaning on the wall or someone after the first week. By the end of the second week, I was able to do a couple squats and push-ups every time I got out of bed. I was determined to get fit and healthy as soon as I could.

I learned about customs and courtesies during this time when I asked about how to help in the store. Handshakes were unknown here, with a small bow being the most common acknowledgement. "Sir" or "Ma'am" were still correct forms of address, though using the person's title was also acceptable. There was not a distinction between men's and women's work aside from caring for young infants, as was seen on Earth. The talent to gather was not affected by gender, so women could be just as strong as men here.

I was also given a quick overview of everything they would have talked about in the "school," which was only a half day, half of the week kind of thing. The basics of arithmetic and reading were taught, along with a very quick overview of recent history, the geography of the surrounding area, and some introductions to major trades. With my education on Earth, we skipped over math. I was debating about introducing Jordan and Elena to calculus. *Nah, I like them, though it'll definitely help later on. I hope, anyway.*

Reading and writing translated as seamlessly as speaking did, with my brain fully interpreting and outputting the correct words, even as I felt a small weirdness to it. The weirdness was trickling away. It seemed that the more I used the translator, the more it added a new set of language files into my brain. This made the transition easier, since I didn't have to work on learning a new language along with a new culture at the same time.

Jordan and Elena also talked about their business. It was very interesting to me. I got to learn about how they made ink and the process by which they transcribed and copied books. Thankfully, I was able to use paper and start working on figuring out writing in this new language. I found that I enjoyed calligraphy.

Over time, my hands steadied and my endurance improved. I started taking over a couple of small tasks in the store, mostly mixing black and red inks. The black ink had only three ingredients and was very forgiving in mixing. The red was a little more difficult, so I made a couple small boxes. Each box held one of the four ingredients, and I could balance the boxes to have the right amount to mix. This helped me, especially when my hands shook, and let me make the red ink needed for some of the commissioned works in Elena's backlog.

Jordan and Elena had a number of commissions that they had been unable to get to during Aiden's sickness, and I did my best to help them get caught up. The bills had piled up too, and they were essentially bankrupt when I woke. I tried to think of inventions from Earth's past that would help. *I never really studied old inventions. At least, not well enough to draw a design. They don't have a printing press, which I can kind of cobble together, I think. Shouldn't be too complex, right?*

When I wasn't helping in the store or sleeping, I was trying to get my strength back. I worked on push-ups, squats, leg lifts, and other bodyweight exercises first, along with walking around the store. Moving books around and stocking shelves helped me get back in shape as well. After the first two weeks I was feeling almost normal, able to function most of the day without feeling like I needed to collapse.

I didn't leave the building for a couple weeks after I arrived here. I was irrationally scared of screwing up and being found out as a body snatcher. Somehow, Jordan and Elena had accepted it and me, but I wasn't willing to risk it with anyone else. Eventually I might tell close friends, if I made any, but not right away.

Even though I didn't leave, I was able to interact with customers, even if briefly. Many repeat customers would approach me to ask how I was doing, as they knew about the sickness. I told them that I was recovering, but had lost all memories from before. This helped to explain any little mistakes I made, though I still got questioning looks when I used sayings from Earth. I had to pay attention and think about everything I said.

After almost a month had passed, I had gotten strong enough to walk to the end of the block and back. Jordan or Elena walked with me the first couple of times, partially to assist me if I needed it, and partially to introduce me to people. I met a gaggle of acquaintances of my new parents, from the bartender and servers at the tavern on the corner to the baker across the street. I also met their best friends, a couple named Alexander and Holly. Additionally, I found out that the culture used the same naming convention as the Chinese. So I was Kupiec Aiden, not Aiden Kupiec as I would have been in America. Noptep Alexander and Holly had a son a couple months younger than me named Jonathan, called Jon, who quickly became my best friend here. He filled me in with lots of stories from his time with Aiden before.

The evening of the next Darkness Day, one month Zemian time from the day I arrived, I was given the go-ahead to try and start gathering. "Normally, you would have started trying already. Most people take a few weeks or months to start, and they don't advance quickly until they can find out their element. The Azyl Academy does their test every three years for free, or you can go to the City Hall and get tested for a significant cost. The Azyl test is in five months, so you have plenty of time to get started," Jordan told me, giving me the book on gathering he had shown me on the first day.

I had not looked at the book since then. I wanted to listen to my new parents' advice about not gathering until I was ready, and I knew that I'd try as soon as I read how. *Now is my chance. Let's do this!* I left the living room and went to my room. Inside there was a bed, a small dresser, and a chair. Solid looking with lumpy cushions on it, the chair was my destination. I sat down and opened the book. I flipped through it quickly, just skimming the pages to start with.

The first chapter contained a description of the elements and went into a bit more detail than Jordan did on that first day. The second chapter had a series of drawings that showed the various known meridians. "There are 30 known meridians, and it is suspected that there are a total of 42. Meridians cannot be seen directly, their presence is more metaphysical than real? Weird. The suspected meridians are based on symmetry with known ones, but have not been detected ever," I mumbled to myself as I skimmed through. "Your talent level is just the number of meridians you were born with that are easily openable, with the second number being the amount openable with known alchemical means. What does easily openable mean? Oh, it means that you just need a small amount of Aether to open them.

"Ooh, alchemy. I wonder how the rules compare with chemistry from Earth. Wait, how does chemistry work here? It can't be too different or we'd all be dead, well unless the magic fixes the problems. I'm going to get tired of saying, 'except magic,' aren't I?" I muttered as I flipped through the book. The next chapter gave a description of meditation practices and a guide to trying to sense Aether for the first time. Following its directions, I sat up straight with my feet curled under me in a lotus pose. "Breathe in for a three count, hold, release with a three count, hold. Focus your mind on your center. Feel your breath, your heartbeat, and seek out the Aether that is flowing through your center."

I sat for a while, focused on my breathing. My first goal was to get the breathing pattern down to the point of instinct, so I could then focus on feeling the Aether. Surprisingly, it only took about an hour to get to the point of maintaining breathing in a three count without actually counting it out. From there, I focused on building an image of multicolored motes of light flowing through me, a pulsing flow that increased with breathing in and decreased with breathing out. Then I focused on the point where the Aether would be flowing through my center, a spot just beneath the diaphragm, about where you were supposed to push when doing CPR. I felt like I could see myself in a third-person view, like a video game. *This is like having an augmented reality view of my own body! Pretty awesome!* At that location I was supposed to imagine a rune with a single vertical line and another, shorter, line that went from the bottom left to the top right at around a thirty-degree angle. I'd done enough trig to get the lines just about perfect.

I immediately felt the difference, and my mental image changed without my input. Small multicolored specks began to slow down and curve around the rune, slowly forming a circle. As they came together, a few would rebound directly off the rune, often zigzagging through my heart and lungs. I could feel each one, a tiny jolt that was not too unpleasant. The first stages of Aether Gathering were supposed to help increase the capabilities of your respiratory and circulatory systems, though that was not described in so many words. All the book said was it strengthened your heart and lungs, but I'm sure that it did something to the arteries and veins connecting them as well. If it didn't, the stronger heart would damage your normal arteries. As the Aether circled, I was supposed to now direct it up through a meridian that went from my center to my brain, circling through the heart and lungs on the way. This was the meridian that everyone had open. A person who had the life meridian forcibly closed died almost immediately.

Nothing happened. The Aether just kept circling, slowly increasing in quantity. Collisions between the specks of Aether would occasionally push one out of the circle, at which point it would just fly off. I focused my mind on a single speck, watching it slowly progress around my center. Just before the place I was supposed to start from, it collided with another bit of

Aether and I grabbed it with my will, forcing the rebound to be in the direction of the meridian. It slowed as it neared, and I pushed with my entire mind. With a non-audible, but rather felt, pop, it entered and flowed up the meridian, giving slightly larger jolts every time it hit an organ on the way around. When it rejoined the group circling, I noticed that it had grown slightly larger. After it rejoined, it circled around once before going back into the meridian. As it did so, I grabbed another dot and forced it to follow the first dot. This was significantly easier than the first one. I spent the next while forcing more and more dots to circle through the meridian. I discovered I could only add about half as many as circled before to the rotation on each attempt. I didn't stop working on this until I got shaken out of my meditative state by Elena.

"Ok, that's enough trying. It is supper time and you need to eat. You can try to grab your first Aether again tomorrow. Getting it by the weekend will leave plenty enough time before the test."

"But I already grabbed some. I was following the directions in the book and managed to grab some specks of Aether and get them circling through the life meridian as described here. I feel like I've got slightly more energy now than I did earlier this afternoon, so it should be helping to heal the damage I've still got in there."

"What, already? In only three hours you've got the basics down?! That's astounding. Everyone I know of took weeks before they could get even the tiniest bit of Aether to flow through the life meridian. Come to the table and describe what you did over dinner." I followed her out of my room into the main living area, where the table had already been set.

Jordan looked up from a ledger, holding what seemed like a stick of charcoal in his hand. "So, I heard a shout of surprise. I'm guessing you already gathered some Aether. That is astounding. Sit and tell us about it. Maybe it'll help us or our friends' kids." He seemed to nonchalantly accept that I'd have found something amazing.

We sat down and Jordan passed a soup bowl to Elena, myself, and then served himself. Inside was a thick stew made with vegetables I didn't recognize, though maybe one was a blue carrot, and some meat that looked like beef. After taking the first bite, Elena stopped and spoke up. "Gathered Elements, we thank you for this meal. Now, Caleb, tell us what you did." I described what I had done, starting with the meditation, then going into the visualization of the flow of specks of light.

"Wait," Jordan interrupted me, "you imagined tiny specks of light, not a liquid flowing through you as the book describes? Why?"

"Well, back on Earth we discovered that just about everything is quantized, that nothing exists on a continuous basis. This was especially true and especially important for energy and light, as this allowed us to discover and use many of the quantum principles to make life better for people. For example, you mentioned a liquid. Let's take water, like in this mug." I lifted up the mug I was holding.

"Water is made up of water molecules, tiny little pieces of water that are lightly connected to the other pieces around them. If we look even closer, we find that water molecules are made up of two hydrogen atoms and one oxygen atom, and even further, those are divided into protons, neutrons and electrons, and so on. At the smallest level, there exist only certain amounts of mass or energy that can be used to build up everything else in the universe. I guess with that knowledge I just assumed that Aether would work the same way. This let me focus on grabbing only a single speck of Aether to redirect it around the meridian, which the book said was the hardest part. If I was able to do it so fast, I'm guessing it's because most people are grabbing too much. I could barely manipulate two tiny motes at first. I guess whatever you use to manipulate Aether gets stronger with use, so it won't work until you are strong enough to grab a huge handful."

"That sounds correct. I was going to advise you to try to move the smallest amount you could, but I guess I don't need to do that anymore," Elena mentioned, a look of concentration taking over her face. "I think this will help me to be able to move forward some more. We'll have to think about how to share this knowledge. Hopefully we can get it into the next scribing of the Guide and help out the next generation." Elena turned to Jordan, who hadn't touched his food since I started talking. "Isn't Holly and Alexander's son Jonathan just about ready to start gathering? He's taking the test at the same time as Aiden. We should invite them over so he can hear what to do." I had asked them early on to only call me Aiden, rather than Caleb, to make a clean break from Earth and get used to the name change.

"Okay, I can ask Alexander if they would want to come over in a couple days. It's too bad we don't know your affinity yet, though. Once we do you can refine the rune in your center to be more effective. The one in the guide is the weakest and simplest, and thus it can be used by anyone regardless of affinity."

"Is there a way to tell besides taking a test? The Aether specks are colored, at least in my mind, so I wonder if that can be used to tell."

"Maybe, though usually not at first. You will gather every element to start with. That is why the starter rune is so weak; it forces you to gather at the rate of your lowest affinity. Everyone can gather every element, but it's not an efficient use of your time. Unfortunately, it is not safe to use runes for elements you have a low affinity with, just as it's not safe to use more runes than you have open meridians. The test coming up will let us know what your talents are, and then you will be able to improve your speed."

We finished up dinner then, with Elena and Jordan discussing the shop. I was always trying to absorb information about this new world, so I listened attentively to their conversation. After dinner, Jordan told me to go work on gathering some more because the larger your Aether pool before testing the more accurate the results would be. Also, having Aether in my system now would help me grow stronger faster. Just what I needed to finish healing from this body's long sickness and to satisfy the unrelenting drive I felt to improve.

CHAPTER FOUR

A couple of days after I started to gather, Jon and his family came over for dinner. "Have you started trying to gather yet?" I asked Jon about halfway through dinner.

"Well, I've started trying. So far I haven't had any success. Have you?" he asked back.

"Started a couple days ago and had success pretty quickly," I said, and began to describe what I had done. I explained the particle nature of Aether by depicting it as the dust particles you could see in a sunbeam, how I pictured Aether drifting as they did. I noticed the elder Noptep's doubtful gaze at Elena, and her nod that answered the unspoken question of "Did he really succeed in only a couple of days?" Jon just shook his head after the explanation.

"That's awesome. I'll try that tonight, thanks. So I guess I'll be seeing less of you, huh? Knowing your drive for getting stronger, I bet you're going to be gathering every night as best as you can?" I blushed a bit at his words. I'd pushed Jon to work out, walking longer distances and moving boxes around that he normally would let someone else move. The Noptep's owned one of the laborer companies that provided people for unloading and loading the ships in the docks. Jon did some lifting himself, but he usually worked on paperwork and overseeing groups of laborers.

"We've got to get ready for the Academy test, right? The stronger you are, the more likely they will reduce the cost to attend. We need all the help we can get to afford it." I'd given one of the many reasons I had for trying to gather as fast as possible. The primary one was *because I can do magic now!* Which wouldn't make a whole lot of sense unless I explained the truth of the situation I was in, something so different I still caught myself doubting the reality of it.

We finished dinner with Jon telling about a recent escapade where he snuck into the baker's shop and replaced their sugar with salt. The irate baker chased him out of the shop after a batch of cookies failed. Jon did come back and buy the cookies. He would play pranks on people but would always try to make it right later.

A couple days later Jon came by super excited. "I did it!" he shouted as he entered the shop. The other two customers looked over and shook their heads at his exuberance. "I gathered some Aether, and it only took me three days with your method!"

"Great! Let's go out tonight to celebrate, then we can get busy gathering for the Academy exam." Jon agreed before he ran off, probably to tell more people his good news. I laughed ruefully as he ran off.

One of the customers came over and remarked, "You've grown really mature ever since your brush with death."

"Thank you. It has given me a different perspective," I said, before helping him with his purchases. *That's because I'm really six years older, at least mentally.* I occasionally received comments like that, and I just accepted them then moved on.

The next couple of months passed quickly. I continued to help out in the store stocking shelves, moving boxes, and making inks. Jordan let me copy a short manuscript once, with permission from the customer. A discount too, I think. This was hard because we worked to make the script nearly the same, not just the words. I kept trying to create a design for a printing press, but I hadn't really studied history before. I kept redesigning my kludged-together drawing.

Moving items helped get my body stronger and I discovered that Aether aided the body recover from exertion faster. I slowly grew stronger and reached to the point of being a normal fourteen-year-old here. Jon didn't get the "have to get stronger" bug as bad as I had, but by association with me he ended up stronger than he would have otherwise.

Pretending to be Aiden got easier over time as well, especially as the amnesia excuse was used to gloss over all my questions about life in the world. My natural curiosity helped me be seen as younger than I felt, though I was sure that was also the hormones in this new body. I also believed that Darkness did something to both my, and my new parents', minds. We accepted and adapted to this new reality much too fast for it to be otherwise. Though the natural charity and kindness Jordan and Elena exhibited to everyone helped as well.

Other than working around the store and our home above it, my only task was to gather for at least an hour every night. I would usually do this just after supper, leaving about two hours to roam the city if I wanted to. For the first week, I did nothing but gather for those extra hours before heading to bed. I discovered that I had a limit of new motes of Aether I could add to the meridian circle per cycle, with each cycle taking a half hour or so to complete. The number was large enough that I couldn't accurately count it, and when I mentioned this to Jordan he told me that it was limited by my talent and the rune quality. Once I was tested I could increase the quality and number of runes by a couple times, depending on overall talent level. "I've got a third-level Earth rune and Elena has a second-level Metal rune along with the starter rune, so either one of those will beat the starting rune."

"Levels of runes?" I asked.

"Yup, runes go up in level based upon their complexity and capability, with each level being significantly greater than the one before. I know of at least twelve levels, though rumors occasionally pop up of a higher level than that. The craziest one I heard of was a reported level twenty found in a ruin in the Skraj Mountains. That one sent people flocking to search for it, but no report was ever made of anything significant being found. People will always chase after something that will make them powerful or rich. No one really knows how many people died chasing that rumor. The wilderness outside of the cities is not to be trifled with."

"How common are the higher-level runes? You said all you have are a level two and level three, so who would own a level ten? Or a twelve?"

"Well, runes get much harder to find above a two. The three I use was a lucky break, found among a grouping of stuff someone sold when their father passed away. Otherwise, I would not have been able to afford it. Above a four you get to the point where large academies or noble families have them, but no one else does. The twelve I've heard of was the rumor of how strong the Royal Families runes are. It might not be true, but who knows? That is outside my experience."

After the discussion about rune quality and my limitation, I spent an extra hour a day gathering, trying to advance my gathering level as fast as I could. The first stage of gathering was just called Aether Gathering, and it focused on increasing the amount of Aether that you could hold, strengthening your meridians and center to hold more. The first level of this stage was described as "Vapor," where the Aether was barely visible, and when I focused on my whole body the Aether was barely able to be sensed by me. Each level of Aether Gathering was divided into low and high, and I really wanted to get to High Vapor. I had no idea when that would occur, but was hoping to get there before the testing. Only sixteen days were left at this point.

Two days later, I encountered my first bottleneck in gathering. One hour into the two I spent every night, I suddenly couldn't force more Aether into my life meridian. I remembered reading that this signified running into the boundary for the next level higher! I sat up straighter and focused on breathing for a couple of minutes before grabbing a hold of some Aether again and focusing on pushing the Aether into the suddenly not welcoming meridian. The next hour was an exercise in futility, until I thought of particle accelerators. I grabbed a very small group of Aether, maybe ten motes total, and prevented them from entering the meridian. I redirected their rotation to circle my center, pushing them closer and closer to the very middle each rotation. As I did so, they noticeably sped up and became harder to control. I focused, chanting to myself, "Stay on target, stay on target," as I pushed until they were as close to the center as I could force. Before I lost control, I directed them straight at the meridian and they slammed into the barrier holding out the extra Aether. With a pop, they shot right in, and I felt a large increase in the pressure of the Aether in my meridian.

Looking closely, the Aether particles were much closer together than they were before, giving significant extra room. "Wow, that was hard," I muttered to myself as I wiped sweat off my forehead. I controlled my breathing and started gathering, noticing a small increase in the rate I was able to gather. "Nice. I'm ready for the testing. I doubt I can get to the next level, as each level is harder than the one before." I spent another half hour gathering, but my focus wavered after that so I decided to wash up and go to bed.

Washing up was interesting and disturbing. I had a small black film over my head and torso that I had to scrape off. *Oh, right, the book said leveling up reduces impurities in your body. Gross!* The technology of the washroom always amazed me. Mostly gravity driven from containers on the roof, the wastewater was pumped into a sewer using Air and Water engravings. Later on, it would be purified with Lightning, Fire, and Wood engravings before being dumped into the river. This significantly reduced the likelihood of disease, as did the strengthening effect of gathering. *Thankfully, I'll probably never get the flu again! Though no one knows why I got so sick before.* After a quick bath where I scrubbed the grime of the day off, I collapsed into bed.

The next two weeks flew by, nothing major happening. I kept more to myself except around Jon, mostly acting the curious but clueless guy. Whenever one of my questions aroused curiosity, Jon would explain that I had been sick and lost my memory. It sounded truer coming from him rather than me. I ran errands for Elena and Jordan, getting to know people around this area of town. We were in a district that was mostly middle class, with the east of the city being the rich part of town. To the west were the docks and the slums. I typically avoided going to either side, except for the occasional visit to Jon and his parents' workplace over by the docks.

Most of the people I interacted with were normal, everyday, good people, until two days before the testing. I was running an errand to the central market, picking up some food for the next couple of days, when I heard a scream of pain from the edge. I hurried over, ready to help out whoever was injured, when I heard a whip crack and another scream. Pushing my way to the front of the growing crowd, I saw a boy about my body's age lash at a slightly older, sixteen-year-old girl with a whip as she cowered on the ground. Bright lines of blood showed where the whip had hit her already while she sobbed, "I'm sorry I ran into you, sir. I'm sorry!"

"This will teach you to insult my august personage with your bumbling, wench." He raised the whip for a fourth time. Seeing no one else willing to step up, I rushed in and caught the whip, wrapping it around my arm and yanking it out of his hands.

"The young woman's had enough, or do you think it manly to beat on someone with a weapon when they have none?" I said, settling into a combative stance.

"Who do you think you are, interfering in my, Haodha Nicolai, business?" he challenged back, expecting me to know his name.

"Someone unwilling to watch injustice occur while I can stop it," I retorted. "Run back to your daddy and report that someone was mean to you. I'm sure that will increase your power in your family," I snidely taunted him, stepping back slowly, and helping the young woman to her feet.

"You'll regret this. Guards, seize him!" As he said this, two burly men stepped out of the crowd and started moving towards me. *Some guards, let me rush him and steal his weapon,* I thought as I backed slowly up. Whistles came from the edge of the market, and three market guards rushed over to us.

"Break this up!" one shouted, looking sternly at the young noble. His two guards backed off, walking to stand next to Nicolai, who glared at me one more time.

"You'll regret this!" he repeated as he left in a huff.

The lead market guard walked up to me. "Aiden, you should know better than to stick your nose where it doesn't belong. Luckily the young Haodha didn't want to make a larger scene, or you could have been in a world of hurt."

"Thank you, Lucas, I'll let Ma and Pa know what you did. I doubt anything will come of this, it shouldn't be worth the noble's time."

"You don't remember these nobles, Aiden, respect and power mean everything to them. You insulted him in front of a crowd of people. He will try to find you and hurt you. Keep your head low and this will pass, but I'd recommend not coming back here for at least a month. Take care," he said as he turned to keep patrolling.

"Thank you," came a timid voice from behind me. I looked back at the younger woman, although she was probably two or three years older than the current me. *Gah, age is going to be a problem, I know it.*

"It is what people should do," I replied back. "Do you have a place to go, or will that cretin come back?"

"I should be okay. I doubt I have a position at the teahouse anymore, but I can find a place on the other side of town. Thank you for caring. I'm Khadma Acenath."

"I'm Kupiec Aiden. If you need help, feel free to come to my parents' shop, just three blocks north and two west from here. Are you sure you can make it alone?" I asked again, but she nodded resolutely and walked away.

"Well, hopefully this tendency to jump in won't bite me in the butt," I muttered to myself.

CHAPTER FIVE

The day of testing was here. The day when everyone was allowed into the northernmost portion of the city, where the City Lord's Keep and the Azyl Academy was located. I woke up early and made breakfast for Ma and Pa, too excited to focus on gathering. I had grown comfortable enough here to view them as my true family, and had started to refer to them as such. *Today I get to know my affinities and my talent. Hopefully it'll be high, so I can pay back Elena and Jordan for taking me in. I really hope it'll be enough to get into the Academy here.* I was fairly sure my abilities would be high, if for no other reason than I was "chosen" to come here, but anxiety listens to no logic.

After breakfast was ready, I finished up the sketch I had been working on, of the idea of a printing press. *I'm finally ready, or at least I need to be. If I don't share this now I probably never will, so just do it.* I had been looking at the world and trying to think of ways to take the knowledge from Earth and apply it here, but without creating social havoc and upheaval.

Civilization on this world was much more fragile than back home, what with the Beasts and Elemental Beasts that lurked in the wilderness, ready to destroy a non-unified people. While the map I had seen on my first day showed the border between Toprak and Craesti was the Skraj Mountains, in reality, neither country controlled anything within a hundred miles of the mountains except for some small outposts and a single city. Freeing people from tyranny to deliver them to death was not my goal, especially if I didn't really know what was going on. I needed to explore and discover the world even more before making any huge changes, and to involve the people who I trusted in helping to make those decisions.

"Jordan, take a look at this," I said as he walked over to the table.

"What's this?" he said, setting down his plate of food.

"We called it a printing press, or rather it's my attempt at remembering what a printing press would look like. I've been working on this for a while now. Basically the idea is to use these carvings, here, to press ink into the paper, thus copying an entire page from a book at once. The way the letters are set up, here and here, allow quick and easy transitions between different pages, or we could set up numerous boards to quickly swap between. I was thinking of copying the elementary gathering book, since you had mentioned that there were never enough copies and the City Lord would buy them from people who produced them."

"Wow, that's phenomenal. I'll look into getting parts for it. This will change our entire business. Elena, what do you think of this?" He handed her the drawing as she walked into the room.

"Hold on, let me get some of this great-smelling food first. Thank you, Caleb, for cooking breakfast today." She gathered some food and sat down, eating while looking over the drawing. "Interesting. So this will make books very fast? We should be able to build this fairly quickly. I'll talk to the Nopteps about getting materials or borrowing some silver to get this started. We simply don't have the money right now to invest."

Turning to me she said, "Thank you for this. If it works out, we'll be able to get back to a more solvent position." We had recovered some during the last few months but were still deeply in debt.

"I just want to pay you both back for taking me in," I replied sheepishly. We finished the meal quietly, each thinking about the day ahead. I was getting antsy, nervous, and excited at the same time. This would be a defining moment in my life here.

"So are you ready?" Jordan asked.

"I think so. I'm not sure what I want, to be highly talented or normal. I'm worried that I'll end up bringing trouble here."

"Either you will be normal, in which case life will continue here and you can help us with this printing press, or you will be highly talented and bring fortune to us, not misfortune. Life for the talented is usually better than for those of us who are normal. Now go get dressed in your fine red tunic, we have to look our best for today," Elena commanded.

I put away the dishes and went to get dressed. My outfit for today was a red tunic with green trim, accented by a pair of loose green pants. The cloth it was made of was finely woven, but not very precious. The clothing showed we were fairly prosperous but not excessively rich. It was left over from before my sickness. After dressing and taming the unruly mop of black hair on my head, I went down into the store. Elena was waiting for me, wearing nearly the same outfit, just adding a silver necklace shaped like a snowflake. "You look lovely, Ma," I said. She thanked me and we headed out of the building and turned to the North, where the keep of the City Lord and the grounds of the Azyl Academy were. After about a half hour of walking, we encountered the crowd of people all moving towards the Academy. Each group of people included at least one youngster who was headed to take the Academy's test.

"The test requires you to be between fourteen and sixteen years of age and have opened one meridian. The test evaluates your affinity with each element and the number of meridians you have easily openable versus those that can be opened with alchemy. As an example, I was rated as moderate affinity with Metal and low with all others, and a talent level of three of six. Moderate affinity is normal, and a talent level from one of two to four of seven is normal as well. A high or exceptional affinity is rare, especially in more than one element, and anything over seven/eleven is very rare outside of the nobles." Elena was explaining the test to me again, which I took as a sign of nervousness.

Just then a loud voice thundered over the crowd, "All test takers move forward into the square. Family members may line the edges but make space for all the testers. We will begin in five minutes!"

I looked over at Elena and gave her a quick hug. "See you after."

"I'll be watching."

I pushed forward, and the crowd began to thin out. When I reached the square, I saw about five hundred other youths here to take the test. The square was packed full of people, almost all of them as nervous as I was. The majority of people taking the test would be normal, with a normal life ahead of them. The benefit to the test to them was knowing their elemental affinities. By opening a couple more meridians, they would eventually reach the peak of Aether Gathering and be healthier and stronger than they would otherwise. For those with high talents, though, this would be the start of their journey to stardom. Hopefully.

Off to the right, I saw Jon along with two guys and a girl. The others of his group were dressed in rougher clothes, and I guessed they were probably children of the laborers Jon's family employed. Across the square I spotted a group of three boys and three girls dressed in silk and decorated with jewels. Each pair of people was standing just slightly apart from each other. One of the boys was the asshole from the market, Nicolai, and probably a sister or cousin was standing beside him in quiet conversation. She was a tall, beautiful, red-haired young woman, but the look of disdain on her face made her unapproachable. Two young men were standing off to the Haodhas' left, both broad-shouldered, black-haired, and Asian looking. Off to the extreme right were two young women in brown and green dresses, tall, fair-haired and pale-skinned. The group of nobles stood front and center in the crowd, with a space around them as if other people were afraid of intruding on their spot.

As I walked over to speak to Jon, the gates on the other side of the square opened and five adults marched out, carrying various equipment. Two were carrying statues that were vaguely human shaped with a large square base, one was carrying a large clear sphere, one a large stack of papers and writing instruments, and the last a large table. *Holy crap, that table must weigh several hundred pounds. It's made of stone!* I thought to myself. The person holding it acted like it weighed nothing.

The table was set down in the middle of the square, with the papers deposited on it. The statues were placed to the left of the table and the sphere to the right. I noticed that one of the statues was vaguely male and the other just as vaguely female. The statues were pale green, and slightly translucent. Behind the adults hauling equipment, a group of older teens ran out holding chairs, and the adults took a seat to preside over the test.

The man who had carried the table spoke out in the same thundering tone as before, "We are ready to begin. You will first come to the table and get a recording paper. You will then go to the Element Testing Sphere and have your affinities tested. From there you will go to the Talent Statue of your gender and have your meridians tested. Finally you will come back to the table to have the results recognized. Directions will be provided from there based upon talent and affinity. Now, who will be first?"

No one immediately stepped up. I wanted to, but I also wanted to wait until after that young noble from the market had left, as I was getting more and more confident that I would have a ridiculous talent level. As time dragged on, you could see the tension in the kids' faces, trying to psych themselves into stepping forward. After a minute, one of the Asian-looking noblemen stepped forward and proclaimed, "I, Lo Xiao, shall be the first, and amaze all with my talent!" As he reached the table, the Haodha children followed him, with many of the others starting to line up.

I stood beside the line near the end, more interested in watching than participating. At least for now. I heard from the front, "Exceptional affinity in Ice, Moderate in Water and Air. Great, go to the Talent Statue. You, girl, come forward. Ah, a Haodha. High in Fire and Lightning and Moderate in Metal. Very good!" As the Lo kid got to the statue, we heard, "Excellent, the Lo clan never disappoints. Let's see, nine openable, up to twenty-one with alchemy. Excellent! Amazing! Go report to the center! You will of course be offered a place here! Next! Ah, Miss Haodha, let's see. Nine! Nine openable, twenty-three possible! Amazing, this year is already a superb catch!"

I finally got in line, at Jon's urging, near the end of it. The annoying noble child was announced as Exceptional in Fire and High in Metal with eight openable up to eighteen. He had the highest overall affinities until, "Exceptional in Wood and Water, High in Earth, Moderate in Ice. Astounding! Come, hurry, you will skip to the front here. Yes, touch the statue in the hand prints. Thirteen openable, up to twenty-six! I… I am beyond words. Come, I shall take you in to meet the Vice Dean for new students immediately." A fourteen-year-old girl with a shocked look on her face was pulled along by a thirty-something-old man.

My breath caught upon seeing her. "Jasmine?" I whispered. She was nearly the spitting image of Jasmine, my former fiancée. Lightly tanned, with dark brown hair and a heart-shaped face, she was the quintessential girl next door, though her skin was rougher than Jasmine's had been.

"No, I heard her name as Jamila. Are you okay?" Jon said to me, concern on his face. I waved away his question.

Notable results were the other two noble girls, who were from the Volkov family and had Exceptional Wood and High Earth. The older was an eight/seventeen, i.e. eight openable with a potential of seventeen with alchemy, and the younger a nine/nineteen. The other Lo clan member was High in Ice, Air and Water, and eleven/twenty-three, causing another commotion. Finally, Jon was up ahead of me. As he walked over to the

Affinity Sphere, I approached the table for affinity testing. "Name and clan."

"Uh, Kupiec Aiden, no clan," I responded, watching Jon.

"High in Air, Moderate in Ice. Good!" I heard the moderator tell Jon. I grabbed the sheet from the monitor with a "Thank you" before heading over to the Affinity Sphere.

"Place your hands here and here." The moderator gestured. With a deep breath, I put my hands on the sphere. Slowly, lights formed in the center. A bright yellow grew until almost the entire sphere shined brightly enough to make me squint, then vanished. Red filled up most of the sphere, followed by light blue and silver, followed by brown taking up half the sphere. Tiny flashes of green, dark blue and purple occurred, and then the sphere blanked. I looked up at the moderator and saw a face full of shock.

"Outstanding in Lightning, Exceptional in Air, Fire, and Metal. High in Earth. I ... I ... I've never seen or heard of the like. Place your hands on it again, I have to confirm this." I did so, and it repeated the sequence. I heard "Six, with eighteen possible, good!" from where Jon was getting his testing. "Go, uh, go get your talent tested." The moderator gestured to the next kid, who was staring at me with unabashed awe. I flushed at his look.

Jon had turned around when he was finished, and saw the expression on the moderator's face. I gestured at him to move on and mouthed "I'll tell you later," to him. I was excited for him since High affinity in Air was great. "Put your hands on the handprints," the moderator watching the statues said with a gesture. As it had been nearly two hours since the start, he seemed to be lagging in enthusiasm. I put my hands where indicated, and lights started glowing in the statue, tracing out my meridians. Blue lights flared up the life meridian, and then around my eyes, ears, nose, and mouth. More lights went down every limb, with several flowing circles through my torso. The disciple's eyes continued to get wider every second while he stared at the statue. After a minute, the light turned green and traced down every finger, through my torso, upper legs, and head.

"Sixteen. Sixteen openable, up to ... uh, remove your hands, wait for it to clear, and then put them back." I did, and after the sequence repeated he said, "Thirty-five with alchemical assistance. Thirty-five. There are five meridians you have the ability to open that I've never even heard of, much less seen. Remove your hands." I pulled my hands off and he put his on. Lights flared, almost entirely blue. "Ok, it's still working. Come." He gestured emphatically at me, wanting me to follow him to the center table. As we walked, he waved at the gates with a couple of signals.

We got to the table, and the disciple stepped in front of the next person in line. "Mentor Alain, call Headmaster Glav, she's going to want to come down personally for this."

"What do you mean?"

"This"—he pulled my card out of my hand to find my name— "Aiden, has sixteen openable meridians, with up to thirty-five openable. He is Outstanding in Lightning, Exceptional in Air, Fire, and Metal. Holy Light! He's Exceptional or better in FOUR ELEMENTS! Along with more open meridians than I'VE EVER SEEN, and openable beyond what we thought was POSSIBLE. Use the stone to signal the Headmaster. I'll take the punishment if she decides it is necessary." After the moderator's outburst, everyone around was looking at me. Thankfully, the jerk-face noble was gone, but the Volkov girls and Lo boys were still there. The boys were looking at me as a rival, someone who would be able to compete with them, as was the older Volkov. The younger looked at me with interest and curiosity. *That is someone who might be a friend,* I thought as I watched them. Most of the other people around were looking at me with awe, including Jon. I couldn't help but be bashful. Over at the edge, I saw Ma watching me with wonder in her eyes, happiness exuding from her. *Well, hopefully I can turn this into something that will help them too.*

As I looked back at the moderator, the gates to the school opened again. Out of the gates walked three armed and armored people, covered head to toe in plate mail, surrounding a dignified older woman. As she walked up to us, the disciples running the test bowed. "Why did you call me out?" she asked in a grave tone.

"This candidate is worthy of your personal attention, Headmaster Glav," the moderator from the table said, offering her my filled-in card. "He's Exceptional or better in Air through Metal, and High in Earth. I've never heard of a five-elemental affinity before. He has up to thirty-five openable with alchemy as we know it. He is probably the greatest potential candidate anywhere in the Kingdom has seen in many centuries."

"Hmm, amazing!" Her face immediately brightened. "Your potential is astounding. Come, I shall show you the school. You will of course be provided all you need to study here!" She grabbed my arm and started dragging me towards the gate. I looked over at Jon and Ma, who were now standing together with Jon's parents, and shrugged helplessly at them. I followed the Headmaster through the gates.

CHAPTER SIX

I entered the grounds of the Azyl Academy behind Headmaster Glav. In front of me, a nicely paved road led to a square with an ornate fountain in the center. Surrounding the square were nine buildings, four to my left, four to the right and one straight ahead. The buildings to either side were six stories tall, while the structure straight on was only two levels. The buildings looked almost like apartment buildings, though the sides had occasional carvings and decoration on them. Beyond the building to my left was a park, with trees and flowering bushes growing around a series of paths and the occasional small pavilion. The sporadic flicker of a bird or other animal was visible, especially near where some of the plants glowed.

As we walked, she remarked, "Your natural talent is astounding and more than meets the criteria for us to admit you to the Academy without any tuition. I strongly encourage you to accept this. Nowhere else in the city will be able to support or assist you in growing your strength as we can. I saw you had no clan listed, are you affiliated with any clan?"

"Uh, no ma'am. My parents own the Kupiec Scribing Store. We occasionally have some nobles shop there, but not often. We mostly sell to other merchants."

"Good to know. I recommend for most unaffiliated students to stay that way through at least the first year. Give yourself time to grow in knowledge and power before binding your fate to another's. Now, for a tour." She pointed off to the buildings. "The buildings to either side of the road are the student dormitories. Straight ahead is the food pavilion. We require all students studying here to live on campus. The first tier dorms are to the left, which is where you will be living. To the right are the fourth tier dorms, where the oldest students live. Beyond is the Meditation Grotto. You are free to use it anytime you have no other obligations. There are inscriptions on many of the pavilions to increase the density of Aether and purify it. The pavilions are available to the person, or people, who arrives first, though first and second tiers must defer to third tiers or higher after half an hour.

"Beyond the Meditation Grotto is the Physical Training Field. Physical Training is held daily in the afternoon and is a mandatory course for all students in your tier. Your body is just as important to gathering Aether as your talent is. A healthy body keeps your center and meridians healthy as well. Down the road that splits the Grotto from the fields, you will find the classrooms, the smithy, the alchemy workshop, the inscription workshop, and the armory.

"You are allowed into the classrooms at any time, but not in any of the elective workshops without supervision or permission. You will be learning the history of our nation and world, military tactics, gathering techniques, politics and etiquette, and an elective. At the end of every year, you are given a test to see if you can ascend to the next tier. It is very rare to move from one tier to another after only a year, though. Ascending to the second tier requires you to pass a test on history, geography, and politics. You also must reach the high Fog level for gathering and pass the tactics exam." *I'll need to work hard on the tests,* I thought as she explained, *since I'm starting with such a disadvantage.*

"Graduates from here are often picked up for the officer corps and government positions, along with joining many of the top clans. I expect that the rumors of your talent have already reached the heads of the clans and they will be discussing how to woo you to join them."

As Headmaster Glav finished speaking, we reached the fountain. "What electives do we have to pick from, ma'am?" I asked politely, showing that I was paying attention.

"You will take a single introductory lesson of Alchemy, Blacksmithing, and Inscription. If you had Wood or Water affinity you would be able to take Healing instead of Blacksmithing, as they are the only gatherers who can heal others. After the introductory lessons, you will be able to choose which to stay with."

"Thank you," I said. I saw a stream of people entering into the food pavilion.

"If you head in you will meet Counselor Might, who will be the head of the first tiers this year. He will have someone assign you a room and your starter gear. From there, you will receive a pass to get back in tomorrow. You will have tonight to say goodbye to your family, and will be able to visit them once a month for the first year. Passes out are available more often for higher tiers and senior first tiers may occasionally receive permission to stay off campus some nights. I wish you luck in your journey here, and may you astonish us again with your success." With that, the Headmaster gestured to the door of the pavilion and then turned to walk off.

"Thank you, ma'am, for your introduction and help," I called after her before entering the food building. Multiple rows of tables were on either side of a couple walkways between them, and across from the entrance was an enormous counter with platters of food on it. *Wow, this place is huge compared to the other buildings I have seen on this world!* I thought. The dining hall could have easily held five hundred people. A line of young, hopeful students led to the counter. I recognized a couple of them as others with high talent, such as the nobles and the beautiful girl who looked like Jasmine. I started walking to get in line when someone tapped on my shoulder. Looking back, I exclaimed, "Jon, you got in too?"

"Yup, they always offer admission with discounts to anyone with over ten openable meridians. My parents said we will be able to afford the tuition, but to hurry and get to the next tier, as tuition halves again at that point. Still expensive, but worth it. From here we will have great options and connections. Just my attending will get my parents more business. Of course, I doubt they'll charge you tuition at all, Mr. More Openable Meridians Than Should Be Possible." Of course, he said that just as we reached the line for food, causing everyone standing in front of me to turn towards me.

"Uh, um …hi. I'm Kupiec Aiden. I guess we will be classmates," I said, my skin turning red from the attention. *Why am I flushing so much? I was fairly used to standing in front of large groups. Is this some of Aiden coming through? Or is it that I spent so much time basically alone the past six months?* I thought while the two girls in front of me looked me up and down.

"I am Volkov Bet, and this is my younger cousin Volkov Vaya. Put your talent to use and I will speak for you to my father, Volkov Neyka. There is always room for talent in the Volkov clan." With that she turned away, waiting imperiously. The younger Volkov gave me a chagrined look, leaned forward, and whispered, "She's always like that. As the heir, she takes her position very seriously. Don't take it personally. I hope to see you around more." She turned back to Bet and they grabbed plates. We were just about at the front of the line. They filled a plate with food and headed over to a table with the Haodha children. I avoided looking at the table, in case Nicky recognized me.

I picked up a plate and looked at the food. A meat I didn't recognize covered in a red sauce, a helping of vegetables, and a roll completed my meal. I looked around, and Lo Ming waved at me. I walked over; Jon followed behind me, and sat down. "Greetings, I am Lo Ming, heir to the Lo clan, and I'm sure you know my younger brother's name, Lo Xiao, after his entrance today. I heard you say you were Kupiec Aiden. You are…?" He turned to Jon.

"Noptep Jonathan, though I prefer Jon. Um, I have a High Air affinity, six/eighteen talent." *Why is he introducing himself that way?* I thought, but I didn't ask so I didn't embarrass him.

"Welcome, Jon. It seems this is the year for high talents. Dig in; this is Beast meat from an Elemental Boar. Have you had anything like this before?" We shook our heads and started to eat. The meat was amazing, easily the best thing I'd ever eaten. As I ate it, I could feel minuscule amounts of Aether flow through my stomach into my veins. *Holy moly!*

"Whoa, this meat is increasing my Aether. I didn't know that was possible!" I exclaimed.

At the weird look this gained me from Ming, Jon explained, "Aiden got really sick near the beginning of the year, such that he nearly died and as a consequence lost all his memories. He's been learning everything since he woke up a couple of months ago."

"I'm sorry to hear that. You have done remarkably well for yourself if you've only been gathering for a few months. I can sense you are nearing the low Haze level, which is very good. Though you should hold off on breaking through until you have had a few classes here. I've been told that the first few lessons are to correct mistakes and improve the quality of Aether absorbed by us before we get too high up the levels. If you don't have better than a tier one rune, that is."

"Thank you for the advice. I guess I'll hold off. If I may ask, what level are you at?"

"I am in the Haze level myself, hence why I can sense your level. You'll begin to develop the ability to sense others' Aether level starting at the Haze level or earlier if you have a meridian easily openable that passes through your eyes. While they teach us nobles many things in our households that you will not learn, we don't have much more time to absorb or grow before our testing. Most clans in the city like to send their heirs and seconds here, to gather contacts and grow the clans' knowledge because the Academy tends to accumulate more gathering methods, Channeling skills, and other bits of knowledge than the clans' do. Also, a word of advice to both of you, don't tie yourselves too closely to any one clan, not until you get stronger. At the present moment, any agreement you made would be detrimental to your future growth."

"Why would you advise us that? Don't you want us to ally with your clan, and gain them power?" I asked.

"I do, and that is why I am giving you advice that is best for you. When you grow strong, you will remember that I helped you out here, and feel more favorable towards me. If I tried to bribe you or strong-arm you, eventually you would figure it out. When that happened, you would fight back and leave. I'd rather start our relationship off on the right track, don't you think?"

"Thank you. That makes a lot of sense. So I should try and make friends with as many of the clans, large and small, as I can. Though I doubt I'll be able to make friends with the Haodhas, unless I can go around Nicky."

"Nicky? Ah, Nicolai. He will throw a fit if he hears you calling him Nicky. Why would you have to go around him?" Xiao asked, speaking up for the first time. I realized that he had been glaring at me, though for the life of me I had no idea why.

"I ran into Nicky," I said, emphasizing Nicky, "a couple of days ago and told him off to his face. That ass… jerk was whipping a serving girl because she accidentally bumped into him. I put a stop to it, took his whip away, and called him a coward in the center of the market square. I doubt he'll let that slide forever." I finished with a shake of my head.

"Shame though, his sister seemed to not care for him too much. Maybe the rest of the family is better."

"Ah, so you were that person. He's been raving about that for the last two days. Especially as you stole his favorite whip. That weapon is Inscribed; you could probably sell it for one or two gold if you didn't want to keep it. Though the way he tells it, he was defending himself from a thief when you barged in and stole his toy." Ming laughed as he finished that thought. "I've heard his cousin – not sister – is almost as bad as he is, though harder to set off. If you can get on her good side, she might stand aside and not assist her cousin against you. It's not likely, so I'd be wary of them both." As he stopped talking, an older man walked into the dining area.

CHAPTER SEVEN

"Welcome, all of you who are joining us today. You are the future of our city and Kingdom, and will be the shield against the Elemental Beast hordes, Toprak raiders, or Illyrian slavers. You all have great potential, and we will drag it out of you, fighting and yelling if we have to. I am Counselor Might, and it is my job to whip you into shape and teach you the basics of fighting." He then spent about fifteen minutes covering the procedures for the following week and a basic set of rules. An older student came running in as he was doing so and signaled to him.

"There are more rules in the packets, make sure to go over them. The introductory stations have been set up outside, and you need to get up and head out to the square. Go to the First Station and follow instructions from there. I look forward to teaching you all and seeing what you will achieve." With that, he turned around in an about-face maneuver and walked off. Most everyone else had finished eating, so Jon and I scrambled to stuff our faces while Ming and Xiao bid us farewell and headed out the door.

After quickly finishing, we both got up and brought our plates back to the counter. The chef behind looked at me, saying, "You didn't need to bring these back; we've got a cleaning crew that comes through."

"It's ok," I replied, handing over the dish, "I grew up without anyone cleaning up after me, and I doubt I'll break the habit anytime soon. Have a great day." A look of surprise colored his face, and only after I had started walking away did I hear "You too" in response. Walking through the door, we saw a number of small tables set up, with piles of various items on them.

I was about to ask Jon if he knew where to start when I saw a big sign saying First Station, with a large number one circled next to it. "I guess we go there," Jon said, pointing to that station. We headed over. An older student, maybe a third or fourth tier, was there handing out bags. He was wearing a tunic with blue piping around the edges, and I saw another person with red piping at a different table. *Huh, must be tier markings?* I thought.

When there were four of us, Jon, myself and two people I didn't recognize, he explained, "Inside is a pamphlet of the rules of the Academy. If you can't read, speak to Counselor Might over there." He pointed. "Otherwise, go to the tables for each of your affinities and get a memory stone for the highest level you qualify for, then head to the uniforms table to be measured. Finally, go to the lodging table, where you will be given your room number and key. Your rooms will have some basic materials and information about your class schedule in it. Now, here, and good luck," he said, pushing four bags to the edge of the table.

"Memory stones?" I asked Jon, picking up the bag and glancing inside. Just a normal bag. I'd been hoping for a Bag of Holding or other dimensional bag of some kind. *Guess they are even rarer than I thought.* Jon shrugged at me.

"A memory stone is a crystal that holds the memories of a Core Seed level gatherer or higher. Only someone at that level can make the stones and store their memories. Everyone at the fourth tier or higher here is at least that level, and most of the Counselors have reached Complete Core. It's rumored that Headmaster Glav is beyond even Perfect Core, though I have no idea what's beyond," the student manning the first table explained.

Jon looked over at me and said, "It'll be fun to explore what is beyond that, don't you think?" He and I laughed, excited by the thought. *Hah, I did infect him with the grow-stronger bug!*

We both headed over to the Air table, where they had a spread of stones laid out, with placards behind them numbered one to six. Jon asked, "How do we know which we are qualified for?"

The student looked up from his book and asked back, "What was your affinity?"

"High," Jon replied.

"Then you qualify for a five."

"What about an Exceptional affinity? Also, who would get a level one or two?" I asked.

"Exceptional can get up to a seven, but we only have a six. Ones and twos are for people with low affinity who want to try and raise their affinity for some reason. They are mostly for Ice or Lightning Moderates or Highs who want to branch out. I don't recommend it to start with, unless you only have one affinity. Then getting a second might be helpful."

"Ok, thanks!" I said while I grabbed the six stone. It was the last level six stone left; I guess they weren't expecting many people above High affinity. At this point, Jon and I split up, quickly agreeing to meet after the lodging table. I headed over to the Lightning table and saw the same setup. They also had a single seven laid out, though that one had a small metal cage around it. "Can I have the seven?" I asked.

"What's your name?"

"Kupiec Aiden. I'm the Outstanding affinity in Lightning."

"Then yes, it was reserved for you by Headmaster Glav. Be careful with that, it is probably worth more than your family would make in your lifetime. Enjoy!" he said, before shooing me off. The Fire and Metal tables were similar to the Air table, where I grabbed a six, before grabbing a five from Earth. I was the only person to get more than three that I saw. I dumped all the stones in my bag, hoping that I could talk to someone about how to use them before I went home.

"Next stop, fitting. Why do I feel like I'm back in Basic? All we're missing is the older students yelling at us to move faster," I muttered to myself, getting into line for fitting. This station was being run by an older woman, with two men working under her doing the measurements. In front of me was the young girl who had four affinities. I was about to say hi when my face flushed and I suddenly felt very shy. *Great, puberty again, why!* I grumbled to myself. Taking hold of my hormones, I said, "Hi, I'm Kupiec Aiden. What is your name?"

She shyly turned around. "I'm Naanva Jamila." Once again, her beauty took my breath away. *Stupid hormones.* She had lightly tan skin, lustrous dark brown hair, and dazzling green eyes. She was just shorter than my six-foot height. *Wait, am I still six feet tall? I never tried to measure myself.*

"How are you taking this? Suddenly finding out you have extreme talent?" I asked, trying to start a conversation. More friends, especially among the talented, would always be good. *I am much too young in this body to be thinking of romance. Stupid hormones. Even if people in older cultures would get married around my age.*

"It is … overwhelming in some ways. I have already been shown around by the Vice Headmaster, with promises of help to get used to this. What about yourself? Are you another high talent from the non-nobles?"

"Yeah," I said, blushing again, "I'm really high too. I'm not sure what to think, though the appearance of a large number of high talents is surprising." Looking around, there were probably forty or so other non-noble high talents, making the total first tier population fifty or sixty. "Looks like you're up. I look forward to seeing you tomorrow."

"Me too," she said as she turned to the station. The other measurer opened up then as well, so I stepped forward.

"Arms up, please," he said, measuring my height from shoulder down, my neck size, my arm length, and leg length. Nothing too accurate, so I assumed the clothes would be the loose, flowing tunic and pants the older students were wearing. Something easy to move around in. After fitting, I headed over to get my room assignment.

"Kupiec Aiden," I replied to the request for a name. He looked down through a list, tracing my name when he found it, and dug through the key pile. He pulled out a key and handed it to me.

"You are in room 410, first building, enter there"—he pointed to the main door— "go up the front set of stairs in the center to the fourth floor, and head right at the hallway at the top. You'll be the last room on the left. Congrats, corner rooms are always sought after. The washing room is at the end of the hallway across from your room. Do not go left at the top of the stairs. The rooms to the left are for the young women. You will not like what happens if you try to go through that door."

"Thank you," I replied, taking the key and heading over to where I saw Jon standing. He was talking with another young man, who towered over my diminutive, in perspective at least, friend. "Hey, Jon. Hi, I'm Kupiec Aiden," I said to them.

"Travail Louis, nice to meet you," rumbled the giant.

"You as well. I'm in room 410, how about you all?" Louis was in room 206 and Jon in 304. Apparently all the guys' rooms were even numbers.

"Let's head on up," Jon said. We walked in, seeing a lounge area filling the center of the first floor, with two sets of stairs going just to the left of the center, one set a third of the way through the building, another two-thirds. Straight ahead was a door out of the building, and to either side was a door marked either Men or Women, along with a picture of a man and woman respectively. We headed up the stairs, with Jon and Louis peeling off on their floors. The fourth-floor lounge was really nice, with a variety of small couches and chairs laid around. I went through the male door, finding myself in a long hallway, with three doors to either side and one at the end. The hallway was wide enough for three people to walk side by side and was covered in a richly patterned rug.

I opened the door to my room after unlocking it. Inside was a bed, a desk with a chair, a dresser, and a stand next to the bed. "This is more spacious than my dorm at USAFA was," I mused. The bed was straight in front of the door, with the desk to the right of it, pressed against the far wall. Directly in front of the desk was a window that looked out over the Meditation Grotto, and a window on the rightmost wall looked out over the pathway between dorms and the Physical Training Fields. I walked over to the desk, pulling the chair out and sitting down.

"I wish I could say I was surprised by today," I mused to myself. *Unfortunately, I know something is coming. Some catastrophe or invasion or world-ending event is going to happen. I don't know why Darkness grabbed me to play a part when he could have used natives to this world. I'll just have to do my best.* After wallowing in my worrisome thoughts for a couple of minutes, I picked up the piece of paper on the desk.

Tomorrow was the first day of the week. Weeks here were eight days long, with each day corresponding to an element. The week started with Earth Day, and on Earth Day all the new students would have Gathering Techniques, followed by meditation time, to be used to implement the gathering techniques you learned. After lunch was history and politics, followed by Physical Training. Dinner was followed by more meditation time. *Looks like we are supposed to gather twice a day for a couple hours each time.* Just about every day we had Gathering or Channeling Techniques in the morning and PT in the afternoon, with the class after lunch being the only difference.

EARTH	WOOD	WATER	ICE
Breakfast	Breakfast	Breakfast	Breakfast
Gathering Class	Gathering Class	Gathering Class	Gathering Class
Meditation	Meditation	Meditation	Meditation
Lunch	Lunch	Lunch	Lunch
History	Beasts	Herbology	Alchemy
PT	PT	PT	PT
Dinner	Dinner	Dinner	Dinner
Meditation	Meditation	Meditation	Meditation

AIR	LIGHTNING	FIRE	METAL
Breakfast	Breakfast	Breakfast	Breakfast
Gathering Class	Gathering Class	Gathering Class	Gathering Class
Meditation	Meditation	Meditation	Meditation
Lunch	Lunch	Lunch	Lunch
Black-smithing	Inscription	Geography	Tactics
PT	PT	PT	PT
Dinner	Dinner	Dinner	Dinner
Meditation	Meditation	Meditation	Meditation

The first week included History, Beasts Knowledge, Herbology, Introduction to Alchemy, Introduction to Blacksmithing, Introduction to Enchanting, Geography, and Tactics. There was a note at the bottom that said, 'After the first week, you will be able to pick a secondary profession to focus on. This will replace the other two on Lightning, Air, and Ice Days. All other midday classes are mandatory for all first tiers.'

Ok, so everyone will get an introductory lesson in enchanting, alchemy, and blacksmithing to figure out which one they want to pursue. Also, everyone will get a basic introduction to this world and important things to look out for. I wonder what second tier students study. I looked out the window and noticed it was starting to get late. *I should head back home to say goodbye to Elena and Jordan.* I found a locking drawer in the desk and placed the memory stones there.

With that, I left the Academy to head back home. *Hmm, this really did come to feel like home. I'll miss it more than I missed the group home or uncaring foster families.* I opened the door to the store and walked in. Inside was a much larger amount of people then would normally be there. I saw Ma assisting a couple that looked suspiciously like the younger Volkov daughter from this morning. Pa was checking people out at the counter. As I walked up, I could hear the discussions between Pa and the customers, and almost all of them ended up mentioning me at some point.

If they realize I'm in the store, they'll make a scene. Word travels fast and I guess I'm famous now. I pretended to be shopping while moving around to the stairs, and then quickly bolted up them when no one was looking. I stood at the top of the stairs, listening to see if a commotion started. When nothing seemed to happen, I relaxed and headed to my room.

I spent the next fifteen minutes or so organizing my room, cleaning everything I could and packing what I felt I needed. Mostly clothes. A keepsake statue of a dog Jon had given me to thank me for helping him with starting to gather Aether. A set of writing instruments and a small notebook. The whip I took from Icky Nicky. *Hee hee, I bet he'll flip if I call him that.* Everything else I put away and tidied up, leaving the room as close to spotless as I could make it.

After that, I went over to the kitchen area and started cooking some vegetable stir-fry. From the cold box I pulled some chicken – or meat from an animal that was a great deal like a chicken, but also not exactly. Still a poultry bird with little brainpower and little flight power. Still tasted like chicken. *If everything tastes like chicken, maybe this is the Matrix? Nah, I doubt the machines would make up this world.* The store closed just as I was setting the table.

"Good evening, Aiden," Jordan said as he entered the room. "That smells good. Thank you for cooking. Elena wanted to wait for you, but I was unable to deal with the flood of customers we got this afternoon. Most of them wanted to buy the most expensive things I sold, just to get on our good side. Of course, they all wanted to meet you, or introduce you to their daughters, or offer to pay for your education. You apparently made quite a stir?" he finished with a question.

"Yeah, I uh, registered as having thirty-five possible meridian openings, which was more than the examiner had ever heard of. I doubt it's something that has never happened before, but probably not here. And my affinity to five elements, with four Excellent or Outstanding, surprised them as well. I've been offered a full-ride scholarship to the Academy. Hopefully I can use this to pay y'all back for your kindness." Jordan's face registered the same shock and happiness Elena's had at the square when I told him my talent level and affinities.

"Full ride?" Elena asked as she entered, having locked the store up.

"Oh, um, it means that everything is paid for. You don't have to pay anything. They expect big things from me, and want to bribe me at this level. I also spoke to the Lo heirs, who advised me to befriend everyone but favor no one, until I have the power to back myself up." *I'm still using sayings from Earth! I need to stop.*

"That is good advice, and what I would say as well," Jordan interjected. "Also, feel free to come to us if you need anything. Just you being announced as having massive talent has driven numerous opportunities to our door. Your printing press idea will also allow us to produce more books faster, so maybe we'll see more gathering techniques or other information that is hard to spread become more widely known. That is praiseworthy in and of itself. Do your best, and I'm sure everything will fall into place."

"Thanks. I hope I can live up to your trust. There was a girl, Naanva Jamila, who also had very high talent. Jon did as well. All the nobles, of course, and a significant number of others, nearly sixty all told. Is this normal?"

"I don't think so. The last couple of years have only been the standard dozen or so high potentials outside the nobles. Why do you ask?" Elena responded.

"That worries me. Why would the year I show up be the year that there is a much larger amount of talents brought in? Combine that with the words of Darkness and I think something bad is coming. I feel like it won't be soon, but probably in a couple of years some major disaster is going to happen. The little I remember from my discussion with Darkness leads me think we have some time, but not a lot of it. Assuming that is true, we can start planning now, and hopefully build up enough capability to stop whatever it is." With this proclamation, Jordan and Elena frowned and looked at each other.

We fell into eating, and I described the campus and my assigned room. Especially the view out the window above my desk. Finally, we finished eating and I let them know I planned on going back tonight. "Ok," Elena responded, "but we're walking you to the gate." The walk was silent, each of us lost in our thoughts. As we approached the gate, Elena grabbed my arm and pulled me into a hug. "You come back and visit us," she whispered.

"I will. As soon as I can. They said we'd be allowed to leave once every month for the first year. So this is just see you in a month, not goodbye forever," I said. Jordan also pulled me into a hug, then said goodbye. Walking up to the gate, I showed the guard the key I had gotten ealier, and he opened it enough for me to get through.

Jogging up to the dorm, I ran to my room. I saw and heard no one, so either everyone was in their room already or was planning to come back in the morning. Setting the bag of clothing and items on the dresser, I unpacked and organized the room. After finishing that, I read through the rules packet, which was fairly straightforward. Basically, don't steal, listen to the Counselors, and don't kill anyone. Fighting outside of sanctioned duels was not allowed, but you could challenge anyone in the same level as you. If you wanted you could challenge those at a higher level as well. All sorts of minor details about timing and allowable challenges filled a page of the book, of which the key point was that challenges would not start until after the first month. Finishing reading, I got ready to sleep. I left the windows open to enjoy the fresh air. I did not gather, following Ming's advice to hold off until after the first day of classes. As I lay down, I saw a beautiful bird flying by the window, looking as if it was on fire. My last thought as I fell asleep was wonder at this new world.

CHAPTER EIGHT

The sound of a gong woke me up on the first day of my new school. Getting up, I dressed in a loose green tunic and pants since we had not received our uniforms yet. I left my room and went to the restroom, surprised yet again as they looked just like you'd expect back on Earth, though without urinals. Five stalls had stone toilets in them, with a glyph labeled "Flush" on the wall. *Oh, that's different*, I thought as I saw the glyph. *Inscriptions!* Past the stalls was a door that led into a shower, though instead of spraying it just poured out of a couple holes when activated. Three people could shower simultaneously if they didn't care about privacy. Finished with my business, I washed my hands with a bar of soap I brought. *I just realized. I don't know if this world knows about bacteria. Can bacteria gather Aether? Animals can, so maybe? I hope not though, as that means superbugs. Maybe that is what killed Aiden? But then why didn't it spread? Or did it? So many questions still about his sickness.*

"Breakfast time!" I headed down the stairs, wondering if I would see anyone I recognized. No one joined me on the stairs, but a couple of people I hadn't met yesterday were sitting in the lounge area on the bottom floor. I waved and said hi as I headed out the door. Entering the food hall, I saw a number of older students eating breakfast, but no one I recognized. I walked over to the counter and received a bowl of what looked like oatmeal with berries and cinnamon on it. I sat at an empty table where I could see the door, hoping to see a friend walk in. The upperclassmen ignored me as was their prerogative. Just as I was finishing my food, Jon walked in with Louis. I waved them over after they grabbed food. "Ready for our first day?" I asked as they sat.

Louis nodded while Jon said, "Yeah, can't wait to find out new, strong gathering techniques. It'll be interesting to see how different they are from what was in the introductory book."

"Yup. I also hope they tell us how to use these memory stones"— I shook the bag—"as I have no idea." We chatted for a bit longer, mostly about the rooms we received, while they finished breakfast. Once they were done, we again brought our bowls back to the counter and headed to the classrooms. On the walk over, we admired the Meditation Grotto and saw older students running down in the Physical Training Fields.

"Well, we'll be down there later today," Jon commented sulkily, pointing at the running students.

"Yeah, I know how much you like running, Jon, though you were pretty good at running away from people after your pranks." Jon gave me a push sideways after that comment.

The classroom building looked very similar to the dorms, though only four floors. The main difference was a carving of the elemental compass that was two stories tall above the door in the center of the building. Walking through the doors, we stopped in our tracks. Rather than a lounge, the area around the stairs was a library with more books than I'd seen since arriving in this world. Even though I had lived at a bookstore, we only had maybe twenty books for sale at any one time. Here, there were maybe a couple hundred books. This wasn't a lot compared to libraries back on Earth, but it was a significant number all the same. Especially in a world where every book was copied by hand. To our right, a stand with a chalkboard on it proclaimed, "First tiers to the auditorium" along with a large number one and an arrow pointing at the door to the right.

The room we walked into was fairly large, probably able to hold four hundred people. The ground sloped down to the bottom of a small stage, with benches off to either side for seating. When we arrived, the first ten rows were full, with maybe eighty other students there already. We hurried to find seats. After we had sat down, a couple more people came through, gathered around Haodha Nicolai. I thought to myself *"The brown-nosing is strong in them!"* in my best puppet voice. I then kept my eyes forward, trying to keep "Nicky" from seeing me. Mostly I didn't want to have him make a scene. A stream of other people I didn't recognize came through, nearly filling up the auditorium, and as the last few were seated Headmaster Glav came out on the stage.

"Welcome one and all to the start of your formal education to become the pillars of the Craesti Kingdom. Here we will train you to be strong, smart, and capable people, to serve in the Army, in government, and in society. You will train to be the shield that protects our people from the Elemental Beasts that roam our borders. You will be challenged and pushed beyond your limits repeatedly, and through this forging will become the greatest versions of yourselves that you can become. Work hard and you will be rewarded. Fail to do so, and you will be pushed and prodded until you do. We do not suffer laziness here, and will refine it out of you if necessary. Your instructors will come in now and gather you up; taking you to the classrooms you will be in for the rest of the year." With that, she waved to the back of the room, smiled at us, and left the stage.

At her signal, ten instructors walked into the room. The first was a middle-aged man who walked with a slight limp. The second was a grizzled older man, with a scar running down the left side of his face. The third was an older woman who looked almost exactly like Professor McGonagall from the Harry Potter movies. Most of the Counselors were middle-aged, often sporting scars, and had serious expressions on their face. The last Counselor was a middle-aged woman with bright gold hair. As they approached the front, a pressure emanating from them became palpable. I felt like I would be pushed away if I didn't push back against it.

When they reached the front, the younger woman stepped out and called, "When I call your name, get up and form a line facing the exit. You will be following me to room 201. Sihirb Akil…" A young man with black hair and dark skin stepped out from the second row. Fourteen others, including the older Volkov and Jamila were included in this group. When Jamila and Bet walked by, I gave them both a big smile. Bet nodded while Jamila smiled back. After finishing calling out fifteen names, the instructor moved to the front of the line and walked out.

The second instructor moved forward and started to call out names. "Haodha Anberlin. Lo Xiao. Noptep Jonathan. Kupiec Aiden." *Ok, at least I don't have Nicky. Hopefully Anberlin isn't too bad. I've got Jon there to have my back, and Xiao wasn't that annoying yesterday.* Jon nudged me to get into line, so I stood up and started to get into position. I nodded to Ming when a shout of "YOU!" interrupted the instructor after the next name. *Well, Nicky's seen me.* "Boy, do not interrupt me, or another instructor, again," my counselor said, staring at Nicky. Nicky started turning red and squirmed in his seat. The instructor was doing something to push him back down. Nicky's face seemed locked in a state between fear and anger. *Whoa, calm down, Nicky, you'll have a heart attack at this rate!* I laughed in my head. I couldn't help the smirk that came out.

Our instructor finished calling the rest of the names, none of which I recognized. The kids who lined up were between fourteen and sixteen, with a mixture of races and ethnicities. Most of them looked upper class, with only Jon, myself, and two others seeming to be from the middle class. Overall there were only a couple people, like Louis, who came from the lower classes that would be able to attend. The competition for the few scholarships available was fierce and had natural talent requirements that most couldn't match anyway. Those few who did make it became a source of great pride to their whole community, though, and would allow a family to be pulled from the lower class to the middle class very quickly.

The instructor led us to the second floor, where we entered room 203, which had fifteen pads on the floor and two older students already in it. "Take a seat. I am Counselor Sila and will be instructing you in gathering techniques, channeling ability and meridian opening and strengthening. I have taught here for twenty-three years now, after retiring from the Army as a Specialist Captain. I will be expecting perfection from you. All of you have amazing talent and affinity and will display it. If you fail, you will try again. These are Mentors Gutierrez and Lo. They will be assisting me in instructing you. This first week we will be working to open all of your easily openable meridians. This will increase the amount of Aether you can gather in, as well as assisting in strengthening your body and mind. Today, we will be opening the meridian in your dominant arm, if you do not have it open or the off arm otherwise. Now, why are we opening this particular meridian first? You, Falconer Bridget, what do you think?"

"Um... because it is easiest?" a short girl with brown hair, pale skin, and a button nose said, not very confidently.

"Well, not quite. Not the main reason though. Almost everyone has these meridians, and the ones for their legs, as openable meridians. The leg meridians are usually the easiest to open, and in commoners who don't get their training from here, they open those first. Here we open the arm meridians to enable combative channeling, though you won't be able to project Aether past your skin until you start compressing your Aether." The Counselor then walked over to the wall and quickly sketched a generic person's outline. He then traced a line leading from the center, through the right side of the heart, the right lung, then down the arm. It looped through the hand covering the knuckles, then back up. Surprisingly it then went down, looping through the right kidney and stomach area before entering the center again.

"This is the right arm meridian, which will strengthen your right arm, shoulder, lung, heart, kidney, and liver, along with other internal organs. As it does connect to your heart, we recommend only opening it under supervision, which is another reason why we are opening this today. Your leg meridian's only danger is paralyzing your diaphragm, which is scary but you can hit it to free it up. Now, young Falconer, come on up to the front. You will be the demonstration for today. I will be guiding you through the process. First, retreat to your center. Come, come hurry up. Now, I am going to inject some Aether into you, follow its movement and do not resist." He placed his hands on the back of her neck, injecting a small amount of Aether into her life meridian. We saw a brief glow, then nothing. "Everyone else, retreat into your center and follow the Aether flowing in your life meridian. Grab a hold of some just as it is nearest your eyes, and pull it forward. This will sting a bit, but set up a small circle of Aether from the meridian to your eyes."

I quickly obeyed directions. Pulling the Aether forward, it tugged slightly, and with a stinging sensation flowed into my eyes. Still concentrating inward, I discovered that the Aether didn't want to go straight back, but wanted to flow out and around, reentering the meridian behind my left ear. I stopped pulling straight out and felt out for a spot at the reverse of that spot near my right ear. I found a section of the meridian wall that felt thinner and *pushed* at it with a handful of Aether motes. It felt like a screen parted, and Aether flowed into a new pathway, moving through my ears, nose, mouth, and eyes. Suddenly the world exploded with new sounds and scents, so much so that I was overwhelmed at first. Opening my eyes, I saw a blaze of light surrounding the Counselor, and little drabs over everyone else. The air seemed to sparkle, as little Aether motes floated in the air.

Looking closely at Bridget, I saw a speck of glowing light blue Aether moving erratically in her core. Counselor Sila asked Bridget, "Are you following the Aether I injected?" To me it now seemed that he was shouting. "It was pure Air, so you should absorb it fine after I stop manipulating it. Now, gather some Aether of your own, and follow my movements." Suddenly, the speck orbited closer to the center of her center, and shot out on a tangent, before hitting a spot above and to the right, where it sank in and then flowed towards her shoulder. Bridget followed this by gathering a large clump of Aether and attempting to hit the same spot. It took her a few tries, but after she was able to hit it, the Aether flowed through the now open meridian.

She gasped as the wave hit her heart, and the Counselor slammed his hand on her back. "A little less Aether next time," he said to her, "and it won't hurt as bad. You only needed a third as much to open it. That goes for everyone," he said, looking over at us. "Use the minimum Aether required to open a meridian, especially one that impacts your heart, lungs or reproductive organs. Now, we will be dividing you up into groups, and the assistants and I will be walking you through the process. You will pick someone to watch each time since you will eventually be called upon to assist others, whether students here or civilians in the city, with opening up these specific meridians. Now begin!"

As he said begin, I kind of fell over. My head was pounding, and my ears were ringing because my increased sensitivity had made it seem like he was shouting the whole time. My nose was completely stopped up and I tasted blood. The worst migraine I'd ever had fell upon me, and I threw up next to the seat. Suddenly, I felt cool air entering into me, and my Aether stopped flowing through the new meridian. The headache started getting better, and I was able to get up off the floor where I had fallen. "What happened?" I asked shakily, still feeling bad but slowly getting better.

One of the assistants handed me a water skin, and I gulped it down. As I did so, the Counselor said, "You opened a meridian that enhanced all of your senses. This overwhelmed you and you collapsed, so I injected some Aether into it and set up a structure that is mostly blocking the opening, so that your enhancement is minor right now. I'll slowly open it up over the next couple weeks so that you get used to it. Everyone's senses will get enhanced as they grow in strength, and I predict you will grow significantly more. I've never encountered this meridian before. Now, are you feeling up to opening another meridian?"

I didn't answer at first, looking inward to try and assess my condition. The Aether he inserted into me had calmed the inflammation down, leaving only a residual headache. "Yes sir, I think I am."

"It is good that you took your time to answer, as if you had said yes immediately I would have sent you out. Now, into your center and follow my Aether," he said, gesturing for me to sit back down. I sat down, and again felt the cool breeze that was pure Air Aether against my skin. I felt something resist it, and consciously relaxed. "Good, that makes this easier. Follow closely." I watched as his Aether swirled around my center, and I followed it closely with a small handful of Aether. As his Aether shot out, I had mine orbit again and then follow, feeling the Aether enter the meridian. A wave of fire seemed to spread down my arm, though my heart dealt with it fine. My knuckles cracked as the Aether flowed through them, followed by my elbow on the way back up. As the Aether hit my kidney, the pain let me know I'd probably pee a bit of blood later, and then it reconnected to my center with a feeling of being more. "Whoa," I said as it connected.

"Good, now watch others. Push a bit more Aether into your senses meridian so you can see the Aether in others. We'll teach you in a month or so how to hide from others' senses, or to at least dampen your presence. Now, onto you, young Noptep." I was still getting my balance but I watched Jon get his meridian opened. The process took about ten minutes each, so we finished just after an hour or so. "Now you've opened your meridians, the Aether already in your system has been redistributed. The number of meridians you have open determines how much Aether is required to advance, at least at first since each must be filled up. However, by having more open, you will gather faster, so it is beneficial to open as many as possible before you advance. Additionally, more open meridians spread the benefits of advancing throughout more of your body, strengthening and purifying it. Take the next two hours to gather Aether and meditate, imprinting the runes given to you on the memory stones if you haven't yet."

"Sir?" A young man with dark olive skin, dark hair, and dark eyes spoke up.

"Yes, Pescador Philippe?" Counselor Sila paused, looking at him.

"Um… how do we use the memory stones? I've never seen one before," Philippe asked hesitantly. His clothes betrayed his status as a commoner, probably from one of the outlying villages. I felt for him, understanding what it was like being the poor guy in a rich school.

"Ah, yes. Simply hold them to your forehead and pull Aether from the life meridian to that point. Your Aether will enter into the stone and pull the information to your mind. It is not instantaneous, but it is significantly faster than reading a book. Take your time, and come seek me out if you need help. I will be here until lunchtime. Go find a place in the Meditation Grotto or return to your rooms, whichever you prefer. Now, you are dismissed."

CHAPTER NINE

After being dismissed, everyone stood and bowed slightly to the Counselor and headed out. Outside the door waited a couple of youths somewhat older than those inside, probably second or third tiers. Some of them greeted my classmates, recognizing them from family gatherings or other activities, and the resemblance was striking in some cases. An older Haodha was obvious, with the bright red hair they were known for. Seeing him, I looked around. I didn't see Nicky, but I was still worried. "Come on, Jon; let's find a good spot that is open in the Grotto. I want to explore it," I urged, eager to get away before running into the arrogant Haodha.

"You go on ahead; I'm going to head back to my room. I left all my stones there this morning."

"Oh, okay. I've got mine. I'll see you at lunch," I said, watching as all the members of the class split up. After heading out the main door, I turned off the pathway back to the dorms, heading towards the side of the Grotto.

As I walked around the classroom building, I admired the Grotto again. It was essentially a small forest inside the walls, around three hundred meters long and two hundred wide. It had a wild feel to it, though you could tell it was maintained. The dichotomy made the Grotto more interesting. Entering into the Grotto, the path split into three different paths, each winding around the interior. The air was noticeably cooler, and I heard insects and bird calls. I hoped I would see that fiery bird again, or other wondrous creatures. That got me speculating about what we were going to cover in the Beasts class tomorrow. I was lost in thought, marveling once again at this strange world I ended up in. Thankfully, my newly enhanced senses alerted me to the footsteps pounding up the trail behind me.

I turned quickly, accidentally dodging the running punch by Nicolai. He moved past me in a stumble as I staggered backwards. Behind Nicky I saw three other kids from our year. *Ah, it's Nicky and the brown noses.* "What in Light are you doing?" I yelled at Nicolai, turning so that I had both him and his lackeys in sight.

"I'm going to beat you and embarrass you in front of everyone! How dare you talk down to me in the marketplace! I will get my revenge for that embarrassment!" he shouted, moving towards me again. *Wow, clichéd noble idiot. Crap, I am the main character.*

"It's not that embarrassing to be beaten by four people. In fact, you'll just be called a coward for attacking me with your lackeys. Or are you a coward, unable to solve your problems yourself?" I antagonized him, mostly trying to make this a one-on-one. If I could delay until an instructor or others showed up that would also be useful.

"Elric, Stephan, go block the path and make sure we are uninterrupted. I'm going to beat him down myself," Nicolai demanded of his flunkies. Seeing two of the three stooges nod and turn back up the trail gave me some relief. *At least now it's just two v one. That's half as many opponents! Look on the bright side, only two sets of bruises instead of four!* My sarcastic inner thoughts helped to calm me down and I settled into a fighting stance vaguely remembered from Unarmed Combat One and Boxing class from the Academy on Earth. Nicky also took a fighting stance before moving forward at me. I dodged sideways, putting my arm in the way of his punch, and tried to punch him back. He smoothly sidestepped my awkward attack, before a pivot kick slammed into my gut.

Ow, how is he that strong? I thought as I staggered backwards, barely keeping my feet and blocking a follow-up punch from the jerk. He tried to repeat the kick, but I stepped forward into it this time, following instincts from my training. Getting close, I focused on pulling my Aether to the surface of my knuckles, as it looked like he was, and hit him in the gut with a sharp right. When my fist hit him, some of the Aether drained out of me and entered him. As it did so, his whole body seemed to lock up. He started twitching like someone was tazing him. "My liege!" exclaimed the as-yet-unnamed lackey, rushing to his side. As soon as his eyes were off me, I booked it out of sight. I ran as fast as I could, putting as much distance between us before he recovered. I took the first right then the second left, zig-zagging so that my path wasn't straight. *Hopefully those nobles can't follow tracks!*

After a number of zigs and zags, and crossing paths with a few other students, I found an offshoot trail that led past a nice gazebo with solid walls. Rather than go inside, I went around it into the woods slightly, sitting with my back to a tree. I concentrated on getting my breath and panted, "Well, at least I got a good run in today, before PT. I'll be faster than everyone else at this rate. Can't hit what you can't catch!"

After several minutes, I had calmed myself down. I reached into the sack I had under my shirt and pulled out the level seven Lightning memory stone. *So this is more than twice what Pa had, and is apparently worth more money than I'll ever see. Time to see what is so special about it.* I pressed it to the center of my forehead. It was a tad uncomfortable, with its sharp edges threatening to pierce the skin if I held it too hard. Focusing on the location of the discomfort, I pulled Aether from the life meridian to the skin. As the Aether connected, I lost all sense of where I was.

Suddenly I was looking into the center of another person, watching as they dispersed a rune and began to draw another. It started with an eight-pointed star, a straight line up and down, two lines to make an X, then a plus sign. Then a continuous line of circles, looking like a curlicue, connected all of the points, with the circles perpendicular to the original drawing. Next, another star was drawn perpendicular to both the original star and the circles plane. Finally, jagged bolts split the open areas between the stars from the center point to the edge of the circles. *Whoa, that's complicated!* I thought, as he made a small mistake and wiped it out again. I watched what must have been hundreds of repetitions, before my head began pounding and I withdrew from the vision.

Coming to, I was lying on the ground drenched in sweat. When I focused on my center, I realized I had used almost every drop of Aether I had in me. I took a deep breath, and gathered for a couple of minutes, until the headache had subsided. *Crud, I forgot to ask how many runes you can have! Well, that rune was incredibly complicated. But it's also the best one I have. Should I wipe the one I have and replace it, or make a new one?* I decided to gather a bit more and see what the end of the stone said. After another ten minutes, I looked into the stone again, trying to focus on the end.

This time the vision showed him setting the rune up one final time, and then gathering with it. The speed of Aether induction staggered me. It wasn't simply seven times, but more than a hundred times as fast as I could gather now. The scene faded, and then it showed him instructing a young girl in how to make it. She was about my age, and through his eyes I saw two open meridians. He guided her through drawing the sign, off to the side of her current one. I pulled out of the simulation or memory or whatever it was. *That is intense!* I thought. *Time to draw a new rune!*

The first attempt was bad, and I felt bad. I also discovered that wiping a rune hurt. Like stabbing-myself hurt. *Wow, I am more impressed with the guy who invented this rune. I don't think I could do this hundreds of times.* The second time I made it through the circles before getting the angle wrong on the last star. I tried to wipe just that part, but it made the whole thing unstable. Whining about how much it hurt, I successfully accomplished drawing the rune on my seventh try. I immediately started gathering, and noticed a huge jump. Not as much as the guy in the memory did, but something like sixty times my previous rate. I gathered for another ten minutes before the gong for lunch rang. *Wow, I must have been watching memories for only about two hours. I'm glad I didn't miss lunch. That felt like so much longer. That's useful.* I thought to myself, getting up from the tree and heading out to the path. I didn't run into anyone I knew, but I felt safe from Nicky and his flunkies since I was around people.

Crossing out of the Grotto, I saw a small flood of people heading into the dining facility. I was still looking around, loving the sight of the Grotto. I looked over the Physical Training Fields again, and this time saw a series of straw targets set up at one end and arming dummies on the other. Racks of different weapons were set up on the side of the fields by the dummies. *Nice, we'll be doing weapons training!* I thought, excited by the prospect of using a sword

Entering the flood of people, I looked around for someone I knew. Coming from the other direction, I thought I saw Jon and Louis enter the food hall. Hurrying to catch up, I walked around a couple groups of people before I felt a weird sense of being watched. Looking around, I didn't see anyone specifically looking for me at first. Then I saw Counselor Sila moving through the crowd quickly, though he didn't look like he was hurrying. "Ah, Aiden, I was searching for you. Follow me, please," he told me in a quiet voice that brooked no dispute.

"Yes sir," I replied, following him back into the Grotto, this time near the edge by the dormitories.

I followed behind my teacher quietly, looking pensively at him. The silence was eating at me, but I was patient enough to wait him out. After about a minute he took a turn into one of the pavilions and gestured for me to sit. I sat after he did, and looked attentively at him. Finally, he spoke. "Why did you try and start a war in my city?" the Counselor asked.

"I what? How?" The question floored me.

"It was reported that you attacked and nearly killed the heir of the Haodha clan. As you have been seen socializing with the Lo clan, many people assumed you attempted to kill Nicolai on Ming's orders. I doubt that is true, which is why we are having this discussion here instead of the City Lord's prison. So, what actually happened?"

I spent the next couple of minutes describing the fight, at which point he asked why Nicolai had attacked me to start with. I told him the whole story of stopping him in the marketplace and taking his prized whip. "Ok, good, you didn't lie to me once; otherwise we would be having a very different conversation. I will bring this to the Headmaster and he will be punished. However, you will probably be punished as well. You did nearly kill a boy, even if by accident. Thankfully a healer was able to reverse the damage, or the Haodha clan would have been able to demand your head. Do not use Aether as an attack again until you are trained how to and how to defend against it. He didn't expect to be hit by an Aether attack from you and so didn't have a defense in place. Your Aether ravaged his muscles and nerves."

"I didn't know. I thought it would just make the hit stronger, kind of like how we pulled Aether to make our eyes see better," I replied, worried now. What had seemed an annoyance might now become a serious threat, as I doubted the leaders of the Haodha would be very forgiving.

"You are lucky he will be fine and that you didn't know. Unfortunately, we will have to change up the order of classes for the rest of the week to prevent this from happening again. Your punishment, and his, still hasn't been decided. Go to lunch. I will see you and your classmates afterwards." He dismissed me, turning and walking down the pathway towards the classroom building.

CHAPTER TEN

"Well, shoot." I sat and worried for a bit, then my stomach growled at me. I got up and hurried back to the food. No one was on the trail anymore, leaving me alone. I jogged the rest of the way. The smell of grilled meat drew me into the building, though I noticed many people staring at me as I walked in. I quickly grabbed food and found a seat alone. I didn't feel like talking. *Hopefully the punishment is light, and hopefully Nicky recovers fully. I think he's an asshole, but that doesn't mean he should be crippled. Maybe he'll learn not to attack other people?* I thought, and then snorted. I doubted it; he'd have to change quite a lot since he was whipping a girl when I first saw him. *Maybe he did deserve to be crippled.* After musing for a bit, I started to eat, enjoying the richness of the grilled Beast meat. *Put worries off until they come to pass. I can't change what I did, and I can't change what the powers that be will decide. Just accept it and move on.* I finished eating and got up, heading towards the classrooms again.

I waved to Jon as I entered the library at the base of the classroom building. Again a chalkboard was set up, this time simply telling us to return to the classes we had before lunch. "So what happened?" Jon asked. I quickly explained how Nicky had attacked me and how I had stopped him. Then I told Jon about the visit from Counselor Sila.

"I'm assuming we'll probably have a lesson now on defending against Aether attacks, rather than waiting until they were planning on it," I said as we approached the door.

"You're right!" called Counselor Sila from inside the classroom. "Everyone get in here." Jon and I walked in, taking our seats. The rest of the class filed in, with Anberlin giving me a glare as she walked by. I nervously smiled at her. Bridget gave me a surreptitious wink as she went to her seat, sitting next to Anberlin. As the rest of the class grabbed their seats, Counselor Sila started speaking. "We were going to spend some time today discussing some of the major happenings behind the formation of our Kingdom and the various academies, but after an incident with Aether attacks it was decided to move the defense channeling lesson forward. Thankfully, basic defense is fairly simple, so we will spend most of this class practicing creating an Aether Shield. Now, Aiden, you will be my test subject for this lesson and all future lessons. Come up front."

Well, I guess I found out one element of my punishment. I'm probably going to be the test dummy for every not-pleasant thing we do this year, I thought as I stood up. "Good. Now focus on your center. Revolve Aether around your center and pull it out to your chest. It will spread evenly throughout your skin if you do it correctly. No, straight out, hit the point where your sternum ends. Good, keep pulling. See how it is spreading around, evenly coating you? Excellent. Now stop, sit down, and gather some to replenish what you just used. Everyone else, try once, the proctors and I will be watching."

I sat down and gathered Aether. Replacing Aether that was used to do something was very quick, especially with the new rune enhancing me. It felt like there was a vacuum inside me that drew in the Aether from around me, filling my tank quickly, so to speak. "Oh, Counselor, I was wondering, how many runes can you use for your center?"

"Good question. You can use one rune for each element, with a level up to your affinity with the element. So everyone can use eight runes, though they are limited to level zero or one runes for Low or Marginal affinities. Usually people put runes in for affinities that are Moderate or Higher, arranged around their center. Having more runes is better, but each one beyond the first does not provide the full benefit, so you'll always want to make the center rune the strongest you have. You should wipe away that rune from the starter book provided to the citizens of the city. Your mother should have given you a level two rune of her affinity. Affinities are nearly always inherited from the mother."

"I didn't know that. Neither did my parents. That information should be spread much farther around. I'll wipe away both runes and redraw them and put together the others later. Thank you for the information, sir," I replied, trying to keep the annoyance from my tone.

"Good. Also, don't put more runes in than you have open meridians. We'll be opening several more over the rest of the week." A quick nod and he was moving away, going to help Jon get the procedure right.

I took the opportunity to practice again, feeling the Aether move and flow over me. Something wasn't right, as the Aether was bunching up on one side. "Make sure you are pulling straight out for now. Getting good at angling the Aether Shield will be useful, but you should be proficient in basic shielding first," Mentor Gutierrez said, walking up to observe my second attempt. I quickly changed the angle, making the bunching-up feeling subside. Once it was even, I stopped and gathered again.

We spent the next hour repeatedly shielding and resting. I managed to reduce the time it took to summon the shield by nearly half. That helped reduce the lost Aether. After everyone was roughly proficient, Counselor Sila called me up again. "Now, I will call you up one at a time and demonstrate your ability at summoning the Aether Shield. Channel a Shield and do not release until I tell you," he commanded me. I quickly followed his order, pulling the Aether straight out of my center and forming a shield around me.

He looked at me, nodded, and then slapped his palm to my chest, thrusting a small amount of Aether into my shield. I rocked backward, but the shield held. It sputtered out immediately after, and I felt exhausted suddenly, like when I had run out of Aether looking at the memory stone. "Good, your Shield held. Go take a seat. I will be testing your Shields versus what a Low Vapor gatherer could produce, to verify minimum capability. Work on thickening the shield, though much more will not be possible until you advance. Next, Hill Lucas, you are up," he said, gesturing at a tall blond guy from the back row.

The rest of the lesson passed quickly, with each person being tested in the same way. Only a couple people failed, and they were given instructions on how to create the Shield better and sent to practice more. Finally, everyone had passed and we were dismissed to get ready for Physical Training. "Aiden, hold back," Counselor Sila said. I stepped out of the line for the door and waited. After everyone had left, another Counselor came in, followed by Nicolai.

Nicolai looked at me, undisguised hatred in his eyes. "I am required to apologize for attacking you this morning. I am sorry. I will not attack you outside of a sanctioned duel or tournament again," he said through gritted teeth.

"Thank you," I replied coolly. I knew this wasn't the end of it, but it should reduce the threat here at the Academy. With my reply, he jerkily nodded at me, turned, and stalked out of the room.

"I will be watching his behavior for the next month or so, Aiden, so you will be safe. Good luck with your studies, and work hard," the other Counselor told me as he turned to follow Nicolai.

"Now that that is over, head back to your room and get ready for training. You'll need it, because you will be the demonstrator for every lesson from now on. Actions have consequences, even if they were in the best of intentions," Counselor Sila told me after they had left.

"Yes sir. Thank you, sir, see you tomorrow," I responded and left. *I doubt that it is truly over. I need to get stronger to protect myself from him and idiots like him. Not that I needed MORE motivation towards building my strength. Time for PT.*

I wasn't sure how long we had until PT was supposed to start, so I hurried back to my room. There I discovered my new uniforms laid out on the bed. There were six sets of loose, flowing pants and tunics, each a nice jade green with black trim. *I guess black trim is first tiers?* Additional undergarments were provided, along with a pair of boots and a pair of moccasin-like shoes which both laced up. *How did they get new shoes for everyone who joined the Academy in a day!* I exclaimed in my head. I hurried to put on a uniform set and the shoes, marveling at how well they fit. *I can move easily in these and the material is nicer than anything I owned back in town.* After getting dressed, I hurried to the Physical Training Fields.

As I approached the field, a booming voice yelled out, "First tiers over here!" I saw Counselor Might standing near the training dummies, with his back to them looking at the weapon racks. The racks held every kind of melee weapon I could think of, and many I had never seen before. "Get in a line in front of me, hurry up. Move, move!" He continued to bellow at us, chivvying us into place. As I hurried into line, I noticed that everyone else had changed into the uniforms, so we looked like we belonged now. From behind the weapons racks a number of older students came out. *Hmm, I guess the third and fourth tiers spend a lot of time assisting the Counselors.*

"Today, we will start by selecting a weapon. Your training in the first tier will focus mostly on duels and small-group fighting, as those with significant power are usually separate from the full army. In your second tier, you will go train in large-group tactics at Fort Pevnost with the army training command. The second tiers are currently training there now. Here we focus on defeating other gathering experts and Beast and Elemental Beast incursions. Your training will be in the weapon most suited to you and your affinities. When I say, split up and explore the weapons. Once you have made your selection, come speak to me. The Mentors are here to help you, so heed their words. Now begin!"

Nearly everyone rushed to the nearest weapons rack. Many already knew what they wanted, especially the nobles who had been trained in self-defense and specific weapon techniques for years. Those like me who had no idea and had never trained with a weapon just grabbed what looked cool to test out. After ducking under the swing of an overly enthusiastic guy's glaive I decided to back off and wait for a clear space where I wouldn't be accidentally impaled. I saw Louis come out with a ridiculous two-handed sword. *That might be as big as the sword from Final Fantasy!* He seemed to carry it with ease, even though it was nearly as tall as he was. Ming and Xiao both came out with a straight one-handed sword. Jon walked over to the Counselor holding a moderate-sized triangular shield and sword. *Huh, I didn't notice the shields.*

As people grabbed weapons and moved off, it was finally clear enough that I didn't think I'd be accidentally decapitated. I still wasn't sure what I wanted, though I didn't think I wanted to use a large polearm. I picked up a sword like Ming had and swung it around, but it didn't feel right. I kept looking around. "Mentor, I was wondering why there are no ranged weapons here?" I asked as I realized there were no throwing weapons or bows.

"Everyone will eventually have to learn both a close weapon and a ranged weapon. This is to pick the close weapon that resonates with you and your Aether. Ranged weapons are almost always the bow or crossbow and will be dealt with later on. Bows usually only go to those who want to focus on ranged attacks after they reach the second tier and higher or those who have used them before. Otherwise, crossbows are useful until you reach Core Seed level. What is your affinity and talent?"

"Highest is Lightning, with Air, Fire, Metal and Earth, and 16/35."

"Oh, you're Aiden!" she exclaimed. "Come on, I know just the thing!" She leaped to another rack, where she pulled out what looked like long sai. *Those are like what Raphael used in The Teenage Mutant Ninja Turtles.* "These are called trisulas. Try them out," she said as she handed them to me, along with a belt to hold them with.

They were a couple of inches short of two feet, with two prongs coming out from the sides and a single long blade up the middle. Unlike normal sai, the middle blade was sharpened on one side, making the left- and right-hand weapons distinct. When held point out, the blade would be facing away from me, and I could hold it with the short end out to make short jabbing punches and slash with my forearms. As I held them, I felt ready. *These are awesome!* "Why do you think these are good for me?" I asked the Mentor.

"Trisulas are good control weapons, able to both defend and attack. They will be useful when you use Metal or Lightning techniques due to their material, and they are capable of channeling short Aether strikes even at lower levels. They are made from a single material and the way you hold it involves pressure on the metal at all times, so it is easier to channel Aether into and through them. This is important for you with your high talent numbers since Aether will become your primary means of combat once you hit the Core Seed level, or even earlier! Finally, if you haven't trained in a weapon before, you can simply hold them in a reverse grip and punch while practicing using the blades for defense and grow into the full capabilities of the weapon." She held out her hands and I handed them back to her. She then demonstrated the two different grips and punched out with them in the reverse grip.

"I'm convinced, these sound great. I will take these. Thank you." I took them back from her and held them in the reverse grip. Punching forward, they fit my arm and hands just about perfectly. On a whim, I channeled some Aether into the right-hand trisula, stepped away from the Mentor and others, and punched in a direction that no one else was in. I wasn't going to take a chance at hurting someone. The trisula glowed for a second and sparked at the end and that was it, but the Aether flowed through the whole thing. I could feel the Aether as it moved through the weapon, circling back into the meridian in my arm. I pushed Aether out like I was making a shield, only this time from the meridian in my forearm and into the weapon. A shield formed on the weapon, though it was sharp. *Neat!* I thought as I cut off the flow of Aether. I turned back to the Mentor, but she had moved off to help someone else.

Now that I had my weapons, I walked over to Counselor Might as instructed. "Hmm, trisula. Good choice. You'll have to work on forearm and wrist strength along with general body strength. You'll work with Mentor Jameson, over there." He pointed to a group of people surrounding a wiry Mentor with dark brown hair who was holding a sword and dagger.

"Thank you, sir," I said with a bow before walking over to the group. On the way, I noticed that everyone over there had either two weapons or a double-ended weapon. Looking around, I saw a group of polearms, a group of large-weapon users like greatswords, a group with shields and one-handed weapons, and a group with just a one-handed weapon.

When I reached the group, Mentor Jameson looked over at me and said, "Hi, I'm Mentor Jameson Jacob. I'll be teaching you the basics of using multiple weapons. Please introduce yourself to everyone here."

"I'm Kupiec Aiden, Outstanding Lightning, Excellent Air, Fire and Metal, High Earth, 16/35 talent. I chose to use the trisula and haven't trained in them, or any weapon, before," I responded, stopping awkwardly.

The Mentor's eyes opened wide and he mouthed, "Ocean's depths!" before getting control of himself. "Uh, welcome to the dual-wielders. Once everyone over there is ready"—he gestured towards the last few people picking weapons—"we will be able to begin. Join the others and do some stretches. We will be working hard for the next hour."

I looked at the rest of the group. The first one I recognized was Volkov Vaya, who waved as I glanced at her. She had two daggers in her hands, one almost long enough to be a short sword. *What is the dividing line between swords and daggers anyway?* I wondered as I smiled back. Next to her stood Falconer Bridget, who held two curved machetes as her weapons of choice. Standing off to the side of them were some people I had not met yet, followed by Unnamed Flunky Number One and Something Stephan, lackeys of Nicolai, who were both glaring at me. Stephan had a double-bladed sword that looked impractical, while No Name held what seemed like two hollow Frisbees made of metal, with some spikes coming out of them. I winked at them and walked over to Vaya and Bridget.

"Interesting weapon choice," Vaya commented as I approached.

"Thank you. You as well. What did your sister pick?"

"Bet has used a single longsword for as long as we've been training, so I'm sure she went with that. I've always like using two smaller blades instead." We talked a bit about various people's choices, passing time for the last few people to choose. After a couple of minutes everyone had chosen a weapon, and our dual-wielding group had grown to twenty. The sword-and-shield and polearm groups were the largest, by far.

The last to walk up was another member of my class that I hadn't met yet, who introduced himself as "Hunter Brett, High Air, Moderate Ice,

5/17." He was carrying two hooked blades connected by a chain. *Well, that's going to be hard to learn if he doesn't know yet. I saw those in one of Jackie Chan's movies. They looked awesome, but impractical.*

As he joined the group, Mentor Jameson spoke up. "Alright, now that everyone is here we can begin. You'll be joining me every day to exercise and learn about fighting. We'll be together for two to three hours daily, so be prepared and eat well at lunch. And dinner. And breakfast. You'll need the extra nutrition to fuel growth. Everyone, sheathe or put away your weapons on yourselves somewhere, then run five laps around the field."

Everyone took off running. The perimeter of the fields was about a kilometer. After slowly running through the first lap, I noticed the Mentor had disappeared. After two more laps, he was back, this time holding a bag. Finally finishing the run, I joined the rest of the group in gasping for air around him.

"Good. We'll be starting off with this just about every time, and it will grow longer soon. Physical fitness is important. Endurance is highly important, especially as fights take immense amounts of energy in a very short amount of time. This becomes critical if there is a Beast Horde, where often the defenders are outnumbered dozens or hundreds to one. If you cannot last in those cases, you will die. Additionally, the stronger your body, the more often you can gather, as you will be physically able to handle the Aether's pressure. Normally we would do some upper-body exercises, but you are lopsided right now. Tomorrow we will do more once everyone has both upper-body meridians open.

"Now I have two things for everyone. First is a memory stone of some introductory forms for your weapons. Study these closely and practice as you can." He pulled out memory stones from the bag, inspected them, and then handed one to each of us. "Once you have mastered that, you will present to me and Counselor Might. If you pass, you will be able to select a new technique or an advanced level technique of a previous one you have mastered. Secondly, I have a duel inscription. You will place this on your weapons. This inscription pairs with these necklaces, which you will wear AT ALL TIMES." He strongly emphasized the last three words. "These necklaces will prevent lethal damage from the enchanted weapons in almost all cases. This will prevent accidental, and deliberate, attacks upon your fellow students. Additionally, the necklaces will send a signal when they prevent damage, and will need to recharge after a couple uses. This signaling is used in the tournaments held every month, to determine your individual combat ranking. Bring your weapons forward and I will place the enchantments."

Everyone got into a line and gave him our weapons when we reached the front. He pulled out a stack of papers from the bag. Each paper had a glyph on it. He took the top paper from the stack, pressed the glyph to the weapon, and infused Aether into it. As the Aether flowed, the paper glowed and seemed to melt. Afterward, the glyph appeared on the blade of the weapon. "Do not lose the necklace. Counselor Pizar and Headmaster Glav have to work for several days to make each one and they get fairly mad when someone misplaces the necklace. You don't want to make the Headmaster angry. Now spread out and examine your memory stones. I will assist as I am able and can call Counselor Might over if needed."

We responded "Yes sir" and moved apart. I walked about fifty feet from everyone else and sat down. I promptly stood back up and rearranged the trisulas hanging on the belt because I'd just about stabbed my calf with one. *That would have hurt. Need to get used to wearing these.* This time I sat down while holding the handles tight to my side, keeping the blades away from my legs. Once I was seated and properly arranged, I pulled the memory stone out of the bag on my hip and put it against my forehead.

I was a young man, maybe a year or two my junior. I was standing in front of an older woman who was carrying trisulas and instructing the person whose memory I was watching. "Stand with your feet shoulder-width apart. Bend your knees slightly, like that, good. Now, pull your weapons out of your belt and hold them with the point away from you. Long edge out, mirror me. This is called front grip." She stood as she described and moved her right hand to just above her head, holding the blade at a forty-five-degree angle or so to the left, as if covering from an overhead attack. Her left hand dropped down, holding the blade parallel to her left leg, as if defending it from a slash or kick. She quickly transitioned her hands so that the left was up and the right down. "Switch your hands one hundred times." I watched and felt the muscle movements, trying to make sure I remembered everything I could as she fixed my motions.

"Next, switch grips so that the short side is front. This is called reverse grip. The blade should be pointing away from your arm, with the prongs flat to it. Good, now switch back. Careful now, don't cut yourself. Switch one hundred times." Again I watched as she corrected his motions, making sure he was safe and correct. "Good, now go to reverse grip. First finger pressed into the edge of the tip; flex your third and fourth finger to provide pressure. Now punch forward. Again. One hundred times. Rotate your hands as you punch, right as your hand finishes extending." After finishing watching this, I pulled out of the memories. *Ok, let's practice switching grips first.* I stood up and drew my trisulas in the front grip. I then switched grips, and promptly scraped my arms with the bladed side of the weapon. "Ow," I whispered. I discovered that while my skin wasn't pierced due to the enchantment, it still hurt. I adjusted my grip and tried again. This time I dropped the left one and only a quick jerk kept it from hitting my foot point down.

Looking around, I saw that about half the students were having similar issues, while the nobles who had trained for years were moving smoothly through their weapon forms. I shrugged, picked up my weapon, and started again. *Someone will always have an advantage. The only way to make up for it is to work harder.* For the rest of the hour, I worked on switching grips, punching in reverse grip, and blocking in front grip. I kept at it until I was able to smoothly transition from an upper front grip block to a reverse grip that I then punched out with and back again. *Hah, I know Kung Fu! The stones must do something to help me learn faster, because there is no way I'd learn that quickly without them. Memory enhancement helps too.* I was about to look into the memory stone again for the next couple of moves when Counselor Might shouted out, "Assemble around me." We moved and lined up around him.

"Good work so far. Take your time to look through the memory stones. At the end of each sequence is a martial art form that uses every basic move introduced. Once you can perform those forms without error, we will unlock the next section in the stone and give you permission to pick an advanced technique. You are required to carry your weapons with you at all times from now on. You will get used to wearing it and grow stronger by having to carry around the weight of it. Now everyone, run five more laps, then you are dismissed for today." We all took off with a groan, getting used to running with our weapons once more. I felt bad for Louis and Jon. Their weapons must have weighed significantly more than mine.

CHAPTER ELEVEN

After finishing the run, we hurried back to the dorms. I quickly grabbed a towel I had packed and headed to the washroom. Three people were already in the showers, unfortunately, so I stood waiting. Lo Xiao walked in behind me. I smiled and nodded at him in greeting, and he returned it in kind. Neither of us felt like talking, being tired and ready for a shower. One of the showers turned off, and Hunter Brett stepped out. I walked around him and took a quick shower since I knew others would be waiting. Heading to my room, I saw another member of my morning class who I hadn't been introduced to yet but now wasn't the time.

I got dressed and left to go get dinner. I filled my plate to overflowing. I was starving. The food this time was a stir-fry of vegetables and what looked like chicken meat. It was amazing, and that was not just the hunger talking. The Aether that I gained eating the Beast meat and elemental plant vegetables seeped out of my stomach and into my center, slowly making the Aether there denser. Jon sat down as I was halfway through my plate. "Hey, those are interesting," he said, pointing at my trisulas.

"Yeah, I wanted something I could defend and attack with, and a shield didn't feel right. How're you liking that?" I asked, gesturing to the shield that he set down, leaning against his leg.

"So far so good, though I'll have a bruise on my thigh later. Smacked myself pretty good. The edge is good for bashing, so I've got something that can defend and attack too," he said the last part primly. "Though getting used to moving with it is going to take some time. At least yours are small. Not so much extra weight to run with." After that, he dug into his food, and we didn't talk much further. Dinner was more subdued than lunch since the majority of students had PT as the last event before dinner. After finishing eating, we cleaned up our place and brought our plates back to the counter.

The server said, "You know, you don't have to bring them back up to us. Normally the nobles don't even think of helping, while the others copy the nobles. We clean up the whole room once everyone is done."

"I know," I responded, "but this is easier for you all, and I think it is better for me to help out than be lazy. You should put a bin for people to deposit their plates and utensils in, then more people would do this and you'd be able to finish faster!" I suggested. We stacked our plates and left, leaving the server with a thoughtful expression on his face.

After leaving the dining hall, Jon and I headed into the Meditation Grotto and found a moderate-sized pavilion. I sat down at the opposite side from Jon and focused inward. *Ok, first I need to wipe both runes and then redraw the Lightning one. After that, look through the Fire memory stone to figure out the rune and draw it. Then Air. That's all I can do today. Counselor Sila said to only have as many runes as you have open meridians.* I braced myself for the pain of wiping the runes and then did it. Wiping two at once nearly made me cry out.

I spent the next ten minutes slowly drawing the Lightning rune, making it as close to symmetric as I could. I had to wipe it twice to do so, but I got it in the end. Taking a deep breath and then focusing on my center, I gathered for a little while, taking a break from rune drawing to deal with the pain. Putting the level seven Lightning rune in the primary position increased my gathering speed by another factor of four. *This is helpful.* I'd noticed that opening two meridians had diluted my Aether down to the boundary between Low and High Vapor. Gathering for thirty minutes got me a little farther up, but not that much. *Hmm, I guess opening a bunch of meridians will make it harder to advance. It does make me stronger though. I'll talk to Counselor Sila tomorrow about the balance between meridians and levels. Now, let's see how another high level rune helps.* I pulled out the red memory stone, ready to see another person made a rune.

Seeing into the center of another person, I again watched a rune being drawn. This was a little different as the Aether in their center was noticeably red tinted. The rune started off with a single upward-pointing chevron. This was then repeated three more times, rotating 45 degrees between them, to form a teepee shape. After finishing that, they then connected the bottoms of the teepee, forming the ubiquitous eight-pointed star. At this point they made a mistake and wiped the rune. Watching them get to this point again, the next step was to draw wavy, flame-like shapes that connected each branch of the teepee. *They're drawing a campfire!*

I watched them repeat this several dozen times, trying to figure out the best shapes for the flames. It seemed that having the flames come to a point in the middle between the branches allowed for better gathering. That was the shape they completed the rune with. I pulled out of the memory. *Time to draw a Fire rune!* I thought as I settled my mind from the vision. I focused down into my center and began to draw. I decided to place the Fire rune about halfway out of my center in a straight line from the Lightning rune to my heart. Altogether it took me an hour and something like fifty tries to get the flames drawn right. *Why was this harder than the Lightning one! Stupid curved shapes didn't want to go in right,* I grumbled to myself in annoyance.

I decided I didn't want to deal with the pain of badly drawing another rune tonight, and instead focused on the meridian that Counselor Sila had partially blocked off. Looking inward, I saw that he had essentially created a funnel shaped wall that reduced the size of the opening by ninety percent or so. *Hmm, I'd rather have control of this myself. Can I make the same structure and have it hold together? I'll try making it after his first.* I pulled Aether together that made it past the funnel, and tried to get it to stick together.

However, as soon as I relaxed my control, the structure fell apart. I tried over and over again, pushing the Aether closer harder, trying to tie it together with additional strands, and anchoring it to the wall. Finally, I figured out how to make it stay, by building a double-sided funnel such that each piece was pushing on another in a way that forced it to stay in the shape. As soon as I finished that, I noticed my hearing ability decrease to what it was before my meridian opened. *Hmm, I just blocked off even more Aether from the meridian, so the benefits decreased.* I focused on the structure put in place by Counselor Sila, and forced Aether to impact the sides. As soon as I put intent into the impacts, his structure dispersed, and my hearing and sense of smell doubled.

I sat with my eyes closed, slowly breathing in and out, savoring the smells of flowers and trees that I didn't notice before. I heard insects, birds, and animals walking around, and a very low hum of conversation from other students in the Grotto. I reached into the Aether structure, and removed the innermost layer blocking off the meridian. I slowly increased the Aether allowed through this way, trying to get used to the enhanced senses. It seemed to be going well until "Hey Aiden, are you okay?" thundered in my ears. With a soft cry, I fell over. I put my finger to my lips and whispered "shush" to him while I rebuilt the blockage to the starting level.

"What happened?" Jon asked after I stood up and took my finger off my lips.

"I unblocked the senses meridian that I accidentally opened this morning and was trying to get used to the extra noise and smells. I was already starting to get a headache when you asked how I was doing, and that was way too loud for me, at this stage. I've got it blocked off again now, so I'm fine," I answered.

"It is just about sunset, want to head back?" he asked.

"Not right now, I'm going to stay out here another hour or so. You can go on in if you want to," I replied.

"Okay, I'm not surprised you are going to continue. Don't stay out too late. I'll see you in the morning," he said as he got up, stretched, and walked away towards the dormitories.

I focused down to my center and began gathering again, with a plan of doing so for an hour and then working on my first weapon techniques again. Pulling in Aether even faster with both runes available left me feeling full and unable to continue after only half an hour. "Whew, if I can keep up this rate, I'll be able to open all the meridians that are easily openable and still make Low Mist in like a month!" I exclaimed to myself, and then thought, *At Mist you are supposed to be able to sense other people's auras. I wonder what that is like.* I stood up and looked outside. I stopped what I was doing, gaping at the wondrous beauty of the Mediation Grotto at night.

Bugs like large fireflies glowed softly, only in eight different colors, the main colors of the elements. They left streaks through the sky as they flew. Glowing lights hovered over the pathways, illuminating them to help people move around. Flowers I hadn't noticed gleamed in the provided light and the fireflies alighted on them, moving almost like bees. A bright red bird started to fly by, before bursting into flames, though without burning. "A phoenix!" I cried in wonder, awed at the world around me. I sat down with my back to the pavilion and just watched the animals and the forest light the night, feeling the stress that had built up over the day start to fade away. The phoenix I saw came back after a couple of minutes, and landed on the roof of the pagoda, looking down at me. It seemed to look through me, then jumped up and flew off. I watched in amazement. *I can do this,* I thought to myself, ready once again to build on my new life.

Watching nature took away from my weapon time, but that was okay. I needed the de-stressing more than I needed to practice. I headed back to the dorms after an hour of relaxing, ready to sleep after a busy day. I went up to my dorm, waving at Brett and Ming in the lounge as I passed them, and changed into sleep clothes. After looking out at the Grotto one last time, I lay down and went to sleep.

CHAPTER TWELVE

The next morning I got up, got dressed, and checked my schedule. *Today is Wood Day, so we have Beasts, which should be fun.* I then headed to breakfast after making sure my trisulas were secured in their belt. It was a good thing that I did since Counselor Might was off to the side of the dining hall chewing out a couple of people for not having their weapons. I saw them take off back to the dorms to get them, apprehension written on their faces. Shaking my head, I walked into the meal hall thinking, *Just like the Academy, the day after you are told something will be mandatory, they will check it. Gotta learn sometime.* The meal today was fried meat from a Jungle Boar that reminded me of bacon, and scrambled eggs of some kind. I sat down with Brett and Lucas from my gathering class.

"I see you remembered your weapons today," Lucas commented.

"How'd you know?" I asked.

"You didn't come in sweaty; Counselor Might is making people run a lap around the training fields if they forget them, after running back to their rooms to rectify their mistake, of course. I doubt many of them will forget again," he responded with a laugh.

"That's probably the point. We are essentially being trained to be elite soldiers, so we need to be used to being ready to fight at all times," Brett informed him.

"So, where are you from?" I asked both of them.

"I'm from East Village. It is a small village set up in the edge of the Great Western Forest. My family is Beast hunters, selling meat, hides, and cores to the merchants in Pevnost City, which surrounds Fort Pevnost," Brett responded.

Lucas then chimed in. "I'm from Mount Rosly Village, named for the mountain nearby. My uncle owns the iron and gold mines, and my dad manages the iron mine. We are a minor noble house, with my grandfather in charge of the village. Where are you from?"

"I'm from here in Azyl City; my parents own a book and writing store, selling books, binding tools, and writing materials mostly," I told them, and then asked Brett, "What are cores?"

He looked at me questioningly. "Beast cores are what let Beasts gather Aether, and are the equivalent to our centers. They are worth good money, especially for stronger Beasts, as they can be used as power sources or gathering assistance. We mostly hunt level four and lower Beasts." At my questioning look he explained, "Beasts are rated by the equivalent gathering level they would be. Level four is the equivalent to the Foundation Aether Compression level, so my dad and uncle have to be in the group to hunt them. You almost always want more people at the equivalent level to hunt a Beast because they are generally stronger than we are."

"Thanks for explaining. I got really sick and nearly died a year ago and lost most of my memories, so I'm still learning all sorts of information," I explained. "We nearly had to sell the store to pay for medicines, but I got better before then."

"You think the sickness and medication helped you get the ridiculous talent levels you have?" Lucas asked me.

"Maybe. Neither of my parents had anything above normal talent. I wouldn't recommend trying to improve your talent that way, though. It was not pleasant," I said with a shudder. I waved over Jon as he walked in. "This is Noptep Jonathan, though friends call him Jon. His family owns one of the local laborer groups that unload ships at the docks. Jon, this is Brett and Lucas."

"Yeah, I've met Brett already. Good to meet you, Lucas." As Jon sat down, we tucked into the food. *Mmm, elemental bacon.*

After breakfast, Jon and I took our dishes up and found a bin next to the counter. Placing our plates in it, I winked at the server. Behind us came Brett and Lucas with their plates, and they gently stacked them in the bin as well. We headed to the classroom building, with Jon telling a crazy story about how he supposedly helped hunt down a thief by following him across the rooftops. "I managed to stop him from getting away so the guards could catch up, when I slipped and fell off the roof onto him," he finished the story to our laughter while we walked down the hallway.

Walking into the classroom, I waved hi to Bridget and did a small bow to Mentors Gutierrez and Lo. Counselor Sila walked in just after I sat down. Ming and Anberlin walked in after he did, making the classroom full. "Okay, today we will continue the theme of yesterday morning's class, and unlock your other arm. After that, you will spend some time looking through your centers to find other potentially openable meridians, and you will present to me where they are. We will pick one or two to open, and that will be one of your tasks during the morning meditation period. Any questions before we begin?"

As no one was raising their hands, I raised mine to ask, "Sir, why do we only open a meridian or two a day?"

He looked at me and smiled. "Good question. Mostly because each meridian opening takes from your total gathered base, and if that gets too low it can cause problems and cause some opened meridians to close. Additionally, the strengthening that occurs needs resources, so you need to eat a lot and your body can run out of stored nutrients if you open too many too quickly, though that is usually less of an issue. So when you present the meridians that you want to open to me, I'll make the determination as to how many you can open. Now, you get to be the first to open the other arm." I nodded and stood up, walking to the front of the class. I saw the Mentors pointing at two others out of the corner of my eyes, realizing that my peripheral vision was better than it used to be.

When I got in front of Counselor Sila, I focused inward, sensing the edge of my center and found the spot that was opposite my right arm meridian. Grabbing some Aether, I flung it into the spot. The meridian opened with little difficulty, and I felt the impacts as it hit my heart, left lung, kidney, and stomach. The stomach impact riled it, and I felt nauseous. "Good, go on and sit down. Your stomach will quiet down shortly. Find a couple of meridians to open," he directed me before waving at Brett to come up next. I staggered to my chair, holding my stomach and breathing deeply thinking, *Don't throw up. Not two days in a row.*

I sat down and focused on my center. It took me a minute to get back into the right frame of mind. It's hard to meditate when your stomach is roiling. Once I was able to focus, I started feeling around the edge of my center. I quickly found several meridians leaving around the top and bottom. Rather than immediately opening them, I tried to sense where they went. Moving my senses was difficult at first, with me leaving the meditative state rather than succeeding. After a couple of tries, I managed to succeed at sensing the start of one of the meridians coming out the bottom of my center. It immediately veered to my left, entering into the side of my stomach, where it turned to follow the rest of my digestive tract, finally leaving just before the end of my large intestine, at which point it came straight back up to my center. *Huh, one that only goes into my digestive tract. That's useful, I guess.*

After that one, I found a few others that were similar. A second one from the bottom ran to the bottom of my spine, all the way up it until it connected to my brain, then back down to my center. One from the top went into my left lung, up my airway to my nose, moved down the top of my mouth, back down the other side of the airway to my right lung, along the diaphragm then back to my center. A meridian left the side of my center to go through my right kidney, down to my bladder and organs down there, before looping back up to my left kidney and center. The last one I traced, at least before going up to talk to Counselor Sila, was one that seemed to zigzag across my chest and back as it traced my rib cage, shoulder blades, and collarbones.

After I finished tracing that last one, I looked up to see Counselor Sila looking over the class, with no one talking to him yet. I noticed that several people, including Anberlin, Ming, and Lucas, were gone already. I stood up and walked over to Counselor Sila. "Ready?" he asked me. I said yes and described the five I had traced. "So, which one would you want to open if you could only open one?" he asked.

I thought for a couple of seconds, then said, "I really don't know, sir, I'm not sure what the benefits from any of them are. So I'll follow your recommendations."

"Good identification of your lack of knowledge. I would start with the airway meridian. It will help your stamina increase faster and helps you gather faster than most since it'll slowly pull some Aether from each breath. Very minute quantities, mind. Next, open the digestive system. This will help with pulling Aether from the Beast meat and elemental plants we feed you here. It also will help with getting more nutrients and less waste. You can open both of those this morning, though I recommend doing the second one in the restroom. The expulsion of impurities from that meridian will be … explosive," he finished with a laugh. My stomach felt a bit queasy again hearing that.

"This evening you can open up the spinal meridian. It'll strengthen your spinal column, making it more durable, as well as slightly speeding up your reaction rate. If you want to open up that meridian, though, you need to eat a double helping of everything at lunch. They will have significantly more food available for the next two weeks, to help all the new students build capability faster. Make sure to stuff yourself at every meal from now until, well, ever. You are lucky; the airway and stomach meridians are small enough that you can open three additional today. Good luck and you are free to go. Come back if you have any more questions. Look for some more meridians tonight. We'll be opening your legs tomorrow morning, but you'll have the opportunity to open another tomorrow night." He gently shooed me away, and I saw Jon was waiting.

"Good luck," I said and left, heading to the pavilion I spent part of last night at. I reached the pavilion after a couple of minutes and looked around at the flowers and trees again. Sitting down on the cushion provided, I centered myself. *Okay, so let's open up the respiratory tract meridian, then I'll observe and carve the Air rune near where that meridian connects. After that, head back to the dorms, go to the bathroom, and open the digestive meridian sitting on the toilet. Yup, nothing speaks to the grandeur of surpassing nature's bounds like sitting on a toilet,* I mused to myself.

I felt along my center to locate the opening point for the lung meridian again. Once I found it, I slowly spun Aether until I was ready and released it into the opening. Aether flowed into one of my lungs, up my airway, through my nose and mouth, then back through my vocal cords and other lung into my center. After completing the circuit, I breathed deeply, getting even more scents than before. A crazy mish-mash of smells and tastes were apparent, though not as overwhelmingly as when I first opened the senses meridian. Exhaling, I began to cough as my lungs and vocal cords spasmed. A minute of coughing resulted in hacking out a couple of small globules of disgusting black phlegm. I spat a couple of times and pulled out a water bag. I rinsed my mouth again before drinking some. "Ugh, that was gross, especially with enhanced taste buds."

After a couple more drinks, I pulled out the Air memory stone, ready to hurt to get it right. I activated the memory stone and watched as the teacher began to draw. The rune was surprisingly simple. It started with an even spiral parallel to their chest, followed by another, perpendicular to the first that started at the same spot. Two more formed an interweaving eight-pointed star, with a final circle connecting the endpoints of the four spirals. Of course, just because it was easy to describe did not make it easy to draw. The hardest part was to get the spirals to interweave without touching. It took me a good hour and a half to get it down, leaving me with only half an hour or so before lunch. *Huh, I've gotten much better at telling the passage of time. I wonder why? Maybe the senses or life meridian helped? Guess it doesn't really matter, but it sure is useful.*

I hurried back to the dorms, stripped off most of my clothes, and went to the restroom. No one else was there, which was good. I sat on the toilet and focused, ready to strengthen my stomach. *I wonder if this will help me eat spicy food better,* I thought as I opened the meridian. I felt extremely nauseous at first, though the pressure left my stomach and went the other way. After about five minutes and many, many flushes, I felt much better and cleaned out. Focusing on that meridian, I sensed that the workings of my innards were improved. I cleaned up and got dressed. As I did so, my stomach let me know that it had been emptied and wanted filling, immediately.

I nearly sprinted to the dining hall. There were several bins of bread, cheese, and grilled fowl available, along with a large salad bowl. I quickly filled a plate up, sat down at the first available spot, and inhaled the food. Eating helped settle my stomach and replenished the Aether spent on the meridians. "Wow, I don't know that I've ever seen anyone eat that quickly," came a deep, female voice with a slightly disgusted tone. I glanced up to see Haodha Anberlin looking at me.

"Hi. Yeah, I was really hungry after opening some meridians. Would you like to take a seat?" I asked, hoping I could mend some bridges here.

"No thank you. I just wanted to let you know that my house will not press Nicolai to mend his relationship with you, but we will not encourage him to attack you either. We will be neutral in this matter. The clan head asked me to inform you of this. Have a good day," she said as she walked away. *Well, at least it's just me versus Nicolai, not me versus the Haodha clan. At least right now. If I keep embarrassing him, it might escalate.*

CHAPTER THIRTEEN

I got up to get a second plate as Xiao and Ming came in. I waved at them, filled the plate again, and sat down. *This plate I'll eat slower and enjoy the taste,* I thought to myself as the Los sat down with me. "How was your day?" Ming asked politely.

"Good," I responded. "Opened another three meridians so far, hence the second plate. How about you?" I asked.

"Good as well. I'm hoping we get to move beyond meridian opening to gathering techniques, rune craft, or channeling soon though."

Xiao chimed in saying, "I can't wait for Beast knowledge. Our cousin said that the first class of Beast knowledge is when they introduce Wind Wolves, and I want to tame one. He said that taming a Beast can let you form a soul bond with one, which can improve your affinity with their respective element. Also, my father has a Wind Wolf soul partner and he's so amazing."

"Are soul bonds common?" I asked him.

"Not really. There are channeling techniques that can assist in forming one, though I don't know which ones. Dad said it took a long time to build their relationship enough to form a soul bond, and that it requires the Beast to be at least level four or higher. Hopefully, we'll find out more in class today." After that, we finished eating and got up. Xiao gave me a questioning look when I took my plate to the bin. I waved to Jamila and Vaya, who were sitting together with a group of other young women, mostly minor nobles by their accessories and posture. "You know they have servants to clean up the building after every meal?" he said as I rejoined them.

"Yeah, but it doesn't hurt me to be kind to them, so I've chosen to do so. You never know when the kindness you show someone will come back around to you." He nodded at that and looked pensive, but he didn't go back for his plate. *Changing the behavior of nobles will take a long time,* I thought, *but at least the majority of the ones I've met don't conform to my worst stereotypes.*

As we walked to the classrooms, I asked them about life in a major clan. Ming described long days of training, in weapons, history, and economics. As the heir, he had to be ready to take over at any time and lead his clan well. That was why he had been delayed entering Azyl Academy. He had to finish some of his intra-clan training first. "I already knew my talent and affinity before coming here because my clan has a method of testing. They had me attend here more out of tradition than from any expectation that it would let me grow faster. I'm also supposed to make friends with new talents and interact with our rivals in a friendlier manner than we would outside the academy," he finished explaining as we entered the library. "Having some positive acquaintances with the Volkov, Haodha, and Kowalski clan juniors helps keep major conflict down."

The chalkboard was set up again, with another message to go to the same classrooms as before. Xiao excused himself to head to his classroom, while Ming and I went up to ours. At the front of the room was a middle-aged woman with dark skin, black hair, and piercing blue eyes. Next to her stood a fox with silver hair whose shoulders reached nearly to her waist. *Wow, that's a huge fox.* We bowed to her as we walked in and then found our seats. As I did so, I saw an owl at the back of the classroom. It was a deep brown with gray speckles and nearly twice as large as an owl from earth. *That seems to be a theme with elemental animals; I guess the Aether makes them bigger.*

Brett and Jon walked in after we did, and right as they sat down the Counselor introduced herself. "Now that everyone is here, let us begin. I am Counselor Taiga and will be your instructor in Beasts, Elemental Beasts, and soul bonds. With me are Akira, my soul-bound Pokryc Fox, and Cichy, my soul-bound Spedis Owl. Yes, contrary to common belief it is possible to have more than one soul-bound partner. We will discuss how and why when we get to our discussion of soul bonds."

"We will spend the majority of the class discussing different Beasts that are common to our Kingdom, the Great Western Forest, the Skraj Mountains, and the Dividing Sea. These creatures will be the ones that you will encounter and most likely have to defend against if you choose to do so. Today, we will begin with an introduction of the Beast ranking system and give examples of each rank."

Over the course of the class, I learned that Beasts were given a level based upon how strong they were. Level one was roughly equivalent to a person in the Low Vapor gathering stage. There were very few animals that did not reach level one. Some examples of level one Beasts were the Elemental Fowl that we'd been having for dinner for a while. Level two was up to the High Mist gathering level, which was where they started to get dangerous, especially in large groups. Earthen Boars and Horned Rabbits were the examples given. *Horned rabbits. Rabbits with horns. And they could kill me. I ... can't compute.*

Level three was equivalent to High Smoke gathering, and the Wind Wolves Xiao was so interested in were usually at this level. Level four was the same as Foundation Compression, with Shadow Leopards as a prime example. Level five was the dividing line between Beasts and Elemental Beasts, since the equivalent of Complete Compression was when they begin to develop intelligence. Silver Apes were usually at this level in the deeper parts of the Great Western Forest. Level six was equivalent to a Core Seed and seven was equivalent to a Complete Core. Both the Pokryc Fox and Spedis Owl present were level six.

Elemental Beasts went up to level nine, after which they were known as Primordial Beasts and best avoided or appeased since there were only a couple people close to being able to cause even minor damage to them. The Kraken in the Dividing Sea was a level eleven, and to cross the sea required special ships that were heavily enchanted with distraction runes. We couldn't fight the Kraken, just avoid it. *Wow, that would be why the map Pa had simply said "There be Beasts beyond here." At least it seems to be unable to enter shallow water, or it might have eaten the capital, like all of it, already.*

One of the reasons that the Kingdom only had nominal control over the Great Western Forest and the Skraj Mountains was the presence of several Primordial Beasts that ruled over territories in the deepest parts. Mankind only explored the edges of the wilderness on this world since they weren't the apex predator here.

We finished the lesson by discussing Elemental Fowl. One of the few Beasts domesticated, it was unique in that what you fed one would change its elemental affinity. They were raised on farms west and north of the city, with each farm typically focusing on a single element. They were useful as food, especially since they bred very rapidly. They were only a danger to people in large groups since they could project very weak elemental attacks that overlapped each other to grow powerful. *By our powers combined! Heh.* The lesson ended with a task to find a book describing Beasts and do some reading, to grow accustomed to looking up information on targets and threats. We were then dismissed to go to Physical Training.

PT started with a run, along with push-ups and other calisthenics. We were then dismissed to our smaller groups to study. All this week would be was self-guided study with exercises, to help our bodies build the necessary muscles and get used to our weapons. The memory stone showed me a blocking motion in reverse grip followed by a stab-and-slash motion in front grip, along with the important footwork required to keep balanced. Lastly, it tied all of the motions together into a series of motions called a form. I would have to master the form to advance to the next part of the memory stone or to get a new one. *First, let's work through the individual motions, then start on the form.*

I spent the rest of the PT time getting all the individual moves down, and started combining them, such as stabbing in front grip with my right hand while blocking high in reverse grip with my left. I was trying to be able to do something different with each hand without too much focus. *Well, I didn't make any progress on the form, but I'll take some time this evening to work on it. Basics first will give me a better foundation.* We finished PT with a run again. After finishing it I realized that I had just run my fourth 5K in two days, but I was only tired, not exhausted as I thought I should be. *Gathering, opening meridians, and the Aether-infused food is helping us to grow stronger faster. This is amazing! I'm gonna be a superhero when I grow up!*

After PT there was a mad rush for the showers, and once everyone had gotten clean, the rush repeated itself at dinner. *I'm pretty certain everyone got seconds,* I thought as I cleaned up my plate. There wasn't a lot of talking, as nearly everyone was exhausted. Exercising for three hours straight wasn't something most of the students had ever done before.

After dinner, a large group of people headed to the library to find books, but I decided to take the time to open my spine meridian and carve the Metal rune into my center. Then I would gather for an hour and work on my trisula form. *I'll get a book before class in the morning.* I headed out to the same pavilion from that morning. Upon arriving, I found Jamila there, already meditating. I was startled, but there were three positions available so I simply took the one on the opposite side and sat down.

First things first, I thought as I focused into my center. I carefully found the spine meridian I identified earlier because I didn't want to make any mistakes with anything connected to my spinal cord. *I like being able to walk very much, no breaking spinal column, no sir.* As I reached into my center to grab Aether, I realized it was getting easier to manipulate it. Not significantly so, but enough to be noticeable. I decided to try and open the meridian with only a tiny bit of Aether.

I tried to grab only a single mote, but couldn't make the grip of my will small enough. After a couple of tries, I focused on imagining a tiny gripper claw, rather than a hand. Fewer pieces in my mental image made it easier to make the image itself smaller. I still wasn't able to grab a single one, but I was able to reduce the number I grabbed to three. *This should be small enough.* I gently guided the three motes to the entrance of the spinal meridian and pushed them through. They basically flew down the open portion of the meridian, until they reached the bottom of my spine. After they ran into the first bone, they vanished. *Wait, what?* I thought. Focusing as hard as I could there, I realized that the bone seemed slightly denser.

Huh, the Aether was absorbed into the bone. I guess I can't use that little Aether to fully open the meridian. Let's try again. This time I pulled out about half as much Aether as I had used on my breath meridian. As I pulled the Aether from my center, I focused on the leading edge, trying to watch it get absorbed. I was fascinated as I sensed the bone thickening, growing stronger and tougher. As the rush of Aether poured through the joints, a loud series of pops echoed out from me from every joint in my back. It was so loud that it startled me out of my meditation. Sheepishly, I looked around, only to blush at Jamila's incredulous stare.

"Are you okay?" she asked. I blushed deeper. *Gah, why do I keep getting flustered! Stupid puberty!*

"Umm, yeah. I'm okay. Sorry about that, I didn't mean to disturb you. I can leave if you'd like?" I said.

"No, you're welcome to stay. There aren't enough pavilions to keep one all to myself," she replied, somewhat hurriedly. *Huh, she's blushing.*

"Thanks. I'll try not to disturb you again." I was still enamored by her looks. *I'll get to know her better on the walk back to the dorms. Now isn't the time to talk.* I took a couple of deep breaths and centered myself again.

I focused my attention back on the spinal meridian. *Huh, after that initial rush, it looks like the bone is not absorbing Aether. Oh wait, there went one mote in. The rate of absorption is much lower. It's like there were a bunch of open holes in the material, and all the easily accessible ones got filled. Now only a few holes are left open, and it's random chance that has motes of Aether grab onto them. Maybe that is why people at higher levels are stronger, as the higher pressure lets the Aether bond better or more completely.*

I wonder... I thought while I reached to grab some Aether and force it into the bones. Some of the Aether I grabbed was absorbed, until I released my will, at which point it popped out. *Yup, higher pressure in the Aether will let more absorb into the bones. It needs to be in equilibrium. I can potentially use this. I'd have to be able to push more in really fast, but I could use this to take a hit better.* I continued to experiment, discovering that a very tiny amount of Aether stayed in the bones after putting pressure on it, that was similar in amount to the little bit that was absorbed while I was just watching. *I can facilitate the extra little absorption, but I'm not sure it is worth the effort. It seems to be logarithmic, with a very large jump at first followed by a sharp decline in the rate of increase. I'll have to ask Counselor Sila tomorrow about this. Time to work on the next rune.*

I pulled the second-to-last memory stone out, ready to watch the next rune be drawn. This rune started as a simple eight-pointed star, with the last stroke being from up to down. This last stroke extended four times as far as the other three. The vertical line was then used to draw out the shape of a sword, with the star as the hilt. Around the tip of the sword, an anvil was drawn, as if the sword was partially inserted into it. Then placed beside the sword on the anvil was a hammer. *Interesting, the other types were abstract images, while this one is more concrete. I wonder why?*

After finishing watching the drawing, and the various tiny ways it could fail, I was prepared to spend the next hour working on it. Thankfully, I was able to get the rune drawn in just five tries, though each failure nearly brought me to tears. The pain for erasing a rune was increasing for each rune currently drawn. *It's a good thing that I'm going in reverse order of complexity. If I tried to draw the Lightning rune now, I don't know if I'd make it.*

Having completed my tasks for the night, I looked around. Seeing that it was still daylight because it was late summer with moderately long days, I decided to gather for a little while. Focusing in on my center again, I breathed deeply and focused, moving Aether with my mind into my center and making it my own. While it was not restful, it was calming. Gathering required intense focus the entire time, or it would not work, and so it helped you to forget worries about tomorrow during that time.

A slight noise in the pavilion disturbed me out of my focus. I would not have heard it without the enhancing effect on my senses. I looked up and saw Jamila just getting up. It was dark out, with the amazing light show of the Grotto going full swing again. "It's beautiful, isn't it?" I asked her, gesturing at the dancing elemental fireflies and lighted paths.

"Yes, it is. I saw this last night, so I wanted to stay out again," she replied.

"I hope to see the phoenix again," I said, somewhat wistfully.

"Phoenix?" she asked.

"Uh, the beautiful red bird that burst into flames. I heard they were called phoenixes," I said hastily. *Stop using Earth words!*

"Oh, the Crimson Zarorzel. Yes, it is beautiful, and I heard it was a level five Elemental Beast. Maybe someone will bond with it, though I've heard they are notoriously hard to bond with," she said with a questioning look in her eyes. I could tell she didn't want to ask me about "phoenixes" but was curious about who told me the strange wrong name.

She walked next to me as we headed back to the dorms. "Uh... so, what does your family do?" I asked awkwardly, reliving my clumsy high school conversations. "If you want to tell me, that is," I hurriedly said afterward, internally cringing. *I thought I was over this!*

"No, it is okay. My father is a baker down on Navale Lane. I used to cook with him along with my younger sister. We would sell the bread and rolls we made to the dockyard workers. It has only been two days, and I have already started to miss the smell of rolls baking in the morning."

As she was talking, the Crimson Zarorzel flew by. "You are right," she said in wonder, "it is a beautiful bird." As she said this, the Zarorzel turned to look at me and landed. It gazed at me curiously, nodded strangely, and then it flew away again.

"That was interesting," I said cautiously. "I wonder what they eat."

"You should ask the cooks in the morning, maybe they would know. Or your Beasts instructor," Jamila said helpfully. "Oh, I must be going quickly, I have to attend my reading lesson. It is held in the dorm lounge on the first floor." With a sly look at me, she said, "I will race you," and immediately took off running.

"What, hey!" I shouted and ran after her. She beat me back to the dorms. As she reached the door, she turned and gave me a smirk before heading inside. In the first-floor lounge, I saw a group of people seated in a circle, with a fourth tier student near the front. Jamila sat in the back of the circle, picking up a book that had been left for her. The fourth tier student nodded to her and she said, "Now that you are all here, we can begin. We will be going over the letters we use and their sounds, and putting them into words to start with. Go back to the third page in your book."

Half the kids began turning pages. I noticed that Jamila was the only one without a partner. As I looked on, the instructor called out, "You, by the door. Can you read? Yes, good, partner with Jamila there. She is the only one without a partner and learning to read is faster with another. Come now." The instructor gestured imperiously. Jamila turned and smiled at me. I walked over and sat down next to her, working through the reading book slowly. After an hour had passed, we had made it through the alphabet and were working on simple spelling. The instructor called the end of the class and Jamila looked up at me and blushed.

"Thank you for your help, Aiden. Um, would you be willing to come back tomorrow night at the same time to help?"

"Sure. I'm glad that I was able to help. See you tomorrow," I said as we stood up. Her room was on the first floor, so she said "Good night," as she walked to the door into the girls' half of the building. I walked up to my room floating on a cloud. *Gah, stupid youthful infatuation!* I thought, *Though she is really nice and pretty. Welp, puberty, you win again!*

CHAPTER FOURTEEN

After breakfast with my group of friends, we headed to the classrooms. We walked in, bowed to the Mentors, and took our seats waiting for class to start. Over the next couple of minutes, everyone finished trickling in, and Counselor Sila stood up. "Good morning, students. Today we will finish opening your major meridians of both legs. After you have opened your leg meridians, search for others that are easily openable. You should know how many are available from the entrance exam. Come see me if you forgot. If you are having difficulty finding them, talk to the Mentors or myself. After finding more meridians to open, or not, and speaking with one of us, you are free to go. Tomorrow we will be starting to work on channeling and gathering techniques since you will be ready for them. Most techniques we teach require the five major meridians to be open, at least. Are there any questions?"

"Sir, is there a limit to the amount of Aether absorbed into the areas around a meridian?" I asked, rehashing the question from last night.

"Yes, though everyone's limit is slightly different. Over time, the materials that make up your body will become saturated with Aether and no more will absorb into them. Each time you increase in level, this limit is raised as well, and is one of the reasons that those at higher gathering levels are stronger," Counselor Sila explained. "Additionally, each meridian that connects to the same portion of your body, like the life meridian and the Right Arm meridian both connect to the right lung increase the limit for that part. Again, more meridians are better. Any other questions?"

Brett asked, "Are we going to work on the meridians that are partially blocked and openable with alchemy soon?"

"Ah, good question. Not during your first tier. While having more meridians open at each level improves the benefit you receive from them, the side effects of alchemically opening a meridian are detrimental if done before you have started to compress Aether into a liquid. Once you have advanced past the Starting Aether Compression level, then we will begin to open the rest of your meridians."

"Thank you, Counselor." No one else asked any questions, and so we got started. The Counselor and Mentors were watching us, making sure that nothing went wrong. I focused down, as I had done six times already, and found the two meridians. I opened them one after the other, watching the rush of Aether be absorbed into the bones and muscles of my legs and lower torso. *Get a little more Aether in there and I'll have a six pack*, I thought to myself because the left leg meridian also connected to my abs.

After finishing opening up my leg meridians, I began to search for more meridians to open. I started feeling around the sides of my center again and found one meridian that went straight out to my chest, along the path I had used to make the shield a couple days ago. This one was strange.

It just hit the top of my chest and seemed to vanish. I tried feeling around for it, but to no avail. A little later, I found another one just like it that went to my back, directly opposite to it. *That is weird, not sure what that one is doing.*

The next meridian I found turned into three when the meridian went to my heart, circled through every chamber and around, before returning to my center. Two meridians split off from my heart meridian, one going through the left side of my body in every blood vessel, and one in the right. They went through every single artery, vein, and capillary in my body. *That's amazing! Following this one, I can see my whole body. It's almost like following a 3D MRI inside me!*

The last meridian I found, and what should be the last openable one if my math was right, went through my thyroid up to my brain, circled through every part of it, and then came back to the center. *I wonder what Aether does to the brain? I know the senses meridian made my eyesight, hearing, smell, and taste more sensitive. Maybe the brain one will help me to process all that information better. Maybe it'll make me smarter.* I spent a good thirty minutes going over everything I could sense before deciding to go talk to Counselor Sila.

When I asked him about the meridian that came straight out of my center to my chest, he said, "Ah, you've got a skin meridian. Those are useful, makes you tougher. The Aether will flow out to your skin, and then around your whole body to the other side, where it flows inward. What else?" The heart and blood vessels ones he agreed were good, and the brain one he said would simply help me to process more information faster. "A brain meridian will be very helpful with your senses meridian. By the way, good job on the blockage on that meridian, though you should have talked to me first. Hmm, of all the meridians, prioritize the heart, right-side blood vessels, left-side blood vessels, kidney system, brain, then ribs, and lastly skin. Do heart today, both blood vessels tomorrow after eating extra meat, kidney and brain the next day, ribs and skin day after. No faster than that. You shouldn't need supervision for the heart meridian. The right arm meridian made it strong enough to deal with the additional Aether provided. Ask if you have questions; find me or the Mentors if you have problems. Enjoy your day."

"Thank you, sir, I think I'm okay for now. Have a good day, sir," I said as I turned to leave. *I've found all of my easily openable meridians. Once I finish opening them, it's time to really push with advancing in levels. Hopefully, we'll get some neat techniques that will help us grow faster tomorrow, as the easy part is done now.* I left the room and headed to the Grotto, where I found what I was starting to think of as my pavilion. Getting settled on the seat, I centered myself.

Once I located the heart meridian, I gathered my courage and some Aether in the bonds of my will. Taking a deep breath, I slowly fed the

Aether into the meridian and watched as the Aether entered the right side of my heart, came out the left, looped back through and around throughout the chambers, and made several wraps around the outside before it turned back down to my center. My heart stuttered for a beat, and then resumed beating even stronger. I saw tiny bits of Aether from the meridian entering into the blood as it flowed through my heart, making the blood itself stronger and able to hold more oxygen and necessary nutrients. *Whoa, that is amazing!* I thought as I watched it.

Suddenly, a small leakage of Aether flowed into the right-side blood vessels meridian, where it connected to the heart meridian. I tried to stop it because I had been told to wait a day, but was unable to. More and more Aether fed itself from my center into the heart meridian, where it entered into the right and left blood vessel meridians. *Crap, crap!* I thought. *You're not supposed to open too many meridians because your body needs materials to build the strength the Aether is giving you. Food, need food.*

I took off, holding the Aether in my center as best as I could, but not able to restrain it all. *Dining hall has food available. I hope.* I ran, feeling the Aether pump through me with every beat of my heart. I passed several other students, including Louis, who called out, asking if I was okay. I didn't take the time to respond, pushing myself as fast as I could. I ran up to the entrance to the dining hall, to find it locked. I knocked loudly multiple times. After thirty seconds, the door opened and one of the servers was there. "Need food. Accidentally opened two meridians I wasn't supposed to today," I said, panting. I recognized the server as the person who told me I didn't need to bring up the plates.

"Um, you are supposed to wait until lunchtime. Though I can make an exception for you. Come in, quickly," he told me, ushering me into the room and closing the door behind me. He guided me over to the door into the kitchen, and had me sit at a table. He brought out a platter of meat and vegetables that I quickly started shoving into my mouth. I could feel the Aether pulling resources from my body, and thought I could see the little fat I had start to vanish. As I gulped the food down, I asked for juice at which he nodded and ran into the kitchen, having felt my urgency. I finished another piece of meat before he came out with a pitcher of juice and a glass. I grabbed the pitcher from his hands and chugged it.

As I did so, I watched the Aether flowing through my digestive system meridian dissolve the juice and seemingly absorb it. It had already grabbed the meat, and seemed to be feeding them into my center. I was pushing Aether into my stomach meridian, trying to hurry it up and prevent any damage to my muscles. As I kept shoveling food into me, the servant ran off and brought another plate of meat. I finally felt the process slowing down and slowed down eating as well. "Thank you. That could have been bad," I said before slowly getting up. Apparently, getting up was a bad idea, and I ended up falling face first onto the ground.

A little bit later, I awoke to see the servant shaking me, and heard another servant run out of the room. "I'm okay," I said groggily, though I realized I felt incredibly weak.

"Stay still, we sent for Counselor Sojka, the healing instructor. She will be here shortly," the servant told me as I lay there.

"Thank you. What's your name? I'm Kupiec Aiden," I said, wanting to stop referring to him as "the servant" in my head.

"I'm Poko Karl, nice to make your acquaintance. Now don't move. If you end up hurt they'll have my head." I nodded at this and closed my eyes. The spinning had stopped, which was a good sign.

After a few minutes, a wave of Aether swept over me as a hand gripped my upper right arm. I opened my eyes and saw the glaring face of a middle-aged woman, with bright gold hair and piercing blue eyes. "Ah, young idiot. Care to explain why you decided to open five meridians in a single morning?" I quickly explained what had happened, starting with the recommendation from Counselor Sila through the accidental opening of both blood vessel meridians.

"Ok, maybe you aren't as large of an idiot as I suspected. It is rare that the blood vessel meridians are easily openable, so Counselor Sila gave you incorrect advice based on the normal way of opening these meridians, with alchemy. That way you can isolate the three connecting meridians you have, whereas you were always going to be opening all three at the same time. Hold still." As she said this, a wave of Aether greater than I had experienced before flowed through me, moving through each part of my body. Every bit of me that the Aether flooded through felt rejuvenated.

As the Counselor finished up, she instructed me, "Go back to your dorm and eat what you will be given. You will rest there until it is time for your afternoon class, which you may attend, after which you will return to your dorm. Eat as much as you can and rest until tomorrow. I will check on you tomorrow morning after breakfast. Now go." She turned and left as I slowly struggled to my feet. The weakness I had been feeling was reduced but not gone. Karl handed me a sack of bread and meat with a quick "Good luck" as he ushered me out of the dining hall. I saw a number of fourth tier students waiting for the dining hall to open. *Huh, I guess the fourth tier eats before us*, I thought. *Though there are a lot less of them than us firsties.*

I slowly staggered to my dorm, feeling like someone was watching me, where I laid down on the bed and picked at the bread loaf. *I'll clean the crumbs later, too tired.* I looked into my center and throughout the rest of my body. I could see the damage done in my meridians, and saw it slowly healing as the food I had eaten was processed. *Well, that was not good, but it looks like I was able to get food and help fast enough to stave off the worst damage. Nap time, I guess.*

After a short nap, I got up, stumbled to the facilities, and ate the rest of the food that was packed for me. I saw that I still had about thirty minutes before class was due to start by the height of the sun. Taking advantage of this time, I centered myself and gathered for twenty minutes, trying to bring my Aether back up to what it was before I opened too many meridians. The speed at which I was able to gather continued to increase as meridians were opened and higher level runes were drawn. I estimated that I was gathering at a rate of nearly two hundred and fifty times what I had been before I started modifying my runes. *I wonder how fast I'll end up gathering, and how far ahead the nobles like Ming are? I'll catch up; I'll just have to work as hard as I can, and harder than anyone else.* With that thought, I got up from the bed and headed out to class.

On the way to class I ran into Brett and Jon. "Hey, I didn't see you at lunch, what happened?" Jon asked.

"Ah, I accidentally opened too many meridians at once and had to get healed. I've been told to stay in my room and rest except for class for the rest of the day and will be examined again tomorrow," I replied.

"Okay. You let me know if you need anything," Jon told me. Brett echoed him. I smiled and nodded in response. *It's always good to have friends.* We walked together to class, with Brett telling a story about hunting a level 4 Silver furred fox with his dad and uncle. The story ended as we reached the academic building, with his dad and uncle running into each other as the fox dodged and ran off. Laughing, we ascended the stairs to the classroom and saw Counselor Sila along with two new Mentors.

One was a third tier young woman a little taller than me, with tan skin and black hair and eyes. The other was a fourth tier young man, as tall as Louis but half as wide, with blonde hair, green eyes, and skin that looked like he had been in the sun every moment since birth. As everyone got seated, Counselor Sila started off. "Welcome to Introductory Herbology. I will be your herbs teacher as well as your alchemy teacher. These are Mentors Granjer Graci,"—he pointed to the young woman—"and Bonde Sterk. They are advanced students in the Alchemy and Herbology track and will be assisting me."

"We require all students to take Herbology so that you will be able to recognize and utilize elemental plants, seeds, fungi, and other resources whenever you find them. As you advance in your studies, you will be sent on missions, with supervision, and on expeditions as teams. One of the goals of such expeditions is to find resources that can be used to enhance our school's ability, to assist in funding the Academy, and to grow the students and faculty here. We will start by introducing the evaluation system used for these resources and discuss some of the major types." He pulled a variety of plants out of a bag and laid them on the desk in the front of the room.

"Elemental herbs and plants are rated similarly to Elemental Beasts, with the levels being used to identify who would benefit from the herb's use instead of how strong they are. This is a level one Iron Grass, which is used by Metal and Earth gatherers to gain Aether. As a level one plant, it is really only useful to those in the Aether Gathering stage. Most herbs will have a very minor effect on gathering speed if eaten raw, but can be used by alchemists to make concoctions that increase the effects immensely." He held up a stalk of grass about a foot tall that was a silvery green color. He put it down and picked up a red flower. "This is a Firebloom Flower, a level three herb that gathers and purifies Fire Aether around it. This is useful for Fire gatherers up through the Aether Compression stage and is often planted in gardens around their homes. The Meditation Grotto is filled with these and their equivalent for the other elements, which is one reason we encourage all students to gather there."

Counselor Sila spent the next hour describing various different plants and how we could recognize them. The color was sometimes useful, but could be deceiving as well. Some types of plants were poisonous to specific affinities and would be colored to attract them. Just like Earth, plants and animals had evolved to work together or to attack each other to spread themselves. Here, they just had a new tool with which to do so.

At the end of class, Counselor Sila dismissed everyone with a direction to find more information about various level one plants that would be useful for us. As I was getting up, he told me to stay put for a bit. Once everyone else had left, he pulled a pouch out of his pocket. "Counselor Sojka told me what happened today. I am sorry for misleading you. As one of the alchemists on staff, I have a number of powders, potions, and pills available. Please take these Meridian Cleanser pills I made as an apology. Take them just after you eat a large meal and they will help heal any injuries your meridians took because of today, as well as disperse some of the impurities in your center and meridians.

"Thank you for your concern, sir," I said with a slight bow and took the offered pouch. Inside were eight pills, enough to last one week. "I am looking forward to learning how to make these and other alchemical goods."

"Good. I will be more careful with advice based upon your unique talent and capabilities from now on. Take care. Counselor Sojka will find you after breakfast to check your condition again," he told me in dismissal, so I bowed again and left. Rather than go to Physical Training, I went back to my room, where I found a loaf of hearty bread and a spread of fruit placed on my desk. I quickly ate everything and fell asleep.

CHAPTER FIFTEEN

The sound of many people rushing into the bathroom after PT woke me up. I focused into my center and evaluated my condition. It looked like I was on the mend; little cracks in the sides of the meridians were slowly sealing together. *Ok, starting to heal. More food, gather for a while, then sleep.* I got out of bed and stretched, then left my room.

The hallway was empty now, with two people in the shower and the rest getting dressed. I left the building and saw the last few stragglers from the third years leaving the building as I approached. "Good evening," I said as our paths crossed. A few mumbled greetings were returned as they hurried towards the classroom building.

Walking into the building I saw a number of servants gathering the dishes and wiping tables down. I walked to the nearest table and stacked up the plates, with the knives and spoons on top. I carried the stack to the bin that was set out and put it inside. "Oh, you don't have to do that, sir," a young woman told me.

"It's okay, Lola, that's Aiden," Karl said as he walked over with a stack of dishes. "He's the one who was cleaning his place and gave us the idea for the bin. I'm glad you are up and about. We hear some scary stories of people doing what you did and ending up crippled."

"Thanks, Karl. Any chance food will be ready soon?" I asked, getting another set of dishes together.

"Only a couple of minutes, they were finishing the Water Buffalo roast last I checked. Thank you for helping, but you still don't look fully stable. Take a seat and I'll bring you the roast and Watercress salad when they are ready."

"Thanks," I said as I sat gratefully. The damage to my meridians translated to a large decrease in my stamina. Karl came out a minute later with a plate of food. I munched down on the buffalo and salad. I was amazed at the taste again. The Aether from the food absorbed a little, though I saw that most didn't get absorbed. Looking closely I saw that the majority of the Aether in the meat was a dark blue color. *Hah, Water Buffalo is Water affinity. Makes sense. I wonder if they look the same.*

After a couple of minutes, my classmates began trickling in. Brett and Lucas were among the first to enter, and Brett waved at me as he went to get food. They joined me, and Lucas said, "You didn't miss much. A couple of people advanced to the next level, but we are still mostly doing individual practice. Though we were threatened that we need to get it done by the end of the week or else. No one had the courage to ask what the else was." Everyone at the table laughed at that.

Dinner was finished quickly, and we all split up to go gather in our chosen spots. I headed into the Meditation Grotto to my pavilion. Finding it empty, I was a little sad, but I realized that the area probably was not as good for Jamila as it was for me. *There are quite a few different plants around here that are Fire or Lightning affinity, and none with Water. She probably found a better spot with more Water and Earth focused decorations.*

I sat down and got out the container given to me earlier by Counselor Sila. Opening it, I smelled an herbal fragrance that reminded me of basil and thyme. I pulled a pill out and put it in my mouth. It seemed to melt up into a puddle that I swallowed down and I focused on gathering Aether into myself. I felt the pill's liquid reach my stomach and be absorbed into my body, and watched a stream of energy flow out of my stomach into my center and meridians. Everywhere the energy passed the cracks in my meridians healed significantly, and the edges seemed more robust. The wave of energy tapered off after a full circuit through my body, finishing in my intestines. I suddenly had a very strong need for a restroom, and I hurried back to the dorms.

Apparently cleansing the meridians of impurities is a smelly process, I thought when I was finished. I decided that next time I was going to take the pill in my room. I gathered in my room for the next thirty minutes, noticing a small improvement in speed from before to after the pill did its work. *Impurities in your meridians make it harder to gather. That makes sense. I wonder how else you get rid of them besides a Meridian Cleanser pill. Also, how do they get there? There is so much to learn!*

After I finished gathering, I went downstairs to find the reading lesson had not quite started yet. Not seeing Jamila, I sat down at the back of the group and tried not to fall asleep again. She came into the room with a couple of other students. Brett and Bridget came in behind her and headed over to the group. Jamila broke into a big smile and came over to join me. As she sat down, her face turned serious and she lightly smacked my arm. "I was not sure you were going to come. I had heard what happened. Do not do that again, you worried me."

"Sorry. I'm feeling better now, and should be back to full health tomorrow. Shall we begin?" I whispered back, hands up in a placating gesture, before indicating the book I had gotten from the instructor. She nodded and we went through the book. Over the course of the next hour, I was intensely surprised. She had learned nearly the entire book. "You are learning incredibly fast," I commented as we finished up.

"I opened a meridian that connected to my head and it has given me a nearly perfect memory. Counselor Sojka said I was lucky since that meridian is very useful. Though she did say that most of the benefits come after opening and it does not get much better as you grow in strength," she said as she stood up.

"Neat. Um, did you find another pavilion in the Grotto? I didn't see you earlier," I asked.

"Yes! I found a place that is right next to a small pond, with Watercress and Frozen Lilies growing around it. It is beautiful and full of Water, Wood, and Ice Aether. The area where you were gathering is too high in Fire and Lightning for me. Should be perfect for you though." "That's good. I need to explore the Grotto more. Maybe you could show me the area you found?" I asked nervously. "I would be happy to. Good night, Aiden, see you tomorrow!" she said as she walked through the entryway into the girls' side of the building. Runes glared at me from the door frame. *Huh, I guess they enforce the no opposite gender in the rooms with magic. That's awesome!* I thought as I turned to go back to my room. I was excited; I had gotten Jamila to agree to show me around, so I got to spend more time with her. Also, I was excited for tomorrow, with the first explanation of channeling techniques, now that we had the major meridians open.

Even with my excitement, I still slept like a log, only to awaken with the sun. Focusing on myself, I looked into my center and traced my meridians. Thankfully, the damage that had been evident yesterday was now nearly gone. *Should be healed up by tomorrow!* I thought. I grabbed my towel and went to take a shower. After the morning rituals, I went to get breakfast. *I'm starving!* I thought. *I wonder if my calorie needs have increased this much permanently, or if they will decrease once I've reached equilibrium with all my meridians opening. Ooh, today's Ice Day! Intro Alchemy! I can't wait.*

Breakfast was delicious, as always. It was eggs from Elemental Fowl and bacon from Aniyu Elk, both with Ice affinity. *The days of the week determine the affinity of the food we are served. Why did it take me four days to figure this out?* I wondered, smacking myself on the forehead. The Aether from the meal refreshed me a bit, but nowhere near as much as the first day did. *Well duh, my affinity with Wood, Water, and Ice was Low, so I won't get much benefit from those. Tomorrow will be much better for me.*

I mentioned my findings to Jon at the table, and he looked at me questioningly. "Really?" he asked, "How can you tell?"

"Can't you see the color of the Aether when you eat it?" I asked. "You can? That's amazing! No, I can't tell at all. No wonder this tasted so much better than yesterday's," he exclaimed back, after which he went for thirds. After Jon finished his meal, we got up and left for class. Everyone was in a hurry to get to the first class on channeling. As we reached the class building, I noticed Bridget and Lucas leaving the doorway.

"Hey. We've got class down on the training fields today. Let's go find Counselor Sila and see what techniques he will teach us!" Bridget exclaimed as she got close. Shouts of agreement sounded out as everyone turned to follow her. Shortly after that, we were all jogging to where we saw Counselor Sila, full of excitement. This was why many people had joined, and I just couldn't get past how cool doing actual magic was going to be. *I wonder what we are going to cover first.*

Just before we got to our class location, Counselor Sojka called out my name. I turned back towards her as she walked up. "Good, I caught you. Come here, let me look you over," she said as she reached out and took my arm. A pulsing wave of Aether flowed through me, looking almost like radar. "Hmm, much more healed than I expected. That is unexpected, but good. Did Counselor Sila give you anything yesterday?" she asked. I showed her the Meridian Cleanser pills, at which she nodded.

"Good. Based on your condition, I think three more pills should be plenty. You can try to give the other four back, but I doubt he will take them. If you keep them, wait to take them until you reach the Smoke stage of Aether Gathering. They will be more beneficial then, as impurities in your meridians will make reaching Compression much harder. You are cleared to attend class. I will check on you in three days. Good day." She dropped my arm and turned to walk towards another group, calling out another student's name. *Well, at least I wasn't the only idiot to need to get inspected by the healer this morning.*

"Greetings, class, good to see you all in such fine spirits. Come, gather around and we will discuss what we are going to be doing today," Counselor Sila said as we approached him. The group of us formed a semi-circle facing him and the small chalkboard he had brought out. "Today we will be learning a method of channeling Aether through your leg meridians to increase your running speed. Often being able to run faster and longer can make the difference between getting to a town in time to stop a Beast horde, or arriving after it is destroyed. Also, at your level being able to run away from danger is eminently useful. Now look," he said as he gestured to the chalkboard.

On the board he had drawn an outline of a person with the leg meridians. Then he drew an arrow pointing into the right leg. "First you need to push as much Aether as you can into the right leg, as the leg is hitting the ground. Some will be absorbed, while the rest will flow on through, then, as it reaches your center, you must use the same Aether and push it into the left leg. Continue this cycle for as many rotations as you can, and make this rune in your center as the Aether flows back and forth." He drew what looked like two Greek chis next to each other. "Without the rune, this will increase your speed slightly, but the rune changes the Aether's effects to enable faster movement. Now, watch. First I will run without Aether, then I will cycle it without the Rune, then I will use the Rune as well."

He started jogging to the side of the PT field. After about twenty seconds, he suddenly increased in speed by twenty percent or so. This was about as fast as many of us could run, so it wasn't too surprising. However,

I noticed that his pacing didn't seem to change; every step just took him farther. After another thirty seconds, his speed tripled from the second stage. *He's running faster than Usain Bolt could! And this is a low level technique that we can all use. I wonder how fast he is able to move?!* Counselor Sila came back, looking none the worse for wear. "Now you can see the difference. I was just jogging lightly and was able to move that quickly due to the effects of Aether and Runes. Any questions right now?"

I took the opportunity. "Sir, how fast can you run with full Aether support?"

"Well, if I'm just running, I could probably make it to the capital and back in an hour, though the soldiers tasked with patrolling the road don't like it when people run that quickly," he said, and everyone gasped. The capital was nearly a hundred miles away. He could run around two hundred miles an hour! *Holy snikeys!* I thought, amazed. "Of course, if I needed to get there quickly, I would use my flying disk and get there in ten minutes."

A gasp of "Flying" came from several mouths. *Wow, they have flying magical artifacts. I want one!* "Any other questions, related to this channeling technique? No, okay, everyone get started. We will be watching to help correct any mistakes," Counselor Sila said as he gestured to the PT field. The Mentors guided us to start running in a line, so that we weren't in anybody else's way. I tried to focus on my center while running, and ended up tripping. Up and down the line, many people were tripping or stumbling. Apparently, they were having the same issues I was.

Standing back up, I centered myself, falling into that focused state that brought my body into high resolution. In this state, I opened my eyes. The first time I did this, I lost the centered state immediately. After a couple of tries, I was able to stay centered while watching the world. I tried to step forward, and my leg barely responded. I ended up on the ground again.

Over to my right, I saw Mentor Lo coaching Jon through what I was trying to do. Ming, Anberlin, Lucas, and Brett were all running up the field. Anberlin looked like her legs were on fire, while a swirl of Air surrounded Ming. *I don't think they are using the method we were just taught,* I thought. *Probably have techniques that they were taught by their clans. I've got a long way to go to catch up. Well, no time to dawdle.*

I got up and focused again, feeling my body move as I did so. I was able to start walking while holding the centered state. After a couple of minutes pacing, I started jogging. Again I focused on just holding the centered state, moving back and forth across a small part of the fields, watching the Aether and blood flowing through my body. *This is amazing. I can see my form as I run. Wow, I really need to improve my running form. Okay, now*

I need to push the Aether into my right leg, and move it to the left after it circulates through.

I waited until I had just pushed off with my left leg, and then flooded my right leg meridian with Aether. The sudden jump in strength caused me to fall over to the left. I rolled a couple of times, and ended up at Counselor Sila's feet. One of Nicky's lackeys laughed at me, before tripping themselves. *Serves him right.* "Good start. A little less Aether to start with, I think, would allow you to get used to the strength increase. Keep going," Counselor Sila told me.

By the end of the lesson, I had managed to get the Aether timing down, and could now use the technique without the rune. Counselor Sila admonished all of us to work on the technique, and to gather enough Aether to replace what we used. "Continue to gather as much as you can. Once you have opened all the meridians that you were instructed to, you need to focus on moving to the next level of Aether Gathering. By the end of the first six months here, you all should be able to attain the Smoke Aether level and be ready to start Aether Compression. Towards that end, tomorrow we will work on a technique for gathering Aether. I will see you all after lunch for your Introduction to Alchemy class. Good day."

The class bowed to him in response, with most of us covered in sweat. Then I turned towards the Meditation Grotto and began to jog off, continuing to work on keeping a constant cycle of Aether streaming through my legs. I reached my pavilion quickly and took some time to stretch. Afterward, I sat down and began to gather. *Wow, I'm really low on Aether. So I can only sustain a small increase in speed for twenty-ish minutes right now.*

Gathering after using up most of my Aether always made me feel like I had a sinkhole in my center. The Aether around me would be sucked inward, pulling into my center to fill the hole. I gathered for an hour, filling myself back to where I was before class and even a little beyond. *Slowly making progress towards Mist. I wonder how fast everyone else is progressing. Adding more Aether beyond my current max to my center takes so much longer than just filling it back up.* As I stood and stretched after I finished, I saw the Zarorzel watching me. *This evening, I'll bring some fruit or something for it.*

CHAPTER SIXTEEN

Before lunch, I hurried to take a shower and change. Lunch proceeded normally, with almost everyone talking about the new technique. After lunch, everyone headed to the alchemy building rather than the classroom building. The alchemy building was in the far southwest corner of the Academy, with a fairly large open space around it. "The gap between buildings is in case the alchemy building explodes," Lo Ming informed the group we were walking with.

"Is that really a danger?" Jon asked.

"Not really. Especially not for us. I doubt we'll be allowed to experiment with new formulas. Generally, the only danger for us is bad smells and ruining ingredients," he said back, grinning. Jon and a few other people relaxed at that. I was excited as we were getting to learn magic chemistry. *I wonder how much of what I studied before will apply. Probably almost nothing. Though I hope something does,* I thought as we entered the building.

Inside the building was a long hallway and stairs that led up to another floor. Counselor Sila's name was written on the third door to the right, so we filed into that room to see Counselor Sila and Mentors Granjer and Bonde standing in front of a number of tables. Each table had a mortar and pestle, a couple of knives, a small brazier with a pan on top, and some glass bottles on it.

"Everyone come in, partner up, and find a seat." I smacked Jon's shoulder and walked to a seat in the front row.

"Good. Today we are going to start with a description of what alchemy is, why it is important, and we shall perform a simple powder creation. In front of you are the tools of the beginner alchemist. Alchemy is the art and science of distilling medicinal and Aetheric properties from plants, animals, and minerals. Alchemists use these properties to create medicines that heal injuries, cure disease, and enhance the gathering base of consumers.

"This last use of alchemical products is the main product line because most people will require alchemical assistance to open meridians, cleanse their inner selves, and to condense Aether into a liquid or crystal for the next two stages. Alchemy provides the ability for people to catch up to Elemental and Primordial Beasts so that we are able to form civilizations and defend ourselves.

"There are three major types of alchemical products. The first and easiest to create are powders. An alchemical powder is a combination of two or more herbal products that are blended, ground up, and dried in such a way as to encourage the medicinal properties to be brought out. The resulting powder is either added to a drink or sprinkled on a person to use these properties. The second is a potion, which includes the powder from before with additional products in liquid form. These allow for the distillation of the medicinal properties to a more concentrated level while reducing the impurities that can occur during powder making. Finally, potions can be condensed into a pill, which has more impurities but lasts for significantly longer than a potion does. Pills are stronger than potions and powders as well. Each step requires significant Aether and technique to prevent the loss of ingredients or the inclusion of extra hindering impurities."

Most of the students were hanging on his words, with some excited by the prospect of creating pills to heal while others just wanted to get stronger. He spent the next couple of minutes describing various powders, potions, and pills, such as the Meridian Cleanser pill he gave me, a Bloodstop powder used to close cuts and encourage healing, or the Aether Flame potion which could be taken only once to increase one's Fire affinity. The latter potion surprised many. It wasn't widely known that alchemy could increase affinity. "Of course alchemy can increase affinity. It can also increase talent, even beyond what the test showed. It is possible to open any meridian; it just requires extremely rare and expensive materials to open those you are not naturally inclined to. Those ingredients are one reason we teach everyone Herbology, so that you will recognize important plants to harvest.

"Now we will try to create our first powder. This is a simple powder that increases gathering speed by a small amount. In the cabinet below your table, you will find a jug of spring water, a Goldenflame Lily, a Frozen Lilac, an Earthen Groundvine, and a Shocking Lotus. The Goldenflame Lily has Fire and Metal affinity, Frozen Lilac Water and Ice, Earthen Groundvine has Wood and Earth, and the Shocking Lotus has Air and Lightning. Take out the jug and all four ingredients. You can make the powder one of two ways. The easiest, and weakest, is to take the ingredient that matches your highest affinity and balance it with its opposite. You will cut one third of the flower of each, boil them in the water, and grind the result into a paste which will be dried. This is a Simple Flower Gathering powder.

"Additionally, you can try to combine all four ingredients to make the Complete Flower Gathering powder. This is harder as the proportions of Aether from each must be exactly equal, or the result will do nothing but give you a sour stomach. Exactness is incredibly important in alchemy. While this powder has little downsides, some medicines will instead turn into poisons if made improperly. You may choose which powder you wish to create. There should be enough of the ingredients for each person to make several powders. If you run out, come up front to get more. You may begin."

I turned to Jon, "Well, do you want to try to make a simple powder or the better one? I know I'd rather do the harder one first."

"Sure, let's try it one time, then see what happens," Jon replied, and we pulled out all the ingredients. The Goldenflame Lily was a gorgeous red-gold color, the Lilac a deep blue, the Groundvine a green flower, and the Lotus a bright yellow. We laid the pieces down next to each other, trying to gauge how much to cut.

"Hold on, remember what Counselor Sila had us do for opening meridians? Pull the Aether in your life meridian into your eyes," I said, and pulled Aether from my senses meridian into the center of my eyes. The world partially transformed, and I was able to vaguely see Aether all around. Looking down, I saw that the Lily and the Lilac had denser Aether. "We need to use more of the Groundvine and Lotus, they have less Aether," I told Jon.

"I still can't see Aether in objects. I can see the glow of Aether around them, but not in detail, and I can't see it around gatherers. I'll trust your eyes then," he replied to me. I cut the Lily and Groundvine to have close to the same amount of Aether and had him cut matching pieces from the Lilac and Lotus respectively. After cutting three portions, we had just enough Lilac and Lily to make a fourth batch of just those two.

"Okay, we've got the ingredients cut; now we need to boil a portion in the pot, grind it up, and dry it out. Now, how do we get this brazier lit?" I said, looking over it.

"Place your hands here," Mentor Sonde said as he walked up, gesturing to two sides of the brazier where a small circle of copper was inset into it, "and inject Aether into it. The brazier will use the Aether to create flame and heat up the water. When brewing potions and making pills temperature control is very important, so alchemists use Aether-made flames as they are easier to control."

"Thank you, Mentor," I said and placed the ingredients and water into the bowl. Pushing Aether into my arm meridians and through my hands caused a flame to appear in the brazier just below the bowl. The flame covered the entire bottom, and I felt the heat begin to radiate. The water began to boil surprisingly fast, and ten minutes later the ingredients were fully cooked. Jon reached out with some tongs he had found in the cabinet and pulled the sodden ingredients out of the water into the mortar.

I looked in the cabinet and found some gloves for moving the bowl. As Jon started to smash the ingredients together, I took the bowl to a basin at the side of the room and washed it, as I saw several other groups do. When finished, I dried it off and walked back to the table. Jon scraped a paste out of the mortar into the bowl when I set it down and heated it up, handing me a rod to stir with as the mixture dried. Five minutes later, the mixture ran out of moisture and turned into a powder. I picked up the bowl and Jon scraped the powder into a glass jar.

Seeing we were finished, Counselor Sila came over and inspected our work. "Not bad. A little too much of the Lotus and Lily, but not enough to ruin it. This will improve gathering speed slightly. You can do better on the next one. Try again." So we did. The next one was better, with the final one having a good balance. Lastly, we made the simple powder with the final two ingredients. I told Jon to keep the last two Complete powders, while I took the first Complete powder and the Simple powder. He tried to protest but I told him that he had to keep up with me.

As everyone finished, Counselor Sila explained that the best use of the powder was to mix it into a drink. "It will taste fairly foul, so a strong-tasting drink is recommended to cover it up. Make sure to clean up your area and utensils before you leave, and dispose of the failures by dumping them in the area around the Meditation Grotto where you gather. The failures still make a decent fertilizer. Good job on making a simple powder today," he said as he stood and dismissed us. After cleaning up, I went to speak to Counselor Sila.

"Sir, will this react with the Meridian Cleanser?" I asked.

"You can take them both. Take the Cleanser first and finish processing it, then take the gathering powder. That will give the best results. Also, don't open any meridians until cleared by Counselor Sojka," Counselor Sila answered.

"Yes sir, thank you," I said, bowed, and left to get to PT. Jon was waiting at the entrance and gave me a questioning look. "Just had to make sure I could take this and the pills he gave me when I opened too many meridians. Let's get to PT, have dinner, and try these powders out!" I said, responding to his unspoken question.

CHAPTER SEVENTEEN

PT passed quickly, with the majority of people upgrading to the advanced level on the basics of their weapon. We also had to run twice as far since Counselor Might knew we had practiced running with Aether this morning. I didn't quite manage to advance, having missed a day. *Tomorrow you'll advance to the next stage, and learn how to use Aether with your weapon,* I promised myself.

Dinner also passed quickly, with everyone scarfing down their food and getting a glass of something strong tasting, usually juice, to slug down their powders. I filled a water skin up with juice to take later. I was going to take the Meridian Cleanser first.

After dinner, I bid goodbye to Jon and Brett and headed back to the dorm. When I got to my room, I took my Meridian Cleanser pill, and watched again as the swirl of energy released moved through my damaged meridians. Looking closely I was able to see the small amount of gunk pulled from my body. The Aether wave deposited the impurities in my intestines again, letting my body's waste removal system do its job. After finishing up, I jogged down the stairs again and headed out into the Grotto.

This evening, I took my time and focused on finding a great spot. I pulled Aether into my senses and focused on what I could see and feel. I followed Lightning Aether in the air to a pavilion where it congregated. Somewhat surprisingly, it was the same pavilion I normally used, only I now recognized the flowers as Shocking Lotus and Goldenflame Lilies, along with others I didn't know but that glowed with Lightning, Air, and Fire Aether.

"Well, I guess what I have been calling my pavilion is the best place, at least for Lightning, Air, and Fire. There isn't much Metal or Earth here, but I think it will be hard to find someplace with all five of my affinities. I should spend some time tomorrow looking for a Metal and Earth affinity area and gather there in the morning, I mused to myself. "Time to take the powder." I pulled my juice skin out and poured some into a cup I had brought with me. Pouring the Complete Flower Gathering powder into the cup, I mixed it with my fingers because I didn't have anything to stir with.

After a few seconds, the powder had been entirely absorbed into the juice, and I chugged it down. It took every ounce of my willpower not to spit it back out. *Augh, that was disgusting!* I couldn't even begin to describe how revolting that stuff tasted. However, the second it hit my stomach, my body absorbed it into my meridians. It flowed up the stomach meridian to my center, where it suffused the area with a golden radiance. I immediately started to gather in the Aether around me, and I could feel the difference. *A small amount!* I thought incredulously. I estimated that the powder had increased my gathering speed by nearly thirty percent!

The effect only lasted a half hour, but that was enough to have me pressing against the boundary from High Vapor to Low Mist. I stopped gathering when I hit the bottleneck since I didn't want to advance until I had opened the last two meridians. I took the opportunity that the extra time provided to work through my weapon forms again, spending another half hour to make sure I had them down perfectly. Once completed, I still had about half an hour until reading tutoring, so I decided to explore. Before I left I put a couple of pieces of fruit I'd grabbed from the dining hall on the branch the Zarorzel had been watching me from earlier. After about five minutes, near the southern edge of the Grotto, I found an area with benches made of iron ore, completely full of both Metal and Earth Aether, with some Fire Aether flowers and plants around such as the Goldenflame Lilies.

"Those benches are great! I wonder how someone made those." The benches I was looking at transitioned seamlessly from rock to metal and back, with intricate swirls and runic shapes made of metal in the rock. One bench was shaped like a lion, while another like a Chinese dragon, long and skinny. It felt like the benches might come to life at any point. While I didn't feel as large a sense of belonging here as the other pavilion, I knew I could gather here and have great results. "I'll come back tomorrow," I said, patting the lion's head before I turned and jogged back to the dorms to meet up with Jamila.

When I got back to the dorm building, I saw Jamila already waiting in the lounge with a different book. As I walked up, she said, "Good evening. The instructor told me to work through a book of my choice. I grabbed this because I thought you would appreciate it." She held up a book titled "Elemental Birds" which had a Crimson Zarorzel on the front. "You seemed to be really interested in the Zarorzel."

"Thanks," I said, and sat down next to her. She began to work through the book. The first chapter described a Crimson Zarorzel. They were omnivores that usually ate several types of Fire and Lightning affinity fruits and any small animals they could catch. The average level of an adult Crimson Zarorzel was five, with the strongest recorded at a level nine. *Level nine! That's almost a Primordial Beast!* There were only a few recorded instances of gatherers able to soul bond with a Crimson Zarorzel, as they required very high affinity in three elements to join with someone, and they were very picky about partners. Those who did reported increases in both Fire and Lightning affinities. The Lightning affinity was assumed to be the reason that the Zarorzels were fast, as they had not been recorded as using Lightning-based attacks. "Wow, they can shoot fireballs!? That's awesome!"

"They can also cast a fire blast that knocks adjacent enemies away," Jamila finished, stumbling a little on "adjacent." We continued to read, learning a bit about the Lightning Finch, the Bluewhite Swan, and a Vine Swallow. Elemental Birds came in a variety of affinities, with various abilities to defend themselves. The Lightning Finch could turn into a bolt of lightning, traveling vast distances nearly instantaneously to escape from harm, while the Vine Swallow set up traps with its ability to manipulate non-elemental plants around it. Most of the Birds, and most Beasts for that matter, were around level two or three.

By the time we finished the book, every other student had left the lounge. I realized that we were sitting touching shoulders all alone and nearly jumped away in embarrassment. My actions got a wry look from Jamila, who shook her head in amusement. "Um, it's pretty late. You are getting really good at reading; do you still need to meet up again tomorrow?" I said awkwardly.

"Yes, please. I really enjoy having someone help as I complete the reading for class. Also, I owe you a walk around the Grotto. Meet me at the door to the classrooms after morning class?" she responded.

"Okay. Have a great night!" I said. She gave me a wave and a smile before heading towards her room. I went up and took a quick shower before going to bed.

The next morning I examined my center before getting up. *Good! I can't see any damage left. Hopefully I'll get cleared to open the last two meridians today, especially as I am really close to the boundary for Mist. We're not supposed to advance until after all the meridians are open, to get the full benefit for advancing. It's Air Day, so blacksmithing is the class of the day. Air affinity foods will be good!* I hurriedly dressed and went to grab food.

This morning was eggs again because Elemental Fowl were prevalent and easy to raise with specific affinities, along with oatmeal that was made from Windspirit Grain and Williwaw Tree fruits, which looked like a mix of a grape and a kiwi. After getting a large bowl of both foods, I looked around and saw Jamila sitting with Bridget, Bet, and Yu Keai, another young woman from her class.

As I looked over, they all laughed at something Bridget had said, and Bridget saw me looking. She nudged Jamila with her elbow and made a comment that I couldn't hear, but it made her blush while the other two giggled. That almost made me turn away, but I decided to go eat breakfast with them anyway. *I will not be driven off by embarrassment, no matter what puberty says.* "Good morning," I said as I sat down next to Jamila at the end of the table.

"It is," was Bet's reply, giving me a sly grin. "Did you know that the Academy prevents students from being engaged until they complete their first tier?"

"No, I didn't," I replied, "why do you ask?"

"Just wondering," she said. "It is common for many noble families to find those with strong talents, such as you or Jamila, and attempt to tie them to their clan via marriage. To prevent excessive pressure on the young commoners and their families, Headmaster Glav has prohibited first tiers from making any type of engagement promise, or other life-long agreements. Usually, after the first tier is complete, they are capable of making better decisions for their lives. Choosing to marry into a clan carries a host of benefits," Bet explained after a pause.

"Of course, that doesn't prevent talks from starting earlier, just that no decisions can be made before then," Bridget added. "My father wrote to me saying he'd had inquiries into my marriage status already, and it's been less than a week!"

"Wow. Does this only happen to young women?" I asked Bet.

"No. Though I doubt you'll hear anything for a while. Your talent levels are too high, so most of the small clans won't even try. The four main clans usually want to watch someone for a little while before they approach. I would expect you to get approached sometime after the first three to four months," Bet answered me, with a slight frown that I barely noticed.

"She doesn't want to say that her father will probably offer her to you in marriage if you grow fast enough," Keai injected right after with a laugh.

"Ummm…" I blushed and caught her kick Keai under the table.

"Yes, that is a possibility. My marriage, as heir, is something that will most likely go to someone like you, a highly talented commoner, rather than another clan. My sister will probably have to marry the son of a minor clan or merchant house to cement a business or economic relationship," Bet responded mostly emotionlessly, though I could hear some slight anger to it.

"I hope you get some say in your marriage," I told her.

"We usually will at least get to refuse if we absolutely cannot get along with the person. Every child of a clan faces the same prospect, though, since we must do what is best for the clan over ourselves," she said.

"Yeah, my dad wrote that he would leave the final decision to me, at least," Bridget added.

"So I shouldn't write your dad?" Jon asked as he sat down next to me. Bridget just glared at him in response. "Wait, how did you get onto the topic of marriage?"

"Volkov Bet asked if I knew that we were prohibited from becoming engaged or getting married this first year," I told him. He looked at me, then at Bet. Bet shrugged her shoulders at him. I looked away for a second, waving to Brett who had just come in, when I heard Jon go, "Ah, I get it." I looked back at him quizzically. He just laughed and shook his head. I shrugged and we all ate.

The food was delicious, and the Aether in the meal surged into me. After the first serving I felt bloated, only to realize that feeling was in my center as the Aether pushed against the boundary towards the Mist level. *Crap, not supposed to level yet, need to hold until I can open my last two meridians.* I hurriedly excused myself from the table and went to find Counselor Stojka.

CHAPTER EIGHTEEN

I went towards the classrooms because she had said she would find me, and saw her coming over. "Ma'am," I called to her, "am I able to open some more meridians? I'm on the verge of moving to Mist unless I can lower the pressure," I babbled quickly. She hurried over, grabbed my arm, and sent out a wave of Aether. The Aether she inserted pushed a little on mine, and I felt like my brain was going to cramp in resisting advancing.

"You are fine to open some more. How many more do you have?" she asked.

"Four more. I've got a brain meridian, a skin meridian, the rib cage, and my kidney and bladder meridian. Any advice?" I asked.

"Open the brain meridian, it is always useful. Hmm, open the kidney bladder meridian as well, then head back to breakfast and eat more. I will meet you after your first class and check your nutrient levels. If sufficient, this afternoon you can open the rib cage meridian. If not, wait until tomorrow morning for the rib cage. Wait a full day after that to open the skin. It requires significant nutrients so you will need to fill back up. Good, now shoo," she said, waving me away. I thanked her and jogged into the Grotto, sitting down on the first bench I found.

I centered myself and found the entry point to the brain meridian. I pushed a small stream of Aether into it, and watched as it flowed into me. The Aether first impacted my thyroid, and I felt it release some hormones. My heart began to race, and then slowed down again as the Aether flowing into it corrected for the increase in my metabolic rate. I felt energized and ready to move! The Aether stream continued on, flowing throughout my brain. As it flowed in a circle through my brain, it seemed as if time stopped. The feeling ended, but everything around me seemed to be moving slightly slower. *Weird. I think this made my brain slightly faster. Well, this will take some getting used to,* I thought.

Once the Aether made a full cycle through my meridian, I decided to stand up and walk in a circle. Standing up took two tries, as my brain was now moving slightly quicker than my body. *Yup, definitely take getting used to.* I slowly walked in a circle around the bench before sitting down again. *Next one,* I thought as I grabbed some Aether to open the kidney meridian.

Again a stream of Aether left my center, this time leaving the lower left portion of my center rather than the top. The Aether moved through my left kidney and I could see impurities gather into the flow of Aether. These impurities stream down the tubes from my kidney to my bladder, where they were deposited. *Ugh, now I got to pee!* I thought, watching the Aether move through the rest of its cycle. The impurities from the right kidney were cycled through the meridian, and looking closely I could sense that my kidneys were working more efficiently than before. They also produced hormones to increase my red blood cell count, which should improve my endurance even more.

Okay, first bathroom, then food, then class, I thought, hurrying to the restrooms in the classroom building first. I was running, using the skill taught yesterday, faster than I had ever done before. *Hey! I got the rune down!* I passed everyone I had breakfast with on the way back to the dining hall. "Hey, got to eat some more. See y'all at class!" I shouted at them as I sprinted past, only to kick myself as no one I knew of around here said "y'all." A quick second serving of oatmeal and eggs was followed by more sprinting. I was the last to arrive, but Counselor Stojka had spoken to Counselor Sila and he waved me over before I could apologize for being late.

"As I was saying, today we will be learning a series of movements and runic focuses to improve gathering speed called the Eight by Eight Gathering form. First, start in a straddle stance," he explained, showing us how to stand. Everyone imitated him, standing in a line on the PT field. He showed us a series of movements that made me think of Tai Chi, with each position corresponding to a runic shape we were supposed to draw by circling the Aether in our centers.

There were a total of sixty-four positions shown, each associated with an element, eight positions per element. Sixty-four runes needed memorization, and I got them down almost immediately. *Wow, the brain meridian opening has made my memory nearly photographic! This will make studying so much easier. No wonder Jamila learned to read in only a couple days!* I thought, excited.

Of course, just because I could remember them didn't mean that I could draw them, or perform the motions correctly. After an hour of explanation and demonstration, Counselor Sila and the Mentors had us all start trying while they wandered among us correcting motions and watching us draw the runes. It was possible for them to see the temporary runes drawn through Aether flows.

"Good, now move the right arm up higher, just a bit more," Counselor Sila instructed me as I worked through the first eight moves. The technique was able to be separated into sets of eight, with each set having a small improvement in gathering speed which stacked with the gains from the previous set. Counselor Sila proceeded to help me get the first eight moves nailed down along with their Runes. I could feel my Aether refilling, pushing towards the Mist boundary again.

Class was dismissed once everyone had gotten the hang of the first couple of moves and we were informed that we would be focusing on this for the rest of the week. "I want every one of you to have mastered at least the first two sets of this series by the end of the week. Come find help if you need it," Counselor Sila said as he dismissed us. After bowing, almost everyone left the PT fields for the Grotto.

I went looking for Counselor Stojka, who gave me the all clear to open up the rib cage meridian during this meditation period. "Eat a very large lunch and dinner afterward. If you can open up your skin meridian tomorrow you should be able to advance to Mist by Fire Day. That would make you the first to advance here, though seven came into the school already at Mist level."

She pulled a small bag off her hip and reached her arm up to the elbow into it. *Holy moly!* I thought as my eyes got huge. *Where did her arm go!? That bag is only five inches deep!* She pulled a small bottle from the bag and shook a pill out of it, before looking up at me. Seeing my face she asked, "Never seen an extended bag before?" A quick shake of my head caused her to laugh. "An application of a high-level inscription allows for a bag to be extended by up to twenty times its original length. Here, take this before you open your meridian." She handed me the pill she had taken out and shooed me off.

There were only a few people left on the field, finishing up the first eight moves of the Eight by Eight Gathering form. No one I knew was in sight. *Okay, time to go*, I thought as I started jogging, heading into the Meditation Grotto to the Metal and Earth focused area I found yesterday. When I got there, the dragon bench was occupied by someone. *What was his name? Grr, the memory provided by the brain meridian opening is not retroactive. Ah, yeah, Sihirb Akil, he is in Jamila's group class.*

Walking quietly, I sat down on the lion bench and relaxed for a bit, tracing the designs on its back. I pulled out my water bag and swallowed the pill. It felt like I had swallowed a lump of dirt or a brick. *Hmm, I forgot to ask what this pill does.* I quickly circulated my Aether and moved to open the rib cage meridian. As the Aether flowed, a light burning sensation trailed it, and I saw the bones growing denser. Changes to the marrow increased blood flow and red blood cell production. My breathing got slower and deeper as the meridian influenced my diaphragm as well as the bones. The lump in my stomach dissolved into nutrients that moved to the bones being affected by Aether, filling in the gaps of what my body had stored.

Huh, I wonder why everyone isn't given these pills to start with, I thought as I watched the nutrients flow. The sudden spike of pain when the burning sensation dramatically increased forced a grunt from me. *Oh, that's why.* The pain only lasted for a minute before tapering off, but it took all my willpower to keep opening the meridian and not cry out during that time. After the pain faded, I could see the meridian was fully opened and there were no cracks or signs of damage. *Oh, that's another reason why,* I thought as I saw small signs of impurities left over in the meridians that impeded the flow of Aether slightly. *I guess Counselor Sojka thought it would be okay since I have the Meridian Cleanser pills.*

I opened my eyes to find the small clearing empty since Akil had left sometime during my meridian opening. Just before I got up I started coughing and hacked up a small bit of blood. "Ugh, that was not fun. Note to self, don't take pills without asking what they do," I mumbled to myself before stumbling off to lunch.

CHAPTER NINETEEN

After a refreshing lunch with a bunch of my friends, with Louis expounding on how excited he was to learn blacksmithing, we went to the forge building. The forge building was just beyond the classroom building on the main path. *This campus is huge! At least three times the size of the Academy back on Earth.* The forge was squat, only two stories tall, but its footprint was nearly four times as large as the other buildings around it. Numerous chimneys dotted the edge of the roof, with smoke billowing from several. The main doorway was a double door that opened outward, with doors nearly twice normal size.

Opening the doors revealed a single large hall with pillars holding up the ceiling, with a couple of walled-off areas to the left and right. It was surprisingly well lit, with balls of Aether-fueled light set throughout the ceiling. There was a quiet ringing of metal on metal, with the occasional hiss of hot metal meeting liquid, but it was much quieter than I had anticipated. A Mentor was waving all of us to head to the back of the building, where a large group of students was clustered.

As we walked towards the group, I could see people talking but could not make out their words. About five feet behind the closest person, I saw a line of silvery metal embedded in the floor, with copper-colored runes etched into it. Stepping over the line resulted in a rush of sound that staggered me for a second. *Oh, they have enchantments set down to reduce noise. Man, magic solves a lot of problems. Though I'm sure it creates its own set of them. Like magic Beasts that terrorize whole cities.*

Louis was looking over to our left, where a third tier student could be seen hammering away at an anvil. After a couple hits, he held up what looked like the start of a sword. He shook his head and put the sword back on the anvil, then placed his hands on the side of the anvil. A few seconds later, the air around him began wavering with heat and the sword started glowing a cherry red again. *Well that makes things slightly easier,* I thought as he started hammering again.

"Greetings, students. I am Counselor Kowalski and will be the instructor for those of you who wish to take up the art of metal smithing and treasure creation. Today is mostly going to be a demonstration of the various aspects of our craft. Mentor Kowalski, my nephew, over on the anvil there is currently fashioning a sword, and Mentor Hodowca will be demonstrating smelting and ore refining. I will be demonstrating alloy creation after Mentor Hodowca. Mentor Boulan is creating a halberd over there…" Counselor Kowalski introduced a number of different Mentors since there were forty first tiers there to see the introduction. *Well, Nicky is here as well. Going to avoid him as best I can.* We were divided into groups of ten and sent around, where the Mentors explained what they were doing and demonstrated their explanations. I made sure to join a group that went in a different direction from Nicky.

My group was sent to the blast furnace first. *Hmm, they are making pig iron here, and then alloying it afterward,* I thought, remembering back to a chemistry elective I had taken in metallurgy. It was interesting to see how they used inscriptions rather than bellows and to keep the heat at a constant level. After creating the pig iron, they added various different materials to it and smelted the iron again.

One example was Icy Sand, a type of sand permeated with Ice Aether, that made the quenching process quicker. This made a harder material that would channel Ice, Air, and Water Aether better. *This is really cool. There are so many things you can mix together to get different Aetheric properties. Though they haven't mentioned anything that would be like steel. I wonder if they haven't figured that out yet or just have a different name for it. Hmm, how to introduce that?* I mused. *Huh, would it even be an improvement over some of the Aether alloys they have?*

My group rotated over to the anvil where Mentor Kowalski was finishing the sword. He described how he would shape the metal, making sure that the heat was uniform using the heating runes in the anvil, while flowing Aether through the hammer into the sword. "By adding Aether, you strengthen the metal and allow it to acclimate to Aether flowing through it. This way, you can use Aether techniques through the weapon. This is also why making your own weapon lets you use more Aether at a time through it. The weapon you created was attuned to you during creation," he explained to us. The rest of the afternoon proceeded with us seeing different techniques for Aether insertion, learning a formula for smelting, and seeing how polishing was accomplished on the finished sword.

Leaving class, Louis declared, "This is what I want to study. Have any of you decided yet?"

"Not yet," I told him, "as I'm interested in this and Alchemy and Inscription. So many interesting and powerful things you can do. I'm probably going to focus on either Alchemy or Inscription, though."

Jon piped in. "I want to study alchemy. Finding new ways of producing strengthening elixirs will let workers unload and load ships faster, which would help my family's business and all the other businesses in the city." We continued to discuss our plans for classes after the introductions as we headed to Physical Training class.

The group of us walking split up when we reached the PT fields, with some heading to their instructors and others heading towards a set of training dummies set up. I went to see Mentor Jameson to demonstrate the final form on my memory stone. *The memory enhancement from opening my brain meridian definitely helps me learn faster.* I waited a bit for Thomas the lackey to demonstrate his form first. *Dang it, the flunky beat me.* He successfully moved through his form, slashing and stabbing with both ends of his double-bladed sword in a neat pattern that would be difficult to attack through. After he finished, he was sent over to Counselor Might to demonstrate it again.

"Come on over, Aiden, show me what you have learned," Mentor Jameson said. I nodded and bowed to him before stepping forward with my right foot and drawing my trisulas, with a slash from the right one. A series of blocks, parries, and stabs followed as I ended up circling partially around him as I stepped through the form. He nodded and smiled as I continued, and congratulated me when I finished. "Good, now head over to Counselor Might and demonstrate again. Afterward, he'll unlock the next portion of the memory stone and give you a one-time pass to the armory to pick out an advanced technique."

"Thank you, Mentor Jameson," I said with a bow before heading over to Counselor Might. There were two people in front of me, the flunky and Akil, who had a battle axe as his weapon. Watching Akil was a lesson in controlled strength, as his axe flowed through his form. *That thing must weigh fifteen pounds, how does he move it so fluidly?* When it was my turn, I performed the same as before, despite the jitters of acting in front of a group of people.

"That was well done. Let me see your memory stone," Counselor Might said, holding out his hand. I gave him the stone, and he held it up to his forehead. The stone glowed for a few seconds, and then he handed it back to me along with a small token. "Study hard, and practice hitting the dummies with your weapons. You will need to get a feel for how they behave upon impact by the end of this week. Before next class go by the Armory and pick a technique to study."

I took back the memory stone, bowed, and walked towards an empty dummy. When I reached it, I settled into a front stance and drew my trisulas. I proceeded to slash and stab the dummy in both front and reverse grip for the next half hour. The first few times didn't go well. I dropped one weapon on the second hit and had to shake my hand out. I slowly grew used to the feeling of impact, and worked on minimizing it on slashes. Amazingly, no matter how I beat on it, the dummy healed up within seconds of me stopping my attacks.

After that half hour I decided to go focus on studying the next set of motions, mostly from lack of oxygen. *Even taking it easy, slashing and stabbing for half an hour has left me more tired than running a 10k,* I thought as I walked over to an empty spot away from anyone practicing. I took a minute just to breathe, getting my heart rate back down. *You know, I doubt I would have lasted half as long if I hadn't opened so many meridians that help with endurance.* Once settled, I pulled the memory stone out and placed it to my forehead.

I watched as the same student learned a series of moves, starting with combining a block with one hand and an attack with the other. "Two weapons can mean twice the defense, twice the offense, or offense and defense at the same time!" came a shouted line from behind my viewpoint. After they worked through every permutation of attack and defense at the same time, the trisulas uniqueness came into play. A move for catching an enemy's weapon in between the main blade and the outer tines was practiced. You could catch with one weapon to direct the enemy's weapon away from you, or both to attempt to either disarm them or break their weapon. I watched as the instructor blocked a longsword and shattered the blade in the middle using her two trisulas. *Holy crap!*

The next technique shown dumbfounded me though. It was a technique for charging Aether in your hands, sending it into the trisulas, then stabbing forward and pushing to send a pointed burst of Aether straight forward for nearly ten feet. *Sword light! Semi-ranged attacks already!* I excitedly watched as the student would stab and slash at a dummy like the one in the field from about eight feet away. I was so excited that I pulled the memory stone away from me and ran over to the nearest dummy. I positioned myself so that no one was in a line away from me through the dummy, in case it worked and I missed, and started trying to emulate the student from the memory stone.

I centered myself and slowly took a stance, holding a single trisula in my right hand. I dragged Aether from my right arm meridian into the palm of my hand and pushed it into my weapon. It didn't work. I moved the Aether to my index finger, which was resting just before the blade began on the hilt. The Aether slowly moved into the weapon, so I moved my fingers to be touching the metal rather than the hand-grip. This way I was able to flow a steady stream of Aether into the weapon until it was full. With a grunt, I pushed more Aether into it, shoving the Aether forward as hard as I could while stabbing forward.

A blob of Aether squirted out of the weapon and landed about a foot in front of it with a sizzling sound. *Well, that was anticlimactic. Okay, what went wrong? Serves me right for being in such a hurry,* I thought, pulling out the memory stone again. "Hmm, it seems like he is controlling the Aether in the weapon. As he charges it up, some of it is moving in a circle, reentering his hand and flowing back into his meridian. Let's try just making a circle of Aether flowing into the weapon and back out first," I mumbled to myself, before stepping up to the dummy.

I followed my own advice and had Aether flow into the trisula from my first two fingers and out of it through my last two, maintaining my will on it as best as I could to have the Aether flow along the edge of the blade. After about thirty seconds I felt that I had it working slightly well and slashed into the dummy. I felt the dummy break my circuit, and a blast of Aether flowed into it, making the cut about half again as big and smell burnt. "Whoa!" I shouted, surprised at the effectiveness. *I guess that's why it hurt Smarmy McSmarmpants so much when I hit him with my Aether-infused fist.*

I repeated this exercise about twenty times, with the last one taking my breath away. Looking inward to my center, I realized I was running on empty. I staggered to an edge of the field, sat down, and gathered for a bit. *Well, magic gives me more endurance, but the crash when it runs out sure is rough.* I was too tired to do the Eight by Eight techniques. After a few minutes, I was feeling better, but not enough to keep expending Aether. *Let's work on the blocking and attacking techniques.* I worked on these for the next hour, with the occasional break to gather and rest.

At the end of class, everyone took off on our daily ten laps around the field. "Stupid running technique just making us run longer," I grumbled under my breath after the fifth lap. I was running low on Aether again, so I tried to gather while running. It sort of worked. I could slowly gather only when I stopped using the Aether running technique. *Guess you can't have inputs and outputs at the same time, at least with what I know so far.* I alternated gathering and expending the Aether until I finished, thankfully not last, though nowhere near first. As we were dismissed, the entire group staggered off the fields, headed to the shower and then food.

CHAPTER TWENTY

Dinner passed quickly, with some of the kids from the minor noble houses bragging about the cool weapons that their clan blacksmiths could produce. Ming and Vaya both smiled wryly at the group without saying anything. Discussions proceeded with more people declaring what they wanted to study, while others wanted to wait for the Introduction to Inscription class. After finishing dinner, everyone began to drift out, heading for their rooms or the Grotto.

Jamila caught up with me just as I was walking past the dorm buildings toward the Grotto. "Good evening," I said as she came up. She returned my greeting and walked silently next to me for a bit.

As we entered the Grotto, she stepped forward and said, "Follow me," before turning down a path I hadn't taken yet. As we walked, the path became overgrown. "The amount of Wood Aether in the soil and air here has made the growth rate of the plants increase. I have been working on extending Aether into a plant to help it grow. Counselor Stojka instructed me that this was a good first step to being a healer," Jamila said as we walked. A small path diverged from the one we were on, and she took it. The path curved out and ran parallel to a moderately sized pond, with some benches. She gestured at the pond and said, "This is where I have been gathering the last two days."

"It's a beautiful area," I said, looking at the flowers growing on the shores and surface of the pond. We stood there for a bit, just enjoying the night air, before I excused myself to go back to a more appropriate place to gather. As I was walking, I was thinking to myself. *Do I like her for her, or because she reminds me of Jasmine? It's been just over six months since I died and came back, and I thought I had accepted that and moved on. Now I'm not so sure. Darkness, why me? Why can't I remember what we talked about?* "Gah!" I exclaimed out loud, startling a bright blue bird off a branch. It chirped at me and flew away.

All I remember is an admonishment to grow stronger. I will just focus on that until I can get more information. This is my life now. No more mopey introspection, at least for tonight. With this thought, I got to the Fire and Lightning pavilion and sat down. I focused on gathering, refilling from earlier and moving close to the edge of advancing again. After an hour, I was ready to practice shooting out Aether from my weapons. I left a couple of pieces of fruit I had saved from the dining hall for the Zarorzel. *Hopefully, I can see it again.*

As I jogged out of the Grotto, I looked backward and saw the Zarorzel land and start eating the fruit I brought. I laughed, then ran out and looked into the PT fields, hoping there was a dummy left available. Thankfully, it looked like the dummies were all still on the field. Not that weather would hurt them, considering how quickly they fixed themselves after being stabbed and burnt. Stopping five feet back from a dummy, I focused on setting up the circle of Aether. "Okay, I know that I can make this work by striking the dummy, but I want to be able to project the Aether, not just use it to strengthen my blows."

I forced the circle to pool a bit at the tip of the trisula, holding more and more Aether until I was straining to make it stay. As I reached this point, I thrust the blade towards the dummy and pushed a shot of Aether into the circle, so that it would impact the tip at the end of my thrust. I squeezed with my will, and the Aether continued straight, forming an elongated blob that hit the dummy with as much force as a light shoulder tackle. I exhaled with a groan, as that push had taken nearly a third of my total Aether pool. "Well, that kind of worked. Now to make it smaller and pointier. I won't last long in a fight if I use that much Aether each time."

I gathered back up to full, and repeated my steps, making the Aether smaller and thinner at the tip, though not by much. It took me the next two hours to get the result to even a moderately acceptable state. Rather than a shoulder tackle, it looked more like I hit the dummy with a slightly pointy log. Still not enough to penetrate, but it would knock the breath out of someone. It also only used about an eighth of my Aether pool rather than a third. *Yay progress, now bedtime.*

Breakfast and channeling class passed quickly, with Lightning-based food this time that was amazing. *I don't think I lost any of the Aether in that meat!* I thought after eating. Channeling class was just continuing to work on the Eight by Eight Gathering form, and I made my way nearly through the second set. By the end of class, I was struggling against advancing in level again. I rushed away from class with a grimace when we were dismissed. *Just a bit longer, then I can open the skin meridian and stop suppressing my level.*

Sitting down at my pavilion, I centered myself quickly. My center glowed brightly, with Aether pressing against some invisible barriers near the edges of my open meridians. I directed some of the excess Aether to the opening of my skin meridian. A gush of Aether rushed out of my control down that pathway, moving straight out and then fanning across the entirety of my body. *Ahh, tickles!* I nearly lost focus when it started tickling, leaving me giggling and twitching while watching the Aether flow. The Aether gathered at the point directly opposite the opening to flow back through my chest into my center.

Looking down, I saw what appeared to be popped blackheads covering my body. I immediately got up and jogged back to my room to take a shower. *Man, advancing is a dirty business.* I looked in the mirror after my shower, and saw that the little bit of acne that had been on my face had vanished. My skin had become slightly tanner, reflecting the time I had spent in the sun the last few days. Dark black hair and deep brown eyes completed the look. My body had filled out some from the intense exercise and massive amounts of food. *At least I no longer look like I just got off my deathbed,* I thought.

I went to get dressed again and the wooden token I was given by Counselor Might dropped out of my pocket. "Oh yeah, I need to go get an advanced technique. I wonder what options there are?" I picked up the token and hurried out. The Armory was a four-story building just past the forge. As I approached, it seemed to buzz with power, presumably because the building was absolutely covered in inscriptions. There was a guard in front of the door who waved me over as I walked up.

"You got a token from Counselor Might?" the guard asked.

"Yes sir, here it is," I said, handing him the token. He took it with his left hand and waved his right hand over it. I felt a fluctuation of Aether as the guard did something. *Dang it, I don't have my Aether sight up*, I thought as the token turned a light blue color.

"You are clear to enter the technique library on the first floor. After you enter the door behind me, turn right and go into the library. Do not attempt to enter anywhere else. You have one hour to decide. Have fun and find Librarian Livro once you have made your choice or if you need help," the guard explained. "Go on in." I walked through the doors behind him and saw a short hallway that ran perpendicular to the door. I could see a door at both ends of the hallway, with the left one labeled "Armory" and the right "Technique Library." Following the directions, I turned and went into the Technique Library.

The door opened onto a large room with four large bookshelves running down it. These shelves had signs on them labeled, from left to right, "Offensive," "Defensive," "Movement," "Auxiliary." There were a couple of students browsing already. Some third tiers were looking through the Offensive category, and a fourth tier was walking down the Movement one. I stood there thinking for a minute, trying to decide which to look at first.

As I stood there, a very old man appeared next to me. "Good morning, student. Is there anything in particular you are looking for?" I jumped when he spoke, as he quite literally appeared out of nowhere.

"Um, no sir. I'm not sure what I should be looking for, or what I am trying to prepare for," I told him. "Do you have any suggestions, sir?" I asked uncertainly.

"Hmm, you should probably be getting ready for the tournament at the end of the month, I'd think. That is one of the places you earn merit points towards your rank in your year. What have you learned so far, hmm?" he asked. I described the techniques I had learned already and found myself telling him about my meridians and affinities. He kept nodding his head, saying "Hmmm," and gesturing for me to continue for the next fifteen minutes.

"Hmm, that is excellent. You have a good base movement technique and a so-so attack technique. Your skin meridian could use a technique to go with it for defense. Another attack technique would be good, and an agility movement technique, rather than speed. That would be best. Don't worry about auxiliary for now. Most of those require much higher Aether levels," he told me. He gestured for me to follow him while walking towards the Offensive aisle.

"Five affinities ... FIVE," the strange old man muttered to himself, "Hmm, what would be the best offensive he could use? No, no, no. Hmm, when he has moved to Condensation, oooh, hmm, no. Ah, yes, this should be good. You are a dual wielder correct?" He suddenly said while I trailed behind him looking confused. After I answered affirmatively, he pulled a memory stone off the shelf and handed it to me. "This is the Four Twin Lightning Stabs technique. It is an intermediate-rank technique that is able to be learned by Aether gatherers, though its full might cannot be appreciated until you reach Aether Condensation. Now on to defense."

I stared at the memory stone until a "hmmm" from the senior had me look up to see he'd walked off. I found him muttering, "Metal or Earth? Hmm, both are good, oh yeah, that one." He grabbed another memory stone and handed it to me. "This is the Iron Bone, Granite Skin technique that will benefit greatly from your skin meridian and rib cage meridian, along with your dual affinity for Metal and Earth. This should last you through the Condensation stage as well. Now we need an agility movement technique. Come, come." He walked around the end of the aisle and continued down the Movement one.

"Hmm, Air, Lightning, or Fire? Fire is good for unpredictability but can be hard to control. Lightning for pure speed, more straight-line movements, not good for his weapons. Air then? Not quite as fast or unpredictable, but more controllable, yes. But which one?" The librarian continued to mumble to himself as he walked down the aisle. "This one! He seems smart enough, unlike the last kid I let have this. This is the Dancing Northern Wind technique. There are four levels to it, and it will last you through Core Creation. This is one of the very few advanced-level techniques you would be able to learn at your level. It is very difficult, but I believe you can handle it. If not, come back and I will give you a different one."

"Thank you, sir, but I was told I was only allowed one technique. Which should I take?"

"Bah, you will take all three. I am the head librarian and get to decide who takes what. Now you will learn all of these by the end of the month. I want to see you use them all in the tournament." He glared threateningly at me.

"Yes sir. Will do," I responded, too intimidated to ask the old man any more questions.

"Good. Now go study." He dismissed me and disappeared. *Holy moly. That is teleportation or something like it. He didn't blur away, he simply vanished!* Stunned, I stood there for nearly a minute before the old man yelled at me again from somewhere to "Go study!" I quickly left the building and looked up at the sun. *Okay, I've got about an hour until lunch. Techniques or gathering?* I thought, walking away from the Armory towards the Meditation Grotto. With a laugh I thought, *Who am I kidding? I'm way too curious about the techniques chosen for me to not look at them first!*

CHAPTER TWENTY-ONE

I took off at a jog, using the movement technique I knew already to move faster. Every time I used it, I refined how I moved the Aether, how I made the runes, and the timing of the movements. All of which let me use it better, though the benefits were increasing logarithmically. "Which one first?" I mused as I jogged. "Do I want a new offensive power, a new defensive one, or another movement one? Apparently, there is a tournament coming up, so I need to get proficient in all three before then, though I don't know what it will entail. Are we really going to fight each other with these abilities?"

I reached my pavilion and was surprised to see Anberlin gathering in the center of it. I walked towards one of the seats, but stopped about five feet out. I could feel the Aether flowing inward from here. *How much Aether is she pulling in, that I can feel it? Wait, is this strange? I didn't feel anything from Jamila that one time, but we were on either side. I would have felt it then if the flow was this strong, but I've gotten stronger and better since then and I'm sure she has too. I just don't know enough. I'll go to the other meditation spot.* I turned and jogged off, trying not to disturb her. *I may not like her cousin, but that doesn't mean I should be rude to her.*

Thankfully, the benches were clear at the other spot I liked. I sat down on the lion's back again and pulled out the three memory stones I had been given. "I still need to decide which one to look at. Let's see. I've just started learning how to shoot a stab or slash of Aether from my trisulas, so I think I'll keep on that rather than starting a new technique. We haven't practiced creating an Aether Shield since that one lesson, so I should either work on that or abandon it and focus on the new one. The last one I have is for an agility movement technique, whatever that means, versus a speed one. The technique I was taught already focuses on increasing my running speed, and I have that one down pretty well. I think that would be the best one to focus on."

Having decided on the next course of action, I put the other two memory stones away and concentrated on the Dancing Northern Wind. Like all the others I'd used so far, this one put me in the head of a student learning the technique. This time, we were in a large open area, with an older woman instructing the student. "First I will demonstrate each level of the Dancing Northern Wind technique," the instructor was saying. As she did so, she raised her hands and stepped lightly to the side before pushing off to the right again, moving slightly farther and faster than I would have expected. She seemed to drift in the air a bit before landing.

The next time she stepped sideways, she definitely floated down, moving at least five meters before landing. Her third set had her leap upwards in a way that would shame basketball players, then drift down to the side. When she landed, she dashed sideways, moving five meters in a blink. Where she had been, a misty shape hovered for a second and then drifted away. *Whoa.* The fourth movement she jumped upwards like before, but halfway to her landing point, she acted like she pushed off the air and turned ninety degrees. *In midair!* This time when she dashed back after landing, the misty shape was more definite. All of her movements were much faster than the force she pushed off with would indicate.

The fifth demonstration had the instructor jump upwards again, then turn sideways and start running. She ran a full circle around the student, about fifteen feet off the ground. *She's literally running on air. That… that is so cool!* Looking closely, I could see condensation where she stepped, like a cloud was appearing. The instructor dashed back and forth suddenly, creating two pale white images of herself hovering in midair. The last demonstration had the instructor leap lightly up, and air circled around her, pushing her through the skies. *She's flying. She's flying, like Storm from X-Men. Holy crap, I get to learn how to fly!!!* I was literally squeeing in my head.

"Now that you have seen the heights to which this technique can reach, I will teach you the first level. You are only able to learn the first two levels at your Aether Gathering level, then the next two levels can be learned when you reach Aether Compression, unless you are extremely accomplished. Running on Air and Flying with Air can only be accomplished once you have created your Core Seed, as they require vast amounts of Aether." The instructor began lecturing and guiding the student on how to work the first level of the technique.

Similarly to the previous technique we learned – which I just realized they never told us the name, if it had one – you started by circulating the Aether through your leg meridians. This time, however, you had to pull the Aether out of the meridians onto the surface of your legs and draw runes all over the legs. She was explaining what each rune meant, and I realized it was similar to a programming language. You had to define how much Aether to use, how far to drift, and how to divert the air around you, which let you move faster. You also got a small boost from the air behind you. I watched the student move their Aether and work on forming runes for the rest of the hour I had until lunch.

I pulled away from the memory stone more excited than I had been for, like, a day. *Okay, I'm getting excited over and over again here. There are just too many things I get to do that I would never have dreamed possible on Earth. I'm going to become a literal superhero, saving villages from monster attacks.* I started to jog towards lunch before I slowed to a walk. "I should practice Aether Shield," I said out loud, and began to work on creating an Aether Shield. The first time I did it, it worked perfectly, even better than it did before. *Huh, the Aether moved away from where I directed it and went into my skin meridian. Making an Aether Shield is now as easy as pushing more Aether into that meridian. Well, let's keep practicing; get it to come up faster.*

As I walked, I continued to practice the Aether Shield technique, while looking for ways to make it faster and better. As I was reaching the dining hall, I realized that I could focus the shield on a single part of my body, making it stronger and denser there, while weaker everywhere else. *Can everyone do this? Or is it a benefit of my skin meridian?* After grabbing food, I sat down with Jon, Lucas, Brett, and Louis. "Have any of you all picked your advanced techniques?" I asked as I sat down. Louis got a very surprised look on his face, shook his head, and ran off. The rest of us laughed a little as he did so.

Lucas chuckled and said, "Yeah, I went and browsed through the Offensive aisle and picked up an Ice based slashing technique that can freeze people at higher levels."

Jon had picked a defensive technique that made the air around him colder, restricting his opponent's movement speed and Brett had found an offensive technique that let him make blades of Air come off the ends of his weapon.

"So every one of you only got one? Did any of you speak to the head librarian?" I asked. They all said no, and I could see the question on Jon's face. "Hmm, I was trying to decide where to look when I was approached by the head librarian, who had me tell him what I've learned and my affinities. He seemed excited to talk to someone, and gave me three techniques." I told them the names of the techniques and described the Dancing Northern Wind as "making me able to dodge better." I also told them about the tournament at the end of the month mentioned by the librarian.

"That is amazing, dude. A tournament. We will have to work our butts off to do well. I want to beat at least one of the annoying nobles," Jon said, glaring at a table off to the side. I didn't recognize anyone there, but apparently, there was an annoying nobleman, or woman, there. "The most irritating are the minor nobles. They have to lord their status over others as much as they can for some reason. Soooo annoying."

We continued to talk about the tournament and speculate what it could entail the rest of lunch. As we were cleaning up, Louis came in with a huge grin on his face. He announced that he had talked to the librarian, and was given two techniques. One was a defensive technique for his Earth affinity, and one an attack technique using both Metal and Wood affinities. "That's awesome, man," I said, patting his back as we walked out. "Did he say anything about the tournament at the end of the month?"

"No. He did not mention it. He did say he pitied me a bit. I was pretty panicked when I walked in," Louis replied. I told him what the librarian had told me about the tournament and we continued to speculate all the way to the inscription building. The building looked like most of the others, like a few-stories-tall square apartment.

"Do any of you know why the buildings are almost all the same?" I asked.

"They are built by Earth gatherers, and it is the easiest way to build them," Louis told us. "I want to learn how to do that too. I want to build stuff that lasts." The inside of the building was different though. It had a small lounge that only extended a third of the way through the building, rather than all the way. Some books were on a shelf that lined the far wall on either side of a large, reinforced door. A staircase led up to our left and the right wall had two more doors. The second door on the first floor had "Group Two" written on it.

A round of goodbyes prefaced the group splitting up to head to our respective classrooms. The Counselor in front of the class waved us in. She looked much younger than every other Counselor, maybe twenty-five years old. She had strawberry-blonde hair and lacked the scars that every other Counselor had. She was pretty in the girl next door kind of way, and I could see Jon had fallen in love at first sight. *For the third time this week I'm sure.*

We found a seat at the front of the class and waited while the last few members of our group filed in. The Counselor was writing something as she waited. Once everyone was there, she stood up holding the paper she had been writing on. I saw a small flare of Aether and the paper transformed into a ball of light that floated over her head.

"Welcome to Introductory Inscriptions. I am Counselor Whynn. Here we will learn more about runes and how they can be used outside of gathering. The world of inscriptions is vast and covers everything from the defensive runes you've seen on the Armory or the main gate to attack glyphs and auxiliary runes like this Light Ball inscription. If you decide to stick with inscriptions we will learn how to create elemental attacks, shields, and enhancements. In the next year we will learn how to make formations, which are large-scale inscriptions that incorporate thousands of runes, such as the formation around the Meditation Grotto that draws Aether into it."

A couple of Mentors came forward from the back of the class. One young woman who was wearing third tier robes, with dark skin and hair, grabbed a stack of paper and began handing it out. The other Mentor, a fourth tier young man with blond hair and fair skin, started giving everyone what looked like metal quills and jars of a reddish-brown ink. "Inscriptions require special materials. The paper being passed to each of you is produced from ten-year-old Towering Pine trees, the ink from Earthen Willow bark and the quills are treated Elemental Fowl quills from Metal-aligned Fowl. Inscriptions are not cheap, but they can work as many miracles as alchemy," the Counselor explained as the materials were handed out.

"Today we will learn how to make the Light Ball inscription. The set of runes is fairly simple for this, as only four are required. The first"—she started drawing on the board behind her—"represents light. The second defines where it will go, namely above and slightly behind your head. The third defines the intensity of the light, while the last defines shape and size." She finished drawing the four Runes on the board.

"Now, inscription would be easy if all it was was drawing Runes on paper. That is not the case. The hardest part is actually drawing the Runes because you have to insert Aether into the quill while drawing them. For these runes the Aether amount is important only in that it is consistent. In most of the more complicated runic structures, you have to vary the Aether input as you write. Carving inscriptions makes them reusable, but requires even more variation of Aether, as the runes become three dimensional. For now, you have been given five pages. Attempt to create the Light Ball inscription. We will be watching and helping out."

Just like a program. You have to tell it what to do and how to do it. I need to get a dictionary of runes and look at creating high-level ones. Also, I need to figure out the Aether rules to this. Why would the Aether amount need to vary? I pulled a sheet of paper out. *Okay, first I should work on making sure the Aether I put into the quill and flow into the paper is consistent.* I dipped the quill in the ink and watched as it absorbed it. After a few seconds, I pulled the quill out and focused on pushing Aether into it. I set up an Aether cycle just like when I was working on the Aether burst from my trisula. I slowly started to draw the first rune, focusing on the Aether flowing through the quill rather than getting the rune perfect.

After a couple of tries, I made the first rune consistent and had a feel for how the Aether flowed. Now I started drawing the runes, smaller than I would for the final version. I filled the front and back of the first sheet working through them. I set it to the side and pulled out a fresh sheet. This would be my first real attempt. I started to write after getting a fresh pull of ink and made it through the first two runes before a swirl on the third was drawn incorrectly. I looked up to the Counselor, who was a desk away, and asked, "If we mess up on the front, can we try to draw the inscription on the back?"

"Yes, that would be fine for this inscription. For some others that can be detrimental, but this one is very forgiving." I flipped the page over and started again. I almost succeeded but failed near the end of the last rune. The third page came out, and I started drawing. This one was successful. "Good, now, to use the inscription, simply feed a small amount of Aether into the first rune. Probably best not to stare at it as you do so though," Counselor Whynn said as she watched me. I picked the paper up and pushed Aether through my hands into it, and goggled as the paper morphed into a ball of light. Of course, it had the same effect as looking into a flashlight and I was blinking for another minute to get the spots out of my eyes.

"Counselor, what defines how long the light lasts? There wasn't a rune in there for that," I asked her.

"For this inscription, the length is defined by the amount of Aether you used to create it, which is almost always the case. You can put a rune in to limit the timeframe, but that would require you to know how much Aether to put in for that. Too little and it will fizzle early anyway, and too much will leave you a ball of Aether that will disperse violently when it no longer has an outlet. That is why we often will leave the timeframe off until you get much more experience with the Aether required. Good job on the inscription. You may leave if you wish. If you are interested in learning more, browse through the books and memory stones outside. I will see you in a week."

"Thank you, ma'am," I said as I stood up. "What should I do with the quill and ink?" She thought for a moment and then told me to keep them. I bowed to her and packed up, stopped up the ink and wiped the quill off on the failure paper. After I gathered everything into one of the pockets on my tunic, I left the room to browse through the library. I pulled out the occasional book since most of them didn't have names on the spine. The first book was on defensive formations. *Way too difficult to start with,* I thought as I browsed through the book. I started searching for a compendium of runes or something like that. After about fifteen minutes, I noticed several others browsing, including Ming and Bridget.

Finally, I found a book entitled *Introductory Runes and Inscription* of which there were three copies. I grabbed all three then walked over to Ming. "I found this as an introductory, want a copy?" I asked.

He shook his head and said, "Thank you, but I'm fairly well versed in inscriptions already. My clan has a number of inscription and Formation Masters in it. Bridget might though, as well as Alexander over there." I thanked him and headed over to Bridget. She was excited by the book. Alexander thanked me for grabbing it. I suggested we should look through the book, then maybe meet up tomorrow at lunch to talk about what we read.

"Learning as a group can work as we can help each other answer questions, and anything that confuses all of us we can take to the Counselor or maybe Ming," I finished. Alexander looked pensive, while Bridget quickly agreed.

Alexander then told us, "Uh, I'll think about it," before heading off. Bridget looked confused by his answer, and I just shrugged.

"It's okay. It is his loss if he doesn't want to work together," I told Bridget before excusing myself. I lightly jogged back to my room and deposited the book and inscription materials. After that, I headed slowly to PT, debating about what I should focus on. *I'm really curious about both inscription and alchemy, and I really enjoyed the metallurgy class I took at USAFA. I need to pick two at most though, so I'll go with alchemy and inscription. Maybe I'll be able to look into blacksmithing at some point in the future. I need to write down what little I remember about steel creation and see what they know about that here too.*

CHAPTER TWENTY-TWO

When I got to the PT field, I was waved to do my starting run of ten kilometers. I pushed myself, working my muscles and my knowledge of the running technique to get the run done in less than a half hour. After finishing and doing some light calisthenics, I was called over to Counselor Might. "So, what technique did you pick up?" he asked me as I approached.

"I was given three techniques by the head librarian, sir. I started looking into the Dancing Northern Wind movement technique first because I am still working on getting the introductory offense and defense techniques down. The offensive technique I was given was the Four Twin Lightning Stab technique and the defensive was the Iron Bones, Granite Skin technique," I answered as I stopped in front of him.

"Good, you spoke to Head Librarian Narwan and listened to his advice. Though I doubt he gave you a choice in the matter. Let me see the Dancing Northern Wind memory stone." I handed the stone over, and he put it to his head for maybe twenty seconds. "This is a remarkable technique. Okay, follow me." He walked away from everyone else, to a clear spot on the fields about twenty meters wide and forty long. He gestured at the field, and circles of stone rose about a foot off the ground. The circles were staggered back and forth, like you would put tires for agility exercises, though these started at a meter apart and ended at probably ten meters apart as you moved forward.

"This should do for you to train on. Use the technique to move side to side down the field. Each time you fall, come back to the beginning, and try again. Once you have mastered the second level, come back to talk and I will adapt the course. There may be some others who use it, depends on if anyone else took an agility technique. Now begin." I was just staring since he had created an agility course by waving his hand! *Magic!* was resonating in my head. "Now!" came the shout that broke me out of my daze.

I started to circulate my Aether as the technique directed and tried to move down the course. I could physically power through the first eight steps, but the ninth I couldn't quite make. I tried a couple of times before I moved off to the side and looked through the memory stone again. I figured out a trick that let me fast-forward to the point I was looking for and watched the student learning the first level again. After that, I got back on the course. By the end of the first hour, I had managed to make it fifteen steps in, though that still didn't count as mastering even the first level.

I took a break to gather and replenish my Aether. I watched the memory again. I continued the cycle of running the course, gathering Aether, and watching the memory for the next two hours, until it was time for dinner. I had been excused from the end run to continue working on the technique. Not that I was thankful for that. The run would have been easier at this point. I was hobbling with aching knees on my way to the shower and dinner. Thankfully, the soreness mostly passed as I ate, especially as the Aether in the Lightning Elemental Fowl meat flowed into me. *Well, this makes working out to a stronger level much easier. Just destroy my muscles then refresh them with Aether. Especially as my multiple affinities make it much easier to find food that is an element my body can utilize well.*

I was eating alone since I had taken longer than most of the kids in my class, and the third tiers were filing in to eat as I was finishing up. Karl and the other servants cleaned up around me, and I brought my plate up to the bin once I was done. A few third tiers looked at me funny as I did so. I went to leave and a large third tier blocked my way. "What have we here, a young 'un intruding in our space. What makes you think you can take our time?"

"I was late getting back from Physical Training. I need to go now, so please move," I said, not backing down as I felt he wanted.

He stepped into my face and said, "No," then moved to grab me. I immediately circulated the Dancing Northern Wind that I had been working on and dodged to the side. His groping hand missed me, and he stumbled slightly. I moved forward, shoulder checking him, and used the rebound to move around him. I sprinted out the door and ran for the Grotto. Behind me, I heard laughter as the bully shouted at me. I ignored him and kept going. Thankfully, he didn't follow. *Bullies are the same everywhere. They pick on someone weaker, but will back off if you aren't afraid and can back that up*, I thought as I turned into the small cutoff that led to my pavilion.

I sat down and centered myself, using this to help calm my racing heart. *Now, what should I work on?* I thought. *What I need most is more Aether. Time to gather and see if I can advance!* Having made my decision, I stood up. No one else was there, so I was going to use the Eight by Eight Gathering form to gather as quickly as I could. I always felt like I was doing a slow dance when moving through the forms, so I began to dance. I was able to make it through the first and second set, before I remembered I still had a dose of the Simple Gathering powder we made in alchemy.

I jogged back to my room and retrieved it then ran back. Losing the five minutes to get the powder was worth the twenty percent gain in gathering speed I got from the Simple Gathering powder. *Not quite as good as the Complete Powder, but still good,* I thought as I went through the forms again. After an hour of working through the forms, my skin was starting to feel tight and it felt like I had heartburn. *Nearly there*, I thought excitedly. I took a break to drink some water and started again. After ten minutes, I sat down and focused on my center, watching as the Aether in it pushed against my meridians.

The pressure in my center continued to grow until, with a grunt, I finally managed to shove more Aether into it than it could hold. A pulse of Aether flowed throughout my body. I watched as everywhere the pulse went, my meridians became larger and the edges became thicker. The Aether in them was now noticeably thicker, though not as much as I had expected. With a shiver, every muscle seemed to spasm for a second, and I watched as more impurities came out on my skin. *Gross,* was the thought that propelled me from the seat towards my dorm.

Suddenly I noticed the first change. I started using the running technique again, and ran face-first into a tree. The speed I had achieved had been a good twenty percent higher than I expected. That is normally not much, unless you are suddenly accelerating by twenty percent more on a small trail with trees all around. *Well, I'm glad no one saw that,* I thought, then I heard laughter. Looking around, I didn't see anyone. Until I looked up that is.

I saw the Crimson Zarorzel in a branch on the tree and it was cawing with laughter that sounded way too human to be coming from a bird. I shook my head and playfully glared at it, which only increased the laughter. I pulled a fruit out of my pocket and waved it towards it. The laughter stopped and it attempted a contrite look. I laughed and tossed the fruit to it while shaking my head. As soon as it snatched the fruit, it chirped happily at me before cawing in laughter again and flying off. *Stupid bird,* I grumbled light-heartedly at the bird's antics.

I walked slowly out of the Grotto, still blushing from the bird and rubbing my face where I smacked it. I went and rinsed off the grime before heading out to the PT fields. There I saw a number of people practicing various techniques, including someone using the agility course set up today.

Their technique must have been Fire based, as small puffs of flame exploded out each time they stepped.

I watched the person with the Fire technique for a little bit because they were able to make it all the way down the course. After that, I decided I needed to work through my new strength for a bit before trying anything else. I took off on a jog around the fields, using the running technique and getting used to the new-found power it had. After a couple of laps, I felt comfortable with it but I continued to jog. This time around I focused on creating an Aether Shield, getting used to doing so while moving and at my new level.

I was amazed at the changes. The Aether Shield I created at this level felt thicker, while also being easier to manipulate. By focusing, I could direct extra Aether from my center to a location to make it thicker for a second, though that grew expensive fairly quickly. I finished my jog, I was mostly out of Aether, in front of the target dummies. Three were being used by some students I didn't recognize. After taking enough time to refresh my Aether pool, I practiced sending out from my trisula the Aether attacks I had learned.

After a few attempts, I was able to project out an Aether blast that was able to penetrate into the dummy. *Hah, I'm Link!* I thought, watching as I sent what looked like a sword blast from the Zelda games. I continued to send out blasts, working on making them still smaller. I was able to send out twice as many blasts as before I had leveled up, which helped me get the hang of the technique. *A couple more levels and I'll be able to almost continuously fire off blasts like this. I wonder what I'll be able to do at higher levels.*

After half an hour or so of weapons practice, I headed over to the agility course. The Fire gatherer had left at some point, so the course was free. I climbed onto the first step and centered. I called up the memory, and was surprised at how clear it had gotten. *My memory got better again! I'm slowly becoming a superhero. Woot!* I started jumping back and forth between the steps, working on the Dancing Northern Wind technique.

Over the next hour, I got closer and closer to mastering the first level of the technique. The feeling of being buoyed by the air as I did so was interesting. As I finally made it to the halfway point on the course and fell, a voice called out, "You're trying too hard." I looked over and saw someone sitting next to one of the steps near the end of the course. They got up and walked over to me.

"What do you mean?" I asked. I saw that he was a fourth tier student when he got close, thanks to his uniform.

"Air wants to move freely, moving from one place to another with no restrictions. You have to emulate that feeling with your runes and thoughts as you perform the technique. Every element behaves differently and the element-specific techniques have to mirror that. Think on that," he said.

"Thank you, Mentor. I will," I responded. He gestured towards the start of the course. I nodded, jogged back to the start and hopped up to the first step. *Air wants to move freely? But wind is caused by a change in pressure between two locations, where the high-pressure air flows to the low pressure.* As I thought about what I knew about wind and air pressure, I realized what the runes were trying to do. They were runes for increasing pressure, decreasing pressure, and directing the air around me.

I realized that, based on what I thought the runes were doing, I had their placement wrong. The student in the memory stone had a different body shape than I did, and I had to adapt the runes to myself. I needed to move the increasing pressure Rune a couple of inches down and back, and a couple directing Runes needed small repositioning. I concentrated and took the first leap. I could immediately feel the difference, and each step seemed easier. I pushed as hard as I could and nearly floated at times.

I made it two-thirds of the way down before I didn't quite reach the step. This meant I had made a sideways leap of nearly five meters! *That little change took me from the first level to the second. Understanding the runes and reasons behind their placement is what will get me farther. Don't just blindly trust the memory stone is exactly right; everything will have to be adapted to me.* "Good job!" came a call from the senior student who had been watching me. "Keep working on it and you will master this in no time." I watched as he went down the course, Fire bursting from his feet every step. *It looks like he's getting a push from the Fire Aether like a rocket, and using heat to make the air around him less dense. I wonder if there are ways of combining them*

The Mentor said goodbye after he finished one last run. I did the course a couple more times, though I only made it one step farther by the end. By this point, it was getting late. *I'm up later than I have been in a while, but I don't feel very tired. Is this a consequence of leveling up? If so, do Core Seed or higher level gatherers even need to sleep?*

CHAPTER TWENTY-THREE

The next morning I woke up refreshed, eager to talk to Counselor Sila about what the new level meant and how to continue advancing. I quickly dressed and left for breakfast. As I passed into the stairway, I nearly ran into Bridget. Or at least I thought I did. I jumped back from her, but she was still a couple of feet away. "Are you okay?" she asked, looking at me with concern.

"Yeah, I just thought I ran into you. Hold on," I said, stepping closer to her. "It feels like there is a little bit of pressure emanating from you. I've never felt that before," I told her, confused.

"You talk funny, you know that? I have no idea what pressure would be coming from me. Other than my beauty, but that didn't change last night, did it?" she asked, grinning at me.

"Uh, um, uh, no, you are just as beautiful as ever," I said hurriedly, sensing the trap in her question. Maybe. *Even in another world, I still don't understand women. Of course, I doubt she understands me either.* "Shall we head to breakfast?" I said, and led the way down the stairs. We talked a little bit about the upcoming tournament; speculation was still rife among the first tiers about what it would be like. I could feel that little bit of pressure coming from her, and from the others we passed. *This is weird.*

We walked in and grabbed food. I saw Ming, Jon, Xiao, and Bet sitting at a table. As we got close, Ming said, "Congratulations on advancing! That makes you the first one to advance in the class. Everyone else at Mist or above was already there when we started."

"Uh, thanks. How did you know?" I asked.

"The Aether pressure you put out changed. Did you notice that gatherers now feel like they are pushing you away slightly?" he asked back.

"Is that what this is? I was wondering about that," I told him.

"Yes, everyone at the Mist level and beyond can feel the Aether pressure of others; it usually has no effect on you other than being able to feel it. Though if the Counselors didn't restrain their aura some it would make it harder to focus and work in the classes. The pressure is light for those at lower levels, and grows much heavier for those at stages above you," he explained. Then he smiled. "When we are able to leave, I will treat you to a great meal as a reward."

There was a round of congrats around the table, along with questions as to where everyone was and how long to advance. Both Ming and Bet were High Mist already, while Xiao was Low Mist and Jon and

Bridget both High Vapor. Bet then said, "It is really hard to tell how long it will take to advance, but you could talk to your Counselors about it. They might be able to tell you tomorrow or the day after. There is a way of observing the total Aether in you and how much is needed to level. They then compare the amount changed over a day or two to get an estimate."

Ah, good old linear interpolation, I thought, amused. The discussion fell off as everyone ate. Gathering class didn't change. We were still working on the Eight by Eight Gathering form. I moved into the third set that class, and then spent the entire meditation time gathering. I was able to gather twice as much Aether into me before I had to start actively converting it through my Runes. As you advanced in levels, the rate of gathering increased, but the amount of Aether required to advance again increased even more.

"Aiden, come over here," Counselor Sila called as the class was dismissed. "Congratulations on advancing to the Low Mist level. Your talent is noteworthy. If you put in the effort, you will be able to make it beyond Core formation, I'm sure. The Kingdom needs as many people with Perfect Cores or beyond as they can get, and will generously reward any who have the potential to make it there."

"Thank you, Counselor. Should I do anything different with gathering now that I have advanced?" I asked.

"Not yet. Finish mastering the Eight by Eight Gathering forms, which will sustain you through the rest of the Aether Gathering stage. Once you move into Aether Compression you'll be sent to the library to find a more individualized gathering form. Since the head librarian took a liking to you, you should be able to find something interesting. Any other questions for me?" When I shook my head no, he dismissed me.

Lunch progressed as breakfast did, this time with Vaya congratulating me and a glare from Nicky which I winked at. The class we had today was geography. I was excited by this, as I was really curious about this world. The map I saw at my new parents' house didn't have much detail beyond the area around the city and coast. *What is past the sea? Or beyond the mountains? What lies east of us?* As I walked to the class with Vaya and Lucas, I couldn't hold in my enthusiasm. I was just so curious, and I hadn't had the ability to fulfill this curiosity before now.

"You know, if you want a map I can probably get you a fairly accurate one of the entire country," Vaya told me.

"That'd be awesome!" I exclaimed. "I want to explore the whole world if I can!" As we got to the classroom building, I realized that I was acting really out of character. *I know I'm excited, but I usually can control myself better than this. My emotions seem stronger now. Is this also a consequence of leveling? Or is it just being back in a teenage body? I need to get a hold of myself!* We split up and headed to our classrooms.

The Counselor for this class was Headmaster Glav. "Good afternoon, Headmaster," I said as I bowed to her, deeper than I did to the other Counselors.

"Good afternoon, Aiden. Welcome, all, to a look at the world around us. I like to teach one class every week in this or history, and you get to be the lucky students. Today we will be covering our beloved Kingdom and the large terrain groups within it and bordering it. Can anyone tell me where we are?" she asked the room.

"The Azyl Academy is located in Azyl City, ma'am. Azyl City is located along the Craesti River, which reaches from the Central Mountains to the Inner Sea. The area we are in is also called the Central Region or Central Plain," Anberlin said. Headmaster Glav waved at the board, and a map started appearing as Anberlin was talking. A dot was placed and labeled Azyl City, then a river was drawn traveling north and south. The Central Mountains were drawn a good ways south of the city, and the Dividing Sea coastline was traced for a portion of the board.

"Excellent. That is entirely correct. Now to the east of us, we have the rest of the Central Plain, followed by the Zaboj Swamp which stretches the majority of the rest of the peninsula that is the Kingdom. Near the coast, the swamp fades into coastal plains, and the major river, also named Zaboj, exits at the tip of the peninsula at the city of Oddali.

"Oddali is the main point of trade with the Weltreich, one of the major powers across the Inner Sea. It also contains the Oddali Academy, one of the five major gathering academies in the Kingdom. Continuing along the peninsula, the entire southern portion consists of the Central Mountains. The Central Mountains are the Kingdom's main source of iron, copper, silver, and mithril. There are a number of small mining towns along the borders. The Polud river runs south through the Central Mountains, and the city of Poludnie lies on the coast," the Headmaster explained. *Wait, is mithril a thing here? In books it was a super metal, better than steel. That's awesome!*

146

Unaware of my distraction, or uncaring, she continued, "West of the mountains and filling the majority of the west of the Kingdom is the Great Western Forest. The majority of our high-affinity meat comes from hunting expeditions into the interior of the Forest. There are only villages around the edge because the central regions of the Forest are largely unexplored. Most expeditions into the deep interior have resulted in the death of all involved, and the few survivors speak of Primordial Beasts that rule sections of the Forest.

"The Kneija River flows out of the Forest and the headwaters are rumored to be an area of extremely concentrated Aether. Kneija City is located where the Kneija River exits the Forest, and has a very high natural Aether concentration. Kneija Academy is another of the five Academies. Beyond the Forest are the Skraj Mountains, which form the border between the Kingdom and the Toprak Empire. A single pass, Zelec's Cut, is traversable through the Skrajs. Zelec's City is located at the mouth of the pass and is the main point of trade with, and defense against, Toprak. They also have an Academy. The last Academy is naturally in the capital."

The map being drawn behind the Headmaster filled in even more details while she discussed different towns and villages around the Kingdom, from mining villages in either mountain range, farming villages throughout the plains, or the few towns that raised alchemical crops along the edges of the Zaboj swamp. I quickly copied the map, at least in broad strokes, onto a piece of paper.

While the Kingdom was very large, it was able to use less than half the space within its borders. The interiors of the Skraj and Central Mountains, the Great Western Forest, and the Zaboj Swamp were all zones where people could not live. Much of their interiors had not been mapped or explored. Class ended with the Headmaster saying she would be back next week.

Physical Training was running, agility course, Aether Blasts, running. With the boost in my Aether gathering level, I was able to run much faster. This resulted in Counselor Might telling me to take two more laps. Apparently, we were going to have to run for half an hour every class, no matter how fast we got. I wasn't able to improve much in the agility course, with thirty steps still left to the end. When practicing the Aether blasts, I was able to extend my range to nearly the ten-foot limit. This was the extent of the capability, though, as everything in the memory stone suggested that the Aether blast technique was limited to a short range.

After we finished running the second set of laps around the PT fields, Counselor Might called the entire first tier class over to him. "Tomorrow will be your first tactics lesson. I am the tactics Counselor for your class. The class will be held in the Training Pavilion. It is behind the faculty housing. Be respectful when passing the housing area. I will see you there. Dismissed."

After showering and grabbing food, I sat down with Jon, Brett, Jamila, Vaya, and Bridget for dinner. "What do you think we're going to be doing for tactics?" I asked the group.

"I heard about the Training Pavilion from my older brother," Vaya started saying. "He told me that it is a testing formation. I don't know how it works since he wasn't allowed to say, but he did say that we will have to use it many times. He shuddered when he talked about it, like it was not a pleasant experience."

"Huh, I wonder why?" Jon asked rhetorically. *I wonder,* I thought. *Maybe it's a formation that attacks you and you have to dodge? Or maybe they have golems that will attack and you have to fight them?*

"Maybe they will have Beasts that we have to fight as a group. Or maybe they will have enchanted dummies like on the PT field that we have to beat? That'd be awesome, not disturbing, though," I commented out loud. We lapsed into silence, each debating in our heads what it could be. Dinner finished quickly after that. On the way out, I asked Jon, "Hey, how're you doing? You've seemed a bit down today."

"Yeah, I've been having issues figuring out the Eight by Eight thing. Can't seem to get the hang of the first set. Counselor Sila said I needed to work harder and being unable to complete it will hold me back since I won't be able to gather fast enough."

"Well, I've gotten past that point. How about you show me where you gather and I'll help you work through it?" I suggested. He agreed, and we spent the next two hours working through the first stage of the Eight by Eight Gathering form. He was stuck on the fifth move, so I demonstrated it a couple of times and helped guide his hands through a tricky motion at the end. After a hundred repetitions he finally got it. I told him to keep working, and proceed to the sixth move. I then told him I'd help him out more tomorrow. I then left and gathered for an hour before retiring to bed.

CHAPTER TWENTY-FOUR

The next morning I woke excited and nervous. At breakfast, almost everyone was tense, nervous about tactics class that afternoon. We ate quickly, eager to get the day on with. When we got to the classroom building, the Counselors were not outside. Everyone hurried into their classrooms and found their seats. "Today we will be working on a self-healing channeling technique, known as the Minor Wound Closure technique. Watch carefully," Counselor Sila said.

Everyone took this to mean channeling Aether into their eyes to see his Aether flows better. He held up his left hand and slashed it with a dagger. Small drops of blood splattered down. We saw as he formed a film of Aether around the wound, forcing it to run across the blood and in a circle around the edges. The Aether then made a crosshatch pattern across the wound, and we saw it start closing. In less than a minute, the wound was gone. It didn't even leave a scar.

"This technique is somewhat painful to learn because it requires an open wound to work. This means you will have to cut yourself or have a friend do it in order to practice. If you take more than five minutes, wave at myself or the Mentors, and we will heal you so you do not scar. Small cuts only; this technique becomes extremely expensive in Aether cost if the cuts get bigger. Hence why it is named Minor Wound Closure, not Major Wound Closure. To work the technique, you have to surround the wound with an Aether film and build a series of intersecting points. You generally want to make twenty intersections. More intersections will give a faster healing time, but uses up more Aether. You may begin."

All of us looked around, waiting to see who would be the first. Of course, Jon shruged and pulled out his sword. "Anyone? No? Okay, I'll go first," he said, fearless as ever. He made a small cut on his forearm and started trying to heal it. As the ice was broken, most everyone pulled out their weapons and began to gently cut themselves. I started out by trying to use the point of my trisula to make a tiny incision in my palm. When I lightly pushed, nothing happened. I could feel the trisula point on my palm, but it didn't hurt. I pushed a bit harder, and then harder still, before my skin finally parted and I made a much bigger puncture wound than I wanted.

"Whoa there," Mentor Lo said, who immediately healed my hand. "Not so big of a wound. What happened?"

"I tried a small cut, but I just couldn't get it to work, until my skin gave and suddenly my trisula stabbed straight through my hand. Wait," I said, thinking, "I think it might be because I opened a skin meridian. I know what to do now. Thank you, Mentor Lo. That would have been unpleasant if you hadn't healed it."

He nodded and said, "Yes, a skin meridian would increase the toughness of your skin and make it harder to cut," then gestured at me to continue. I rubbed my hand a bit, then picked my trisula up again. I channeled a very small amount of Aether into the blade, and sliced lightly along my skin.

This time, I managed to make a small incision, only slightly bigger than if I poked it with a needle. As the blood welled up, I channeled Aether into a circle around it. This was really easy due to that same skin meridian. However, as soon as I did that, the wound healed. "You'll have to make a bigger cut than that. This technique works on wounds, not pricks," Mentor Lo said, observing me. I looked around and nodded to him.

Taking into account what everyone else is doing, let's try making a one-inch cut. I don't want to make it too big to start with, I thought while I sliced the meat of my palm again. *This sucks!* This time, I was able to surround the cut and start crisscrossing it with Aether. I could feel the Aether drain as the wound started closing. It looked like just circling the wound with Aether would let it heal fairly quickly, but by crosshatching it, the Aether was able to stimulate healing and keep blood and other fluids inside. The Aether acted like stitches, a bandage, and sci-fi healing stimulant at the same time.

I gauged how much Aether that cost me, then did a slightly bigger incision. After healing that—Ow! Ow! Ow!—I did another. *The Aether cost is exponential with the size of the wound. That is why this will only work on smaller ones. I bet I would run dry before being able to close a five-inch slash. I wonder what the advanced techniques in healing are. This one isn't very sophisticated, just throw Aether at it until healed.* After the first five tries, Mentor Lo said I had it down well enough. I looked around, and saw about half of the class was done, and was rubbing their hands or arms where they had been cutting. *Yeah, no one wants to do this again. But this might save our lives, or at least reduce scarring from an injury. This also taught me that just surrounding a wound with Aether will slowly close it, at a much smaller cost. Slowing down bleeding could be just as important as stopping it entirely, especially in a battle condition. Combat first-aid lessons at USAFA emphasized that.*

Class ended and Counselor Sila ran a quick Aether examination on everyone. He looked at me and said, "Good job. So far it looks like you will advance to High Mist in about a week. You might even be able to push that sooner with hard work and powders." Everyone spent the time walking into the Grotto complaining, though I was happy to learn a little bit more about how Aether affected my body. *The Aether made everything happen faster and smoother. Normally I'd have a small scar, but the Aether prevented scar tissue from forming, instead making new normal skin. This also explains why we can run multiple 10ks a day and do workouts without collapsing; it heals our muscles perfectly.*

I spent the next couple hours refilling and expanding my Aether pool. *Getting stronger will depend on my gathering level, so I need to work on leveling,* I thought. The class had stimulated my desire to get stronger, to prevent the catastrophe or whatever was coming in the future. As before, the Zarorzel was watching me as I gathered, and pounced on the food I left it as I got up. *The phoenix is getting more comfortable with me,* I thought. *It's landing on the food closer to me every time. Maybe soon it'll let me touch it?*

At lunch, Jon was regaling a table with his bravery for being the first to cut himself. "That's because you're always doing crazy things anyway, so why not another?" I called as I went to grab food. Everyone there laughed, Jon included, as he agreed with me. Jon then started telling everyone about my accident while I sat down. "Yeah, that sucked," I said with a laugh.

Lunch continued with everyone telling stories from their class. After the first few, it became obvious that we were telling stories to avoid thinking about the upcoming class. Finally, everyone finished up and began leaving. I took my time cleaning up and followed the crowd. The laughter of the dining hall was replaced with silent worry. *This is ridiculous, why are we all so worried about the class coming up?* I thought.

We turned the corner around the housing and saw the Pavilion. It was a large gazebo with an ornate roof. Statues of Elemental Beasts stood above each of the ten pillars holding the roof up. As we got closer, we could see runic inscriptions covering the floor. Ten large circles were lined with silver in between the pillars, with lines of silver running throughout the center. A single circle was also in the center. Counselor Might sat in the center circle. As everyone was filing around the Pavilion, he stood up.

"Welcome to your first experience at the Training Pavilion. This is where most of the tournaments and training in actual fighting will occur because here we can do so without risk of permanent damage. Today we will be conducting a ranking challenge. Ten of you at a time will come forward and sit in the circles there." He gestured around him before continuing. "The formation here will examine you and your equipment and create a copy in an illusory space. There you will fight increasingly difficult opponents until you are beaten. From the center circle, I will be able to watch all of you simultaneously. I will be giving feedback to each of you individually once everyone has completed their ranking attempt. The level you reach will be displayed on the pillars. These levels will be used to determine the initial pairings for the end of month tournament. Additionally, rewards for the top ten, top five, and top three will be given out. You may discuss all that you see within, and how you dealt with the challenges. Learn from your friends to make your attempts better. However, do not discuss what you see today until everyone has completed their turn. Do not discuss what the training entails with anyone not of the Academy and who has not already entered it. The Pavilion is one of the few unique things that an Academy can provide, and we don't want to give this capability or knowledge to others." He then called out ten people's names to start the competition.

Those of us not called out took a seat and watched, wondering what would happen. Ming and Jamila were among the first group, so I alternated between watching them. Jamila walked up to one of the nearest circles and sat cross legged while Ming jogged around to the rearmost circle. Once everyone was seated, a flash of light flew along the silver lines, and a soft humming could be heard. Everyone seated in the Pavilion closed their eyes simultaneously. Nothing then happened for a minute or so, until one of the students let out a gasp, with their face visibly paling. *Huh, what happened?* I wondered.

About a minute later, that same student let out a cry and fell over backwards. The light in the formation around them faded. A small flash occurred on the central pillar, and "Wagner Jonas – 1" was written near the middle in slightly glowing letters. Jonas shakily stood up and stumbled off the Pavilion. Counselor Might called Jon up to take his place. I was worriedly watching Jon and Jamila now since Jonas was pale and shaking.

This continued for about ten minutes, with a couple more people being eliminated at levels one and two. Finally, Jamila was eliminated at level three, and I was called to take her place. As I walked up, I stopped in front of her. "Are you alright?" I asked, offering my arm to help her down. She took it, shaking her head, and I helped her sit.

"Be careful," she whispered to me as I turned back to the Pavilion. Counselor Might gave me a nod and gestured to the circle. I took a deep breath and moved up to the circle. Sitting down, I felt a wave of Aether wash over me. The world faded to black, and then slowly faded in again. I felt like I was standing on a prairie, short grasses waving in the hot summer wind. *Heh, magical virtual reality! So cool!* I thought and looked around curiously. Off to one side, an Earthen Boar snorted and charged at me.

I shouted in surprise and dove to the side, dodging its charge. I stood up and drew my weapons, focusing on centering myself. "Have to use Aether techniques to win this. An Earthen Boar's skin is usually too strong to directly stab," I said, trying to circulate Aether into my trisulas while also setting up the Dancing Northern Wind technique. The Boar charged again, faster this time as the dirt under it buckled with the force.

I slipped sideways using my technique and stabbed forward, lightly slicing its hind leg. As it slowed to turn back to me, I quickly sent out an Aether blast which knocked it off its feet. I rushed forward before it could stand back up and stabbed it through the chest with a burst of Aether. The Beast disappeared. "That wasn't that bad, though that would have hurt if it hit me," I said to myself. "That must have been what happened to Jonas."

I kept a lookout, trying to figure out what was next. *Is it going to be more than one Boar, or something else?* After a minute, I was getting more nervous. I pulled Aether into my eyes, trying to see around me. A flash off to my left had me jumping backwards, and I saw a silver-colored Lion land where I had just been. *Well, this is more worrisome.*

The Lion looked up at me and roared, a wave of sound rolling out from it. Aether was infused throughout the roar, and it smashed me backwards. I rolled with it, sort of, ending up on my back but continuing to roll. The Lion pounced as I fell, faster than the Boar had been. I managed to dodge the first pounce, but the second one put it on top of me. I managed to get my legs up, preventing its back legs from savaging me, while my weapons intercepted one claw. I flared Aether into a shield, holding back its fangs from my shoulder.

I kicked it as hard as I could, and slashed at its throat with one hand. We traded slashes, with its claws ripping into my left shoulder and my trisula opening its throat. I managed to push it off and roll to my feet, left arm dangling. *I guess this is why we learned healing this morning,* I thought as

I surrounded the cuts with Aether. The wound closed, but I didn't have full mobility, as it was really too deep for that technique. The Lion was unable to get up and quickly disappeared. I looked around, trying to spot what was next.

A howling started up a minute later, and two Wind Wolves stalked out of the grass. *Don't sit back, attack!* As I saw the Wolves, I shot an Aether blast at the far one, while starting to strafe sideways. Being the first to attack startled them, and the rear Wolf dodged too late, taking the hit on its right side. With a yelp, it collapsed, seemingly unable to stand up. Seeing it fall, I charged forward, hoping the other one would interfere and I could get it too.

The second wolf charged towards me and flung its head sideways. A blade of Air Aether formed in front of it and shot at me too quick to dodge. I formed an Aether Shield again and took the hit. The force made me stumble and drained a significant chunk of Aether from me. Another blade formed, and I circulated the Dancing Northern Wind, dodging to the side as the Wolf leaped at where I would have stumbled if I took the hit again. I slashed at it, trying to take it out in a single hit, but the Wolf managed to slightly change its direction in midair.

It landed, injured but not defeated, and came at me again. I managed to dodge the next Air Blade and sent an Aether blast back at it, which it dodged. It started to form yet another blade, when a tingling intuition caused me to jump sideways. The first Wolf had managed to get up and attack. By causing it to miss, I had a great opportunity to take it out. As I stepped forward, the other Wolf jumped to intervene, and I managed to get both of them with the next two slashes. As they disappeared, I sat with a huff.

I've got just about a minute until the next level. I'm already halfway out of Aether. But hey, at least I made it past the first three levels. I think. Attacking worked better, though I don't know what will be next. So far it was a level two Beast, a level three Beast, and two level three Beasts. This is why almost everyone fell at level two and three. I got really lucky with the Wolves.

I stood back up, looking around when a voice called out, "Well, look what we have here. A lone wanderer, all banged up from the Beast." I saw two men in ragged clothes walking towards me. They both held swords, and the pressure I felt from them was equal to Xiao's. "Put all your stuff on the ground and we'll give you a quick death!" the one on the right yelled.

"Not a chance, scum!" I shouted, settling into a ready position. Both of them shouted and slashed at me, sending blades of Aether through the air. I intercepted them both with my trisulas, blocking their blasts before sending one back at the talker. I charged behind the blast while they both dove out of the way. The talker rolled back to his feet in time to meet my charge, knocking aside the stab move I made. He tried to counter, but I managed to get my other trisula in the way, and caught his sword in the outer hook.

With a snap of my wrist, I trapped his blade and yanked it out of his hands before stabbing him through the heart. His expression changed from enraged to surprised, and so did mine. I stared at my hand, covered in blood, aghast. *I just killed someone!* I thought, shocked. I was utterly not ready for this, even while I was trying to convince myself, *It's just like a game, it's not real!*

My musing was interrupted by a bloom of pain in my stomach. Looking down, I saw a sword sticking through me. The pain in my abdomen flared as the sword was pulled out, and I collapsed next to the bandit I had slain. I managed to roll as I fell, landing on my back with a cry of pain. "Die!" shouted the other bandit, who was slashing down at me. With the last of my strength, I redirected his slash to the side with one hand and stabbed with the other, taking him through the throat. I tried to use Aether to stabilize my wound, but blacked out before I could finish.

CHAPTER TWENTY-FIVE

With a gasp, I woke up from the illusion and clutched at my chest. I could still feel the pain of the sword. *Okay, that was too real. I'm gonna go throw up now!* I got up and staggered off the Pavilion. A couple of steps into the grass, I bent over and threw up. Looking around, I saw several other people had done so already, and one of the Mentors came over and washed the vomit away with a wave of his hand. He handed me a cup of water and said, "Take a drink, it'll help." I took a sip of the drink, an herbal tonic to help my stomach, and walked over to sit next to Jamila and Jon. I saw my name, saying I made it to level five.

Huh, guess it counted when I got that last guy. Apparently we will also have to fight other people. I, uh, guess I never thought of that. Fighting the Beasts was exciting, but the bandits bothered me. I don't want to become complacent with killing. I need to make sure it keeps bothering me, even as I grow used to it.

After another hour and a half, everyone had gone through the test and been eliminated. I was seventh on the list at level five. Two others, Nicky and Xiao, had been eliminated at level five but were ranked higher than me. Vaya, Bet, and Anberlin made it to level six, and Ming was top at level eight. *Holy crap, how strong is he!* Brett, Bridget, and Weber Lea, someone I hadn't met, rounded out the rest of the top ten.

10	Weber Lea	Level 4
9	Falconer Bridget	Level 4
8	Hunter Brett	Level 4
7	Kupiec Aiden	Level 5
6	Haodha Nicolai	Level 5
5	Lo Xiao	Level 5
4	Volkov Vaya	Level 6
3	Volkov Bet	Level 6
2	Haodha Anberlin	Level 6
1	Lo Ming	Level 8

"Congratulations on completing your first experience with the Training Pavilion. You will be going back in next week, so you have time to refine your ability and train some more. If you wish, you may request to enter the training one additional time this week, beyond the weekly ranking session. I recommend you use this. Training in actual battles is always helpful in engraining your skills into reflexes. The opponents you fight will be different each time, though their relative strength will be nearly the same at each level. Additionally, there are rewards available for every five levels you reach. Now, the top ten come on up."

Everyone in the top ten got up and formed a line in front of him. The Mentors walked over and handed all of us a pill. "Brett, Bridget, and Lea take a seat. Everyone up here has passed to level five, and so receive a reward." Again the Mentors handed out the reward, this time a crystal badge. "By passing to level five, you have shown basic aptitude and the minimum required to advance to the next tier, and you receive fifty merit points. The total number of received merit points will be stored on the crystal badge. Your total merit point accumulation determines your rank in your class, and you may spend the merit points to get additional Techniques, alchemical pills or powders, or weapons made. Aiden, Nicolai, take a seat."

I walked back over to sit down, examining the pill I was given, barely noticing the angry grimace from Nicolai. The top five received a small bottle with a healing powder in it, and the top three got ten additional merit points. One of the Mentors came over when he saw my questioning look at the pill. "It is a Minor Gathering Enhancement pill. Its effect is similar to and stronger than the Complete Gathering powder you should have heard about in your first alchemy class."

"Thank you, Mentor. Um, how many merit points would it be worth? We haven't heard much about them yet," I asked.

"About ten merit points for this. Techniques cost around fifty, usually, though there are some higher-grade techniques that would cost more. The healing powder given out to the top five is usually sold for twenty merit points," he explained.

"Thank you. Uh, how do we get more points?"

"Right now, only by advancing in the Pavilion. Soon, I don't know when, you'll be given opportunities to take on missions or perform services that will also earn merit points. As an example, all Mentors receive merit points for assisting instructors with classes. You will probably be able to earn merit points through whatever specialty you focus on. With alchemy as an example, if you become proficient at making the Minor Gathering Enhancement pill you have there, you could sell it for three to five merit points, depending on purity." With that explanation, he left to talk to Brett and Bridget.

A couple of minutes later, Counselor Might announced, "Good job, everyone. From here, run to the Training Fields and work on your techniques. I will be going around to everyone to discuss what you did well and what you did poorly. Together with your Mentors, we will start new training regimens tomorrow. Go!" Everyone got up and took off. I stumbled a bit for the first few steps, still drained and weirded out, but got my stride fairly quickly. The run back was only a couple football fields, so not as bad as our normal starting run.

As I jogged, I began going over how I did. *So, the lion nearly got me because I let it have the initiative. Or it took it anyway. That roar knocked me over and I don't know how I could have blocked it. At least I managed to get my Aether Shield up before that wind blade thing hit me. That would have sucked. I did okay on the Wolves. Maybe I should have used more Aether blasts? They only worked the first time, after that the Wolves could dodge. The blasts aren't fast enough. I should work on making them faster.*

160

Getting stabbed sucked. I never want that again, but it's probably going to be a weekly occurrence. Or getting mauled, or bitten, or poisoned, or some other way of dying, as it seems that death is the only way out of the Pavilion. I guess if we get used to wounds and fighting on through them here, where the only damage is mental, that's better than elsewhere where it will leave scars. Even in a world of magical healthcare, there are still Counselors who limp and have long-term injuries. Magic, like science, is not a panacea. It has its limits, I just don't know what they are yet.

I got to the PT field and jogged over to a training dummy. I pulled out the memory stone for the Aether Blast technique and watched through the process again. I saw a couple of places where I could work, getting the Aether more consistent, more uniform, and having thinner streams. I spent the next twenty minutes just circulating the Aether, working on making each second have the same amount of Aether flow through at the same speed. Once it was as uniform and consistent as I could make it, I sent a blast at the dummy. The blast was slightly smaller, but it rocked the dummy back just as much as I did earlier. *Nice!*

"Good job, though the Aether is too thick. That is what is slowing your projections down. You should work on moving finer strands of Aether, as thin as you can make them, and then join those up until you have enough to send out," Counselor Might said, approaching me from behind. "That is one of your tasks as feedback from your Pavilion run. You did very well for a merchant's son. Normally the top ten are entirely either nobles or those whose family are hunters. You did especially well when you attacked the Wolves. Though you need to watch for when Beasts are going to attack at range since if that had been a level three Wind Wolf, as is more common, you would have died there."

"They weren't level three, sir? What was the progression, if I can ask?" I asked him.

"You can only know up to where you have achieved. The first level was a level one Earthen Boar. The second a level two Silverfang, and the third level was two level two Wind Wolves. The last level was two bandits, one Vapor and one Mist. You did well against them until you froze. That was your first time fighting a person, wasn't it?" he asked me.

"Yes sir. Or at least the first time I seriously injured one," I responded.

"That is what I thought. Freezing is not an uncommon reaction to the first time you kill a person, and that is a good sign of character. Feeling nothing when destroying a bandit group often causes as many problems as it solves. You will have to work through that, though. One of the main jobs that graduates from here do is hunt down bandit groups or defend merchant caravans. There will always be people who think that stealing from others is the easiest way to get rich. As the sword of our Kingdom, we have to be ready to put an end to that behavior."

"Yes sir!" I said. I had wanted to be my nation's sword in my previous life, and here I was going to be as well. Of course, in my last life I was planning on being in a fighter jet, not stabbing someone.

"Now, your reaction times for the Aether Shield technique were pretty good, though you can improve them. You have a skin meridian, so you should be very fast with that technique. Your reaction times with your agility technique were poor, though. You should work on getting that first sideways motion to be quicker, not just on getting distance. I'll make a second course for that. Other than that, one additional benefit of breaking into level five is that you can use the Pavilion four times this coming week, including the ranking session, rather than two like everyone else. Additionally, you will be able to start at level five rather than one. While it is allowed, I do not recommend you do that the first time."

"Thank you, sir. Um, are the enemies the same every time you enter the pavilion?" I asked.

"No, though their levels are. There could be up to four bandits, all at Vapor, or only one Smoke level bandit. Let me know if you would like to run the Pavilion again. You will have to come during your evening Meditation time. The second agility course will be done tomorrow. Continue on," he said before heading over to speak to the next student.

I spent a minute digesting what I had been told before I resumed working on the blasts. After the next hour, I had managed to get the Aether threads a bit smaller, which had a noticeable effect on the speed of the blasts. After that, I went over to the agility course. There were two other people using it, Brett and a young woman I hadn't met yet. I didn't know what element she was using since there were no visible effects from her technique, but she was fast.

After she had taken off down the course, I hopped up and worked on moving down it. Trying to work on my speed of calling up the Dancing Northern Wind technique, I stopped on each step and relaxed, before flaring the technique and stepping to the next one. Like this, I was only able to make it halfway down the course. *Well, I still have a lot of work to do on this.* We alternated using the course until it was time to go to lunch.

"Hi, I'm Kupiec Aiden, I don't think we've met," I said to the young woman. She was slightly shorter than I was, with dark brown hair and bright blue eyes.

"It is nice to meet you, Aiden. I am Skipari Maove." I chatted with Brett and Maove on the walk back to the dorms. I found out that she had Exceptional affinity in Water and the technique she was using mostly relied on sudden bursts of strength in her muscles. Which was awesome. Her family owned one of the trading ships that traveled from Azyl to the capital and back. They sold alchemical and Inscribed products from and to both cities.

When I asked her about the whip I took from Nicolai she said, "Bring it to me the next time we are allowed to leave and I can get my father to appraise it and sell it for you if you wish. It will take longer than just selling it to a shop in the city, but you can probably get more for it."

"Thank you! I'll think about it and let you know before then. What is the capital like?" I asked. She described a city much like Azyl, though bigger in every way. The walls were a hundred meters tall around the keep, which boggled my mind. *Only with magic is that possible!* The Academy there was apparently not as welcoming of non-noble talents. There was a much higher concentration of nobles in the capital, so they didn't accept as many commoners. If commoners had the choice and talent, they went to a different Academy. Hence why Maove was here and not there.

"I can't wait until the All Academy Tournament at the end of the year!" Maove said. "The Capital Academy likes to lord it over all the schools, but with Ming, Bet, and you, we should be in a good position to beat them in the first tier category. I especially want you to wipe their noble faces in the dirt, jerks lording over normal people," she finished with a growl. Brett and I both looked at her confused and she explained. "At the end of every year there is a tournament held in the capital, sponsored by the King. Every academy sends their best students in a hope to win awards and resources that the King puts up for the prizes. Last year the prize for the top first tier was to have the King's armorer make a weapon just for them. Nearly every year, the Capital Academy takes all the top spots. Now we can take back the lead from them!"

"Thank you for the vote of confidence," I said, "that sounds amazing. We will all have to work our bottoms off to get strong enough for that. Do you know how they pick the competitors from here?" I asked.

"No, but it probably will be done with merit points, or the tournament that rumors say is at the end of the month. Though that is really early. Maybe there will be a tournament here to decide who goes there." We all agreed that made sense, and that we would find out later. As we did so, we split to shower and go to dinner.

At dinner, I went to sit with Jamila, Vaya, and a bunch of others, and we talked about the Training Pavilion. Jamila had made it to the third level, but ended up fighting two level two Fire-tailed Hawks and she had ended up losing to them. She didn't say how she lost, and she shuddered a bit when she mentioned it. I grabbed her hand and squeezed it, which got me a smile. I told her about my trial to the third level, describing how the Wind Wolves had fought. When asked, I told them about the bandits and how I froze and got run through. Jamila squeezed my hand back, and Vaya patted my shoulder in support. We all agreed that going in again was going to suck, but was probably necessary for advancing and graduating. "We should ask if there is a surrender ability next time, or see what other types of simulations it can do," I said.

"Simulations? Is that another word for illusions?" Jamila asked, confused.

"Uh, yeah. I heard that word in relation to this type of illusion before," I said awkwardly. *Watch out for strange words, Caleb— Aiden,* I thought, smacking myself mentally for the slipup. "Counselor Might said 'Today we are conducting a ranking challenge' which implied that there are other types of illusions. Hopefully there are some with less pain involved." We finished eating and I walked her to the Meditation Grotto.

After saying goodnight, I jogged to the pavilion where I usually gathered. After laying out some fruit for my bird friend, I pulled out the gathering pill I had been given, and examined it curiously again. A faint whiff of mint and other herbs came off it. "Here goes nothing," I said as I popped it into my mouth. As the last pill did, so this one seemed to dissolve instantly into a liquid that I swallowed. I could feel the energy of the pill as it entered my stomach, and the Aether inside was dissolved into my meridians and center.

I stood and worked through the Eight by Eight Gathering forms, and the pill's Aether seemed to explode within me. My gathering speed had nearly tripled from this morning. This boost lasted for an entire hour, giving me three times as much Aether as I normally would have been able to get. "Well, that was useful. Three hours' work for one hour actual time.

This is also twice as much Aether as I normally would be able to absorb without resting, so the pill essentially saved me half a day's worth of gathering. Let's go find Jon and see if he managed to get past the moves that we worked on yesterday."

I jogged to where Jon and I had worked yesterday and found Jon assiduously going through the first six moves of the Eight by Eight. He still had a small flaw in the position of his arms for the sixth move, so I walked up and helped him adjust it. After two tries he got it down, so we moved on to the seventh move. I spent the next hour doing this, then said goodnight when Jon was nearly falling asleep on his feet. Even though I still had energy, I walked back with him. I spent the next hour studying Elemental Birds, especially the chapters on the Crimson Zarorzel.

CHAPTER TWENTY-SIX

The next morning I woke up and lay in bed for a minute. "It's been a week now, Earth Day again. Though I guess the concept of a weekend is foreign here. Only the end of month Darkness and Light days substitute for a rest period. Everyone seems so driven, so you don't hear anything like 'Man, I've got a case of the Earth Days, '" I mused, sending myself into a fit of snickers. I got up and hurried to breakfast. After breakfast, we all ran to the classrooms, where there were four Mentors and Counselor Sila. The two new Mentors for this period were Mentors Bonde and Granjer from alchemy.

"Today we will be discussing the courses you will be taking for the next month in addition to continuing to work on the Eight by Eight Gathering form. Bridget, Travis, and Ming please stay here. The rest of you, head to the front yard and work on the form. Mentors Lo and Bonde will assist you. As we finish with those who stay, they will come get the next person to discuss. Head on down."

Everyone not named got up and went outside. We lined up where we had the last week and began to work. As I was working through, Mentor Bonde came over to watch. I got to the seventh move of the third set when he corrected me on my form. We worked through it and the eighth move, when he complimented me on getting so far already. In less than ten minutes, I had finished understanding the first three sets. "That is probably enough for a while, if you want to work on something else. The fourth set is usually not mastered before getting to the Fog level, or later," Mentor Bonde told me.

"Thank you," I responded as he walked over to another student. *I think her name is Qingshan.* I worked through the forms again, making sure I had the first three sets fixed in my mind. After that, I looked over and saw Jon was still working on the seventh move of the first set and the Mentors were all working with other students. So I went over and asked if he'd like help.

I ended up helping Jon through the seventh and eighth moves of the first set, and Lucas asked for help as well. We worked for about twenty minutes when Brett came over and told me to head up. Lucas and Jon both thanked me as I went to speak to one of the advisors. When I got to the classroom, Mentor Gutierrez waved me over. As I got closer, I passed through a thick layer of air, and my ears popped. I reached up and rubbed at them as I sat down in front of Mentor Gutierrez.

"The Wind Wall is set up to make sure our conversation isn't interrupted," he explained. "Now, nothing we decide here is permanent. As a first tier, your classes can change on a weekly basis for the next month or two. The first week you got to see a quick overview of most of the classes we offer here. Now, again as a first tier, there are some classes you will have to take for the next month. History and Geography are together as one class starting this afternoon, and you have to take that. Beasts and Herbology are mandatory, though your other classes will decide which version of each you take. You get a choice between Alchemy, Smithing, and Inscription, and Tactics is again mandatory."

"I'm really interested in both Alchemy and Inscription. Is it possible to take both?" I asked.

"Yes, it is. You can take two days of each. Most people pick one crafting area to focus on, so you'll have to work harder to not fall behind. The Counselors may ask you to come in on some of the evening periods as well, so you may have to give up sleep or gathering time. Though with your talent that won't hurt you that bad. Having chosen those, you'll be put in the Herbology and Beast classes that focus on alchemical properties. That should suffice for the next couple of weeks," Mentor Gutierrez told me, writing down my choices in a notebook.

"Thank you, sir," I told him.

"Go grab Jon and have him come in. Good luck," he told me as I stood to leave. I went down to the front yard and told Jon to head up. Mentor Lo saw me and waved me over.

"Good job on helping out your classmates. You were teaching Jon and Lucas well. Do you have your merit point crystal on you?" he said as I approached. I pulled it out and he took it. Afterward, it glowed for a second and then he handed it back. "I just awarded you ten merit points for helping out without being asked and doing so successfully."

"Uh, thank you, sir. I was wondering, how do I check the value that I have? Also, how do I spend them?"

"To check, you should just run some Aether into them, similar to memory stones. Go on and try it," he said. I held the stone up and pushed some Aether through my hand into it. It glowed for a second before showing 60/60 on the crystal. "It tells you the current value along with the total accumulated. The total accumulated is the value used to determine your place in your tier and how you advance. The current value is how many points you have after all the subtractions for spending on equipment and consumables.

"You'll be able to spend the points at the Armory for techniques or available equipment. On the second floor of the alchemy and inscription labs is a small area where you can purchase pills and inscription papers. Alternatively, you can ask for a specific pill or equipment inscription to be made and commission it for points. The forge has an area where you can commission weapons or armor to be made as well. Now, you are free to leave, as is everyone else who has already spoken to the Counselor or a Mentor."

I thanked him as he walked off. I decided I wanted to go by the alchemy lab to see what was available for purchase. Upon entering the lab, I went up the stairs to the second floor. This floor was different. On one side, there were still doors into rooms, but the other side was an open area, with a number of tables set up. There were around ten third and fourth tier students sitting around the tables, discussing various things. I heard recipes and gossip mostly. The walls were all chalkboards, and there was a counter that led into a storage area on the wall.

On the chalkboards were written all sorts of pills, powders, and potions along with a price next to them. These went for as little as two points for a Complete Flower Gathering powder to eight hundred thousand points for something called an Aether Crystallization Catalyst. I saw the Minor Gathering Enhancement pill for ten points as the Mentor from the Training Pavilion had said. There was a Small Gathering Enhancement pill for fifty points. There was also a Major Gathering Enhancement pill for eight hundred and fifty points. I didn't think I'd see that one for a while.

I was surprised, however, when I saw that the Meridian Cleanser pills I had been given went for one hundred points each. I went up to the counter, and a third tier student came out from a small lab space after a minute of waiting. "Good morning, what brings a first tier to the alchemy shop? Ah, you just had your first pavilion run, didn't you? That means you made it to level five on your first run. Congrats! I didn't make it to level five until my fourth try," he bubbled at me.

"Uh, yeah. We had the run yesterday and I barely made it to level five. I was also given some merit points today, so I have sixty right now. I was wondering, is it better to get five Minor Gathering Enhancement pills or one Small Gathering Enhancement pill?"

"That depends on what you mean by better. Five Minor pills will let you get about half again as much Aether as a Small pill, but the Small pill has fewer pill toxins than three Minor pills, so you come out ahead unless you spend more points on a Meridian Cleanser or other similar pill. Of course, if you can craft pills and make a Meridian Cleanser, it is probably better to use the Minor pills. At least for a little while. But if you can make Meridian Cleansers, then you have enough points to just use Smalls and not have to worry about damage to your meridians. Or even use Moderates. Though it is also not good to take more than a couple of Meridian Cleansers per level, especially at your stage. So I guess better is very subjective." *How did he not take a breath while saying all that?*

"Oh, I didn't know that. They hadn't mentioned what pill toxins were in alchemy yet."

"I would think not. That is one benefit of powders, as they have very little toxins in them. However, they lose much of their efficacy due to the roughshod nature of their production. Of course, at your level you don't have to worry too much about pill toxins. It is only when you are ready to start Condensing your Aether that you need to make sure your meridians are clear. Though having clear meridians is always good since it helps you gather faster and prevents issues as you advance. Though your meridians clear some of their blockages as you advance past bottlenecks and levels." *Wow, this guy loves the sound of his voice, or doesn't get to talk to people very often. It is good information, though.*

"Thank you for the information. So, in your view, I should buy two to four Minor Gathering Enhancement pills instead of a single Small one? In that case, I'd like to buy three."

"Okay. Let me see your point crystal please," he said while he pulled out a larger crystal. He inserted Aether into the larger crystal and put mine on top. They both glowed for a second. When he handed mine back, I checked the value and it said 30/60 now. *Useful, it's like a credit card.* He then walked into the back, and came out with a small glass jar holding three pills. As he handed them to me he said, "No more than one at a time, and probably best not to take more than two in a day. First tiers have a morning and an evening gathering time. That is separated enough. Have a great day."

"You as well!" I said, more informed and three pills richer, though thirty points poorer. *Oh well, easy come easy go.* I left the lab building and ran to my lion bench. Akil was there again, still on the dragon across the path.

I pulled a pill out and took it, before starting to move through the first three sets of the Eight by Eight Gathering form. The rush of Aether was intense.

Over the next hour, I gathered as fast as I could, just repeating the first three sets over and over. With each set completed, my gathering speed doubled for nearly five minutes, then slowed down again. *If I can get all Eight forms done, for the last time period I would be gathering at two hundred fifty-six times as fast as before I started. That's insane!* Adding that to the pill that tripled my speed and absorption threshold, and I was able to get three days' worth of gathering in an hour. *I wonder how quickly I'll advance at this speed.*

CHAPTER TWENTY-SEVEN

Once I finished, I rushed to lunch, waving at the Zarorzel as I passed it on the trail. Lunch had already started. *Oops!* I ate quickly. After lunch, I walked with Jon and some others towards class. We were supposed to have History and Geography combined now, so I assumed we would learn about a place and its history. "Most of this will be new to you, won't it, Aiden?" Jon asked suddenly.

"Yeah, I don't remember anything about history, and getting used to the world again took most of this past year. Thanks for sticking with me through it, though," I said.

"No problem. Maybe now I can help you some more."

"Hah, you've helped me more than I could ever help you. Let's head to class." As we walked into the classroom, I noticed most of the students were not excited. Only Qingshan and I seemed even remotely interested in history. Headmaster Glav was back as our instructor. For the next hour, I was fascinated by learning an abbreviated version of the Kingdom's history.

The Kingdom of Craesti was formed by King Craesti Aurel three hundred and forty-seven years ago. King Craesti arrived on the shores of what was now the Kingdom at the base of the Craesti River. Aurel was the leader of a group of refugees, nearly fifty thousand strong, from across a large empire. They were fleeing what was only described as a calamity. No books described what happened, and the few people who survived from that time refused to talk about it. The King did say, however, that they did not come from the land where the Weltreich was nor from the Illyrian Empire.

At their landing point, they decided that they had traveled far enough to escape. After a decade of establishing the capital city and spreading to the surrounding countryside, a Primordial Beast known as Jormung attacked the city from the south. It was defeated by the King after a long battle that tore up portions of the city. The capital was then redone to be a large fortress, and an outpost was created on a bluff overlooking the Craesti River. That outpost was now the Azyl City Lord's keep.

After fifty years, groups of people began to explore the Central Mountains, the Great Western Forest, and the Zaboj Swamp. Many small towns were formed, and sources of minerals and resources were discovered. However, Beast attacks grew rampant. This led to the series of forts established near the borders of the Kingdom, at the time, and the establishment of the Academy at the capital and at Azyl. The most critical of these was at Kneija, and eventually it too became a city and established an Academy.

Ten years after the forts were built, a series of explorations into the Great Western Forest were conducted to try and discover why the Beast attacks were occurring. This resulted in the deaths of over ninety high-level gatherers. A small group led by Barakat Zelec found a way through the Forest and discovered the Skraj Mountains. After some exploring, they found a pathway through the mountains that, in Zelec's words, "Looked like a giant sword had cut the mountains in two." This pathway became known as Zelec's Cut. The exploration team circumnavigated the Forest, moving north in the boundary between the Forest and mountains. They then followed the coast back to Kneija and then Craesti. Zelec was elevated to the nobility and given several hundred soldiers and settlers to create a town at the cut, and explore the mountains for resources.

It was nearly a hundred years later when a party of people from the Toprak Kingdom came through the mountains. These were very high-level gatherers, and they attacked Zelec's City immediately. Nearly a tenth of the city was destroyed before they were driven out. The resulting war would last for ten years, and deplete the Kingdom of nearly twenty percent of its soldiers. Small skirmishes and attacks came occasionally, though we traded with them as well. The traders were most likely black marketers since the hard feelings between our two Kingdoms had lasted even through today.

At the same time, expeditions into the Zaboj swamp had made it all the way down the Zaboj River to the sea. Large amounts of medicinal herbs and rare plants grew in the swamp, but it was full of dangerous creatures and maze-like inlets. The Zaboj Gateway was a moderate-sized city established at the entrance to the swamp on the Zaboj River, and Oddali was established at the tip of the peninsula. This was the discovery that the Kingdom was on a peninsula. Over time, Oddali became specialized in building large sea-going ships using materials from the swamp.

Eight months after the founding of Oddali, a sailing vessel from the Weltreich arrived. They were ecstatic to discover us because they normally had to hunt for food to replenish themselves before the trek home. Our settlement let them just trade for food. This was our introduction to the Weltreich, the Illyrian Empire, and the Free City of Monster Island. Trade between the Free City and the Weltreich had been happening for several decades, and Oddali slotted into the perfect position in the middle. Oddali quickly grew, becoming the second-largest and the wealthiest city in Craesti.

The Illyrian Empire was a nation of slaves who would occasionally raid our coastal villages. They were hated by everyone around them, but were in a nearly unassailable position. The Empire was bounded by two large mountain ranges that were full of extremely hostile Beasts, and their coast was small, with only a single harbor that was heavily fortified and surrounded by cliffs. The largest raid ever sent out was just over ninety years ago, and they succeeded in capturing over two thousand of our citizens. There was no telling how many people they had kidnapped from the Toprak Kingdom or the Weltreich, and fighting them was one of the few things that we could agree with the Topraks on.

So, this Kingdom has two allies, one antagonistic relationship, and one ongoing war with a different large power. I wonder what calamity the original settlers experienced, and why they won't talk about it. Wait, that was three and a half centuries ago, how are people still alive from then!

The last thing discussed in class was eighteen years ago, when the Free City established a multinational competition for the outstanding youths from themselves, the Weltreich, the Topraks, and ourselves, which occurred every five years. The last competition, three years ago, was won by the Weltreich and the winners received amazing equipment and medicinal pills. "So get ready, as you all and the second tiers will be the prime candidates for the junior level of the competition, where I believe we have a good chance of winning everything." Headmaster Glav said, finishing her lecture.

"Headmaster," Jon asked, "What do you think happened in the calamity that King Craesti was fleeing from?"

"Sorry, I won't answer anything about the calamity. Speaking of it is potentially dangerous," she answered him. *Potentially dangerous to speak about? Should I mention the warning given to me before I got here? How would I do so? I need to think about this, and figure out some way of communicating it, hopefully without revealing my origin. Wait!*

"Ma'am, were you in the original group of settlers to arrive in the Kingdom?" I asked, awe leaking into my voice.

"Yes, all the Academy Headmasters were, along with the City Lords of most major cities." *Holy moly! She's over three hundred fifty years old! She barely looks like she's forty!* "Yes, I am nearing four hundred years old now. If you can ascend to the Perfect Core stage or beyond, you'll be able to live for potentially a thousand years. Now, it is time for your training. Shoo!" she said, and then turned and walked out.

I was lost in thought as we all moved to the PT fields. *A calamity is coming, and the Kingdom was formed by people fleeing a calamity. This can't be a coincidence. I need to—we need to—grow stronger faster. I need to get more information too. Need to think about what to do later, but for now just focus on the here and now. Okay, now what do I need to work on for PT? I've got the Aether Blast mostly down now. Let's look at the Four Twin Lightning Stabs today.* As I was musing over the lesson, Jon looked at me and said, "Are you okay? You've been very quiet since the lesson."

"I got a really bad feeling when Headmaster Glav told us that speaking about the calamity was potentially dangerous. Like something bad was coming. I feel a real need to train faster now."

"Train faster? You're already speeding past everyone other than the nobles. You should relax sometimes. I haven't seen you at the first tier pagoda yet."

"First tier pagoda? What's that? Why would I take a break? Everything is so amazing here. I want to learn as much as I can as fast as I can. Why would you not want to work as fast as you can?" I asked Jon back.

"Yup, same old Aiden. Always working. Come on, after dinner come with me to the First Tier Pagoda. It's for us to relax and not explode."

"Fine, if it'll get you off my back, sure. I'll go to the pagoda tonight. But now it's time to train, and if I'm going to take a couple hours off I'll have to work even harder now." I jogged ahead, getting to the PT field and starting my warm-up runs. I pushed as hard as I could, finishing a 10k in just over twenty minutes. *Well, I'm literally superhuman now, though only slightly. I wonder what it'll be like to run a 10k in ten minutes. Literally a kilometer a minute, or something like fifty miles an hour.* After rushing through the calisthenics and working up a good sweat, I jogged over to the training dummies and pulled out the memory stone for the Four Twin Lightning Stabs technique.

I watched as a student learned the technique, which involved using the arm meridians to create an almost circular technique. *This won't work in front grip. The trisulas are too long, and won't create the right sequence. So I won't be stabbing but bashing since it will work in reverse grip,* I thought, watching the student use twin daggers. The result of the technique created what seemed like a very quickly changing magnetic field. It made the weapon flash back and forth in quick stabs that all had a similar power.

The technique was named after the first stage, where you would be able to stab four times in the time it would normally take you to stab once. Watching the technique demonstrated was like the scene in the Matrix when Mr. Smith beat Neo down with superfast strikes. At the highest levels, the instructors' arms were barely able to be perceived.

I pulled out of the memory, and walked up to a dummy. As I called to mind the sequence of Aether flows and runes, I realized yet again that my memory had become just about perfect. *Opening the brain meridian has been amazing for my progress on these techniques.* I flipped my trisulas to the reverse grip and began cycling the Aether. I pounded on the dummy for the next hour, slowly getting the hang of the technique. By the end of the first hour of PT, I could feel the technique start to work, and my hits became faster in the instant before contact, with extra rebound that was cancelled and propelled forward. I was maybe at one-and-a-half-stab technique, not yet enough to say I had mastered the first level. *Good progress so far.*

I went over to the agility course and started working on start-up speed again, making good progress. I heard a snicker as I did so, and saw Floozy and Flunky laughing at me. I enhanced my senses meridian and was able to hear Floozy, a.k.a. Builder Thomas, joke that I was slower than a "Frozen Fire Ooze." *What is a Fire Ooze? I guess the flunkies of Nicky are still holding a grudge. I haven't seen Nicky around recently either. I wonder why?*

Ignoring the onlookers, I continued to focus, getting my reaction time down as far as I could. I continued this until just before the end of class, when I went back to the beginning and did a speed run down the course. As I formed the runes and moved as quickly as I could, I realized that there were places where I could put some of the Lightning Runes from the Four Twin Lightning Stabs technique. *I'll have to try that sometime, though I think I'll run it by Counselor Might or Sila first. Don't want to blow a leg off or something,* I thought as I jogged over to the Counselor to finish up class.

CHAPTER TWENTY-EIGHT

After the final run, I went to shower and eat. I joined Jon, Brett, Ming, and Xiao at a table after waving to Jamila, Bet, Vaya, and Keai. As I sat, Brett commented, "So, you're finally going to come by the Pagoda after dinner and relax some? I think you're the only one who hasn't come once yet. Though many people have only come once or twice. Finally giving up on working every second you are here?"

"Well, I know Jon would only keep bothering me until I agreed, so I preempted him by saying yes to start with." We ate quickly, starving as only teenagers working out daily could be. *I bet we are eating five thousand calories or more. Maybe Elemental Beast meat has more calories? I don't really know how to build a calorimeter, though I bet I could figure it out. I don't think it matters enough to do so. Hmm, I wonder if I could make one to test how many motes of Fire Aether would equal a calorie.*

"Hello! You awake in there?" Jon's sarcastic call took me out of my thoughts. "You've been staring at the wall for a minute. What were you thinking about?"

"I was just wondering if there is a way to tell how much Aether is required to do things, like heat water or push a rock," I said.

Ming then asked, "How much Aether? That would be hard to measure because everyone has a different amount."

"Well, I think that an Aether mote is the same for everyone, so we could measure something that way. Though that could get unwieldy as they are tiny," I answered.

"Aether motes?" Xiao asked, "what are those?"

"You know, if you look really closely at the Aether in your center, it looks like thousands to millions of tiny, colored dots. I call those motes. Since Aether comes in those motes, I think they are all the same."

"I've never heard of such a thing," Ming said. "Hold on." He then closed his eyes and took a deep breath. It was obvious he was focusing intently, trying to see the Aether motes. "Whoa!" he gasped, opening his eyes. "That's amazing, how did you know that?"

"Uh, I've always seen Aether that way, ever since I started gathering. I just thought Aether would be like ... that," I finished lamely, realizing that I hadn't really made a good reason. I had started to say air, but I didn't think they knew air was made of gas molecules. Nor water of water molecules. *Crap, what did I use before? Divert, divert!* "Well, shall we head to the Pagoda?" I said, standing up with my plate. Xiao and Jon stood up too, while Ming had a questioning look on his face.

I walked to the door, with the group following behind. Just after I stepped out, I stopped. I realized I didn't know where to go. "Uh, where is the Pagoda?" I asked. Jon burst out laughing, and to our surprise so did Ming. That was the first time I'd seen him lose his composure the entire time I'd known him.

"Follow me," Jon gasped, still laughing as he walked past me away from the dorms and the Grotto alike. We walked past the third and fourth tier dorms, and I saw a series of pagodas that butted up against the wall of the school compound. There were a number of people in three of them, and one completely empty. I saw Lucas and Louis talking animatedly in the Pagoda to the far right, near the corner of the wall. *Guess that one is ours.* The empty pagoda was next. *Huh, I just realized I haven't seen any of the second tiers around campus at all. I wonder where they are. Oh, wait. Counselor Might said they were at the large-group training at some fort.*

My eyes were drawn to the far-left pagoda, near the gate, as a burst of color and sound came from it. What looked like a serpent made of fire bloomed into life, raising its head almost twenty feet off the ground. At its base, I could see someone gesturing, and the serpent moved along with the gestures. With a whooshing noise, the serpent vanished into the figure. I could see then that the person was a fourth tier. "That was amazing!" I said, wonder evident in my voice.

"Yeah, there is almost always someone from the third or fourth tier showing off over here. Makes for good entertainment. Especially when they screw up," Jon said, still chuckling. As we got closer to the First Tier Pagoda, I could hear light music playing. It sounded like a harp or zither, a gentle plucking of a string. Small groups of students were chatting or sitting and playing a card game. Another couple of people were playing some board game that looked a lot like Go. Near the center of the pagoda, I saw the source of the music.

Anberlin was playing a zither-like instrument, with a group of people around her. After a minute she finished with murmurs of appreciation from the group. Two guys, neither of which I recognized, took over afterwards on a set of drums and a lute. They started playing a fast song, and several of the students began dancing. I got pulled into a dance with Bridget, and then with Bet.

The dance style reminded me of swing dancing, though it had a four-count beat to the movement. I looked around after dancing with Bet to see Jamila, and walked up to her. I bowed lightly, saying, "Would you like to dance?" She agreed and we danced a song together, and then Vaya grabbed my hand and I danced with her. I think over the next hour I danced with every young woman I had talked to at any one point here, and several I didn't know.

After the last dance, when I finally managed to escape, I went and found Jon. "Is there dancing like this every night?" I asked.

"Not always. Depends on if Stephen and Andrey play or not. Anberlin is usually here playing the zither for a couple of songs, then she leaves. I always feel more relaxed after she plays. There are usually more people playing games, or just talking. So, what do you think?"

"Well, it was fun. I might come back, but probably only once or twice a week. Thanks for bringing me, but I need to go gather," I said, starting to leave. I stopped when I had a thought. "Hey Jon, have you seen Nicolai around? I don't recall seeing him for several days."

"Uh, now that you mention it, I don't think so. That's strange. Not that I want to see him anyway," he replied. I shrugged and jogged off. My speed jogging was now equivalent to my fastest sprint from two weeks ago, which made traveling to the Grotto take only a minute. After arriving, I pulled out another pill and took it, leaving me with one left. I started working through the Eight by Eight Gathering form, focusing to make my movements perfect and pulling Aether in as fast as I could. After almost an hour, I started feeling tight inside. *I'm getting close to breaking through to high Mist! These pills are amazing. I thought it would take another seven days to get here!* I pushed harder, filling my meridians to their maximum capacity.

As I got close, I focused on pushing Aether into the sides of my meridians, slowly stretching them wider, until they suddenly jumped outward, increasing in diameter by twenty percent. I exhaled as the pressure inside decreased. I had broken through and gained a larger Aether pool. I slowly gathered enough to fill my Aether pool up to its new limit. *So I need to gather enough Aether to condition my meridians, and then use Aether to stretch them to a new width to break through. At least at this level. Neat.* The pill ran out just after this, so I sat down and examined myself. I again was covered in gunk, my skin meridian being used as a garbage disposal by the rest of my system.

I got up to leave and remembered I had put a piece of fruit in my pocket for the Crimson Zarorzel. I jogged around a bit, looking for it. When I couldn't find it, I went back to my pavilion and left it on a tree branch nearby. "This is for the Crimson Zarorzel," I called out, hoping to see it again, but the bird wasn't around. I then left and went to get a shower.

CHAPTER TWENTY-NINE

The next day passed quickly. Gathering class covered the Eight by Eight again. I got the first of the moves from the fourth set down, then helped Jon and Brett finish up the last two moves in the first set. Finishing the set let them double their gathering speed, which was always helpful. After class, I decided to gather without taking my last pill, saving it for when I knew I could get more points. The Zarorzel showed up again, this time landing right next to me as I gathered. "You are a beautiful bird," I told it. It poked my arm, expectant, so I pulled out the fruit I'd brought and it ate from my hand. I quickly stroked its head, which caused it to glare at me and hop away. I laughed and said goodbye as I left for lunch.

Lunch passed quickly, and Beasts class was filled with students describing one Beast or Elemental Beast they had studied over the last week. I went to speak to Counselor Taiga after, who encouraged me to bring some meat to the Zarorzel as well. "Encouraging trust is a good way to start working towards a bond. Zarorzel are usually very picky about soul bonds, though, so it may not lead anywhere."

"I understand. It is just a beautiful bird, and you said they are intelligent, so I'm just trying to be friendly."

"Okay, come and see me if you have any more questions, otherwise I'll see you next week." She dismissed me, and I headed to Physical Training.

During PT I practiced on my Four Twin Lightning Stabs technique up almost to mastery of the first level and the Dancing Northern Wind technique to nearly mastering the second.

I was ready to go back to the Training Pavilion. After dinner, I ran to the Pavilion, both eager and nervous about the upcoming challenge. When I arrived, there was a Counselor sitting cross-legged in the center who I had not seen before. There were also two positions taken, one by a third tier, and one by a fourth tier. As I approached, the Counselor opened her eyes and beckoned me forward. "Good evening, student. What is your name?" she asked.

I answered her and she nodded, saying, "Elements welcome you, Aiden, I am Counselor Chokhmah. I am the senior Counselor for the Training Pavilion and the Martial Arts instructor to all third and fourth tiers. Now, this is your first extra training time, so you have the choice of running the ladder again, or picking a level and staying there until you choose to leave or perish. Also, you may surrender at any time to leave. It is only the official ratings that you must continue until you perish. Those will happen weekly for the entire time you are a first tier. Which method do you choose?" she asked as she finished explaining.

"Can I change my decision after I've entered? Or exit and reenter?" I asked, trying to figure out my limits.

"Since you asked, I'll let you reenter once if you start with a ladder. Then you can enter again by picking a level to start at and work in for a time. Now, hop on up." She gestured at me, and I found myself bouncing into the Pavilion. I landed awkwardly, slightly stunned by the casual use of magic. After a quick shake, I sat down and took a deep breath. As I let it out, I found myself in a clearing in a forest. Looking around quickly, I saw a large chicken. *What? It's a four-foot-tall chicken. Seriously. Is this what an Elemental Fowl looks like?* I thought.

It looked at me and clucked, just like a chicken. I laughed, shaking my head until it clucked three times rapidly and spat a ball of fire at me. Diving sharply to the side with a shriek, the fireball missed me. *At least it's not a D&D fireball, those explode,* I thought as I rolled. I pulled my trisulas out and flipped them to reverse grip. I sent an Aether blast at it from the short end. Blasts from the short end were smaller and did almost no damage, but were much faster than the larger blasts from the pointy end.

Well, they did almost no damage to the training dummies. The Elemental Fowl was knocked over, but it quickly regained its feet and shot another fireball at me. I sent an Aether blast at nearly the same time, and they collided in the middle. The fireball exploded, knocking the chicken and I down. I shot to my feet before taking a potshot at the fowl, which barely dodged. I started closing the distance when it clucked rapidly again. I quickly shot a blast and managed to hit the fireball just as it cleared the bird's beak, causing another explosion. This one ended the level as it detonated too close to the Elemental Fowl for it to resist.

Well, that was really useful. Birds are lighter weight, so it reacted more to the hit. Or my leveling made the blast stronger. Most likely both contributed. Now, what's next? I thought, looking around warily. As I thought that, a bunny hopped out of the trees. Not a normal bunny though. This rabbit was probably twice the size of a normal rabbit and had a unicorn horn on its head. It still looked cute and cuddly, like all rabbits though. *I guess it's time to fight no-longer-helpless prey animals today,* I thought with a laugh.

As I was laughing, it hopped towards me, only for sparks to crackle down its horn. Halfway into the hop, it suddenly shot towards me like a missile. Only the practice Counselor Might had suggested, of working on getting Dancing Northern Winds going as fast as possible, saved me from being impaled through my chest. I was able to turn a mortal wound into a glancing injury, but its horn still ripped right through my enhanced skin. Of course, I didn't have a shield running at the time, stupidly.

I circled the injury with Aether and started an Aether Shield running while I staggered to the side. I turned to see the bunny flip over and cock its head at me. "Come on, fluffy rodent, I will show you why that was a bad idea," I taunted the non-sapient simulated creature, mostly to make myself feel better. *I nearly died to a bunny! I can't be Elmer Fudd. I refuse!* Sparks flew again, and the rabbit lunged at me. This time, I met it with a slash, already dodging as it jumped. *Batter's up!* The bunny tumbled as it hit the ground, knocked off course and deeply injured. As it staggered to its feet, I sent a full-power Aether blast into it that ended the level.

The cut down my side healed quickly, draining a small but significant portion of my Aether pool. As did the blasts I had sent out. I continued to look around, waiting for the next level. A chirp from my side caused me to dive forward into a roll. I looked and saw two praying mantis-like bugs that were around three feet tall and shimmering green. Having learned my lesson, again, about not waiting, I sent a full-power blast at the rightmost mantis. It blocked with one of its talons, taking some damage but nothing major.

They both charged, chirping at me. I blasted several times at both before they got close. I tried dodging, but they were faster than me. I was suddenly blocking hits with my trisulas and taking them on my shield, which was failing quickly. A quick flip put the trisulas in reverse grip, and I tried out my new technique. My shield failed at the same time, causing me to take a couple of light slashes on my arms and torso.

I activated the Four Twin Lightning Stabs as I stepped into the slightly more injured one, and my arms blurred into a series of strikes. Its torso exploded outward, all that force directed into a single point, and it dissolved as all defeated simulations did. To do this, however, I exposed myself and took several more deep cuts. I managed to repeat the process against the last mantis as well. As it popped, I shouted, "I'm done here. I won't make it past the next one. I surrender." When I did, the world faded and I woke up in the circle.

"Good job recognizing your weakness. You did fairly well, though you underestimated the first two enemies and it cost you. Time and Aether for the first one, and an injury for the second. Good attempt on the Wood Mantises, they are some of the tougher level two Beasts, especially for someone with a short weapon. Now, do you want to go back in? I'd recommend going to level two and working on your techniques."

"Yes ma'am, that sounds exactly like what I would like. May I go into level two?" I asked. I spent the next hour fighting a number of level two Beasts, getting more proficient at Aether Blasts, Aether Shields, dodging, deflecting, and stabbing. I practiced every technique I knew in a battle setting, which helped engrain them into my reflexes. I only stopped when I was running on fumes, both physically and in my Aether pool. When I awoke, I was covered in sweat.

"You pushed harder than almost everyone does, especially for your first time. Keep up this work ethic and you will be incredibly successful. You're allowed two more visits before your end of week exam, so I will see you in two days. Be back here at the same time. Go gather and come back stronger," Counselor Chokhbah said.

I bowed to her and left. I went to the lion statue bench and gathered, making sure to gather in an Earth and Metal area to keep the elements in my Aether pool balanced among my affinities. After an hour and a half, I went to the PT field to practice more. *Advancing in level let me gather for longer, but I'll need even more to advance again. The amount of Aether I need is increasing faster than my ability to gather is. Pills and other enhancements are going to become increasingly necessary to advance. At least in any reasonable amount of time. I need to ask Counselor Sila about getting more merit points, and about getting ingredients and alchemy supplies.*

I practiced until my tiredness started impacting my ability to practice correctly. *Remember, practice doesn't make perfect, it makes permanent. Only perfect practice makes perfect. Bedtime.* I left the PT field and headed to my dorm. I was quickly asleep.

The next morning flew by. Breakfast was interesting since more people said hi than just the small group I had been talking to. This was especially true of the young women, as everyone I danced with said hi. This made me self-conscious. After breakfast Gathering class was more of the same. Counselor Sila did say that we would work on a new technique tomorrow. At the end of class, I went to speak to him.

"Sir, I just advanced again, and I have come to suspect that I'll need more pills or powders to keep this speed up. Is there a way I can earn merit points to purchase pills or powders? Also, can I purchase just ingredients and make powders?" I asked.

"That observation is correct. You are going to either take longer to advance or use increasing amounts of resources. Unfortunately you are still too weak to be sent out on missions for the Academy, and the missions aren't available until after your first month anyway. You should be able to purchase ingredients at the same place you purchased pills, and craft powders for a minor profit. Hmm, if you want I can meet you after dinner at the alchemy lab and will teach you a new recipe. You will need to spend five merit points for ingredients, and if you are successful you will be able to make significantly more than that back. That is the best way to make points here. At least at your level."

"Thank you, sir. I will take you up on the offer," I said before heading into the Grotto to gather with the Zarorzel. After that and another awkward but fun lunch, we went to Herbology. We were introduced to a number of herbs that were able to cure poisons or enhance healing by themselves or as ingredients in a powder. Counselor Sila let us know that anyone in alchemy would be learning a recipe for a healing powder tomorrow.

PT was more training, with some guidance from Mentor Jameson on punching with the trisulas, followed by more exercises. I was fitter now than at any other time in either of my histories. Even with the benefit of Aether, I was still working harder than ever. I loved it.

Dinner was good. I was starting to feel like I fit in, at least among a group of friends. Though they did make fun of me a bit when I said I was going to get tutoring in alchemy rather than go have fun during the free time after dinner. I waved it off, though I did promise to go tomorrow. Mostly because Bet, Vaya, and Jamila all asked me to. It's hard to say no to three different beautiful young women.

Leaving the dining hall, I ran to the alchemy lab. *Being able to jog faster than the old me could sprint makes this huge campus seem much smaller.* I found Counselor Sila waiting in the main hall, and he directed me into a smaller lab off to the side. "Good evening, Aiden. Ready to get started?" he asked.

"Yes sir. Here is my merit crystal to pay for the ingredients."

"No need, I'll collect five points' worth of finished product and only deduct anything if you don't succeed enough. Tonight we're going to work on enhancing the Complete Flower Gathering powder by adding another ingredient. These are the leaves of a Balsam Tree grown in a neutral affinity valley. They aren't extremely common, but are not prohibitively expensive either. By mixing in an equal portion of these and refining it properly, the Complete Flower Gathering powder becomes an Enhanced Flower Gathering powder and nearly doubles in potency. The process only adds about thirty percent costs while doubling value, so it is well worth your time. Now watch as I prepare the first dose."

Counselor Sila then divided all four flowers into equal amounts, and measured out about a third more Balsam leaves than the flowers. Looking with Aether vision, I saw that the density of Aether in the leaves was less than the flowers. The Aether was an off-white color until I picked up a leaf and held it close. I saw all colors of Aether in a near-balance with each other. *Ah, so it's only quasi-neutral, like plasma,* I thought, *though the colors of all of the motes seem muted, so maybe there is a difference?* After dividing, Counselor Sila ground all four flowers together and dumped them in the wok. He then got out a second mortar and pestle and ground up the leaves. Once ground up, he pushed Aether into the wok and it heated up. After slowly drying out the flowers, he sprinkled leaves into the mixture while flowing Aether through the wok. The Aether wrapped around the flower powder and seemed to grab the leaves, slowly merging them together. A rune was being traced along the side of the wok as well.

Over the next three minutes, the ingredients slowly mixed under the guidance of Counselor Sila's and my watchful eyes. This was the first real alchemy, to me at least, that I had seen. The resulting powder was an off-white color and let off a strong flowery smell. "Do you think you can repeat that?" Counselor Sila asked after scraping the powder into a bottle.

"Uh yes sir," I said firmly while I took the tools to wash. I cleaned and dried them, before setting out ingredients and beginning the process. I was able to get the first part down pretty easily because I had already made the Complete Flower Gathering powder successfully, and grinding the leaves down didn't need any special techniques. I slowly tried to copy the rune and move the Aether through the mixture, but had trouble getting the ingredients to merge.

"Use less heat next time, slow the process down, and get a feel for how the ingredients mix. Try again," Counselor Sila instructed me after the ingredients became a burnt mess. I tried again, taking nearly twenty minutes this time, but I started to get a feel for the process. This still ended in a burnt mess, this time taking me another ten minutes to clean off the wok. *Back to scrubbing pots for me!* The third time was the charm, though, and I managed to successfully make an Enhanced Flower Gathering powder. "I didn't expect you to be successful this quickly. I have ingredients for another eleven doses. They are worth half a merit point each, so nine more to pay off the ingredients. That will leave you with either two doses or one merit point. For your level, these powders are good. You can use them twice a day with no real drawbacks. Also, the powder I made is for you to take, not sell. I want to see how quickly you can advance," Counselor Sila directed. "Just leave the powders here, and I will collect them tomorrow morning."

I spent the next two hours making powders, slowly increasing the speed until I could make one in ten minutes. I burnt one last one, leaving me with only two powders that I could keep, one I made and one made by Counselor Sila. "I'll do this every night I'm not at the Training Pavilion. Spend five merit points, make six and keep three powders to take in two days. Then I'll see if I can maintain this speed. If I can, I'll spend ten points to make thirteen and have four doses left over. After a week or so maybe I can learn a more lucrative recipe. Let's go use one dose and gather for a bit. I'm still going to save the pill for later."

I jogged out to my pavilion and washed down the powder with some water. I gathered, using the Eight by Eight Techniques, and noticed an increase from the powder of just over fifty percent, which was great as the unenhanced version only gave a boost of thirty or so. *Now, I can use these all the time, though I still have to worry about toxins building up. I think. Maybe that's just pills? He said they have next to no toxins, which isn't any. Uh, I'll ask tomorrow,* I thought, yawning as I finished gathering. The powder had run out after forty minutes or so, and I had finished out the hour unassisted. By now it was late, and I needed sleep, even with my enhanced constitution.

CHAPTER THIRTY

The rest of the week passed quickly. I spent time at the First Tier pagoda twice, dancing, playing games, and talking with my classmates. In Alchemy we learned a healing recipe that took most of the class two days to get. When I had achieved it the first day, Counselor Sila told me to just make powders and gave me three doses' worth of ingredients for both the healing powder and the Enhanced powder he taught me for the class. The second class was more practice for me, along with helping a couple of classmates out in how to make it.

In Gathering we learned a general enhancement channeling ability, which made every muscle something like thirty percent stronger, but ate Aether quickly. By focusing the ability, it was possible to just increase strength in the arms or legs or torso as well. This was mostly used for physical labor. Using the ability let you chop trees, haul boxes, or dig ditches faster. In inscription, we learned how to change the ball of light into a ball of fire or ice and send it shooting straight forward into a target. *Fireball! Fireball!*

After that, I spent time in the library studying the runes some more, this time with Bridget. We decided that we could make a ball of just about anything and send it flying with the inscription, but it still wouldn't be very powerful. Still, we made a couple more inscriptions, one that shot Fire, one Ice, one Lightning, one Metal, and one a combination of Wood and Water that was labeled Acid in the book. *Not trying that one indoors*, I thought, not wanting to destroy part of the building or release toxic fumes into the air.

PT was more of the same since I still had not managed to fully master either technique. I did, however, start on the Iron Bones, Granite Skin technique. It was good I had spent time on the Dancing Northern Wind because the defensive technique slowed me down significantly. I did ask Jon to hit me with it active, and he punched me as hard as he could. I staggered back a bit, but he broke his hand and needed healing. "Sorry!" I said, wincing as he shook his hand.

"Well, that technique works. Too bad I don't have the right affinities," he said. After dinner that night he tested it with a large branch he had found, and it still didn't hurt. Then he tested it with an Aether blast, and that knocked me down.

"Apparently this needs to be done with an Aether Shield," I said, recovering from the blast, "as it didn't stop the Aether you sent very effectively at all. It's very good at dispersing force, and probably at preventing being cut, but ineffective at Aether protection."

"That's good to know. So I should smack and blast you occasionally to test your reaction times?" he asked mischievously.

"No, I'm good," I said hurriedly, not wanting to have to watch my back against him too, though he would do it only in jest. I still worried about Nicky, as I still hadn't seen him. He didn't seem the type to let bygones be bygones. *I wonder if he's avoiding me, or if he left the Academy. Just how much does his house value my potential? I doubt they'd censure him over me. I worry that he's plotting something.*

Geography was a lesson on the coastline, covering major cities in all five known coastal kingdoms, including the fortified city of Borgby in the Illyrian Empire. The discussion on the known fortifications made all of us wonder how anyone could possibly take it. *I guess that's why no one has successfully attacked Borgby yet. Someday, someday that evil will fall.*

Gathering had proceeded smoothly, and Counselor Sila said I should reach the Haze level, one above Mist, by the end of the month. Many of the nobles had already reached Haze because they were able to use pills all the time. *Gaining strength is much easier when you are rich. Well, to catch up I'll just have to work harder.* I was holding my own, keeping pace with them, but they so far had an insurmountable lead. I resolved to make points faster, and would talk to Counselor Sila after the next ranking challenge about another recipe that was worth more.

The two times I went back to the Training Pavilion I stayed at level three and worked on tactics for dealing with two enemies. I slowly discovered another benefit the brain meridian had conferred. I had become much better at multitasking, and had become entirely ambidextrous. This led to an awesome scene where I skewered one Silverfang while slicing through another as they both leapt at me. I stood in awe, feeling more like a superhero at that moment than I had at any point before it.

That is, until a duo of Wind Wolves took me out of that session. I discovered that I could not reenter for a day after losing. Something about trauma to the psyche and soul damage. This was the main reason behind the limit of four times per week, to give your soul a chance to rest and heal. This was the first I had heard about the soul needing rest or being able to be damaged. When I inquired about it, I was told that it wouldn't be important until you started to develop your Core.

Finally, it was time for another ranking challenge. *This is going to suck, but I wonder if I'll be able to beat level five? I haven't tried going above three since last week. I've definitely become a lot stronger since then. I still don't know what the fifth level is. Is it more enemies? A stronger one? How did Ming get to the eighth level?*

The crowd of students was solemn as we approached the Pavilion. Everyone was excited, but we all knew that we would die today, at least virtually. That took the spring right out of our step. As we arrived around the Pavilion, I finally saw Nicky again. He seemed even more nervous than the rest of us, with his group of sycophants around him laughing cautiously at something he said. The push of Aether I felt from him had grown significantly since I had last seen him.

I guess he leveled up too? I thought. Counselor Might called out, "Today we will use a slightly different order. You will be called up in reverse class order, so the bottom ten will go first. Use this to improve yourselves. The goal for everyone is to advance over your previous result. Rewards for increasing your level and especially for reaching level five will be provided. Now come, let us see how much you have improved over this last week."

The lowest ranking ten were called up and sat down. Jonas, the guy who failed quickest last time, had a determined look on his face. Over the next five minutes, no one was knocked out. Finally, a student stumbled off the pavilion, having reached the second level. A Mentor met him and congratulated him on advancing to the second level since he had only made it to the first last time. It looked like the reward he received was a bottle of powder. *Huh, that's Enhanced Flower Gathering powder. Are they using the powder I made for the rewards? Neat!* I thought proudly.

Over the next two hours, the class cycled through the Pavilion. Everyone who had lost in the first level managed to pass to at least the second. I congratulated Jon on making it to level four, from level three last times. Jamila was still in when it was my turn to go up. *Okay, go all out every step of the way,* I thought as I sat down. *Never give up, never surrender!*

The world faded, and I awoke in a rocky glen, standing next to a small stream. I hopped on top of a rock and looked around. Flapping towards me was a goose from hell, the frozen one. "Oh Darkness no," I said, sending a full-power Aether Blast into its head as it started to dive towards me. It crashed to the ground next to me and dissolved. *Well, that was easy,* I thought, while still looking around carefully.

After a minute passed, I started to get really uneasy. I kept searching, even using Aether to enhance my eyes, but I didn't see any creatures. *Wait, did that rock move?* I stared at a boulder that had seemed to move a couple of feet diagonally towards me. *Let's not chance it,* I thought, and blasted the boulder. A roar sounded out, and what looked like a giant, stone-covered armadillo pounced towards me. I dodged off the rock I was standing on, and the creature dropped into a roll. It started rolling towards me like a granite-covered Sonic the Hedgehog. I blasted it, which did very little.

"Need blunt trauma," I whispered to myself, flipping my trisulas to reverse grip to use Lightning Stabs. It picked up speed, and I slipped sideways past it, slamming both trisulas into its side as it passed. Rock cracked and it sprawled out, trying to recover quickly. I flipped my weapons again and was on it before it could stand. A couple of stabs later, and this level was complete. I kneeled down, taking a rest. "Whew, that was intense." Even with my stamina, narrowly dodging enemies got my heart pumping. *Stupid adrenaline making me winded when I'm not. Now what is next?* I thought, standing straight.

Howls announced a pair of Wind Wolves, again. *Again!* I sent a series of blasts into them, taking down one almost immediately. Blocking an air blade, I charged the second one and finished it off quickly. "Wind Wolves are all offense and dodging. My Aether Blasts were faster though. Having fought them before also helped," I pondered, getting ready to fight people this time.

From behind a large rock in front of me, two men stepped out. They were wearing ragged clothes, but had functional weapons. The taller of the two held a longsword in both hands while the shorter had a short spear. "Surrender and we'll make it quick," shouted the shorter one. I answered him with an Aether Blast that knocked him sprawling.

"Same to you!" I shouted back, charging toward the standing enemy. I had pulled my Aether into a shield and started circulating both Dancing Northern Wind and Iron Bones, Granite Skin techniques. This saved my bacon. I was jolted forward by an arrow that shattered on my skin. I tried to turn the jolt into a roll, but ended up sprawling. The longsword opponent rushed at me, sword raised to chop. He received a blast to the face for his troubles, and I jumped to my feet. The spear opponent was coming, and there was at least one guy behind me.

I dropped to my knee and threw another blast at Spearman while slicing at Sword Guy as he was standing. He cried out as I got his arm, sending him to the ground again. Spearman had dodged, and I was barely able to parry his thrust. I slid the spear down to the cross guard of my trisula and struck it with my other one, knocking it out of his hands. A quick step forward left the unarmed bandit on the ground, defeated.

A subconscious alert had me diving forward, dodging another arrow. This one was Aether powered, and it pierced into a rock ahead of me. *Crap, that would have hurt!* I was starting to feel the burden of using so many techniques and blasts, my Aether pool drying. I sent one last blast at sword guy, and took him out of the battle. Afterwards, I dodged behind some rocks, trying to focus on gathering a bit to partially refill my tank.

I listened intently, trying to hear the approach of the archer, but couldn't hear anything. It reduced my gathering speed, but safety was more important. *Is he just waiting for me to leave the rock? Or is he moving around farther away to get a better vantage point?* I stopped gathering once I had absorbed enough for a couple more blasts or a minute of Dancing Northern Wind. I had maybe two minutes total fighting ability left when using techniques. *Good thing fights take less time than that.* I knew I had to get out and close in to win this, but wasn't sure how to do so.

I guess this is the time to try it, I thought as I started doing both the running technique and Dancing Northern Wind at the same time. I had to coordinate the runes and timing to make sure they didn't interfere, and I knew I couldn't maintain the focus necessary for long. I sprinted out from behind the rock, moving faster than I ever had before. I saw the archer, a ragged woman holding a longbow, fire an arrow at me. I was moving so fast it missed. I closed quickly, my limbs blurring as I approached and used the Four Twin Lightning Stabs to batter her down. As soon as she collapsed, she disappeared.

I quickly gathered, very nearly out of Aether. *Well, I definitely did better than last time. I'm not dying right now, so that's a plus. Hopefully I'll be able to take the next one, but I have no idea what it could be.* I gathered slowly due to keeping an eye on my surrounding, as I was unable to focus enough on gathering to be efficient. Several minutes passed, and I still hadn't seen anything. *Does level five give you more time to recover?* I wondered.

After five minutes, a form started moving towards me. *Okay, level five gives a five-minute break, ha.* I jumped onto another rock, and saw what looked like a rolling blob of lime-green jello slurping towards me. "Uh, what?" I said out loud, surprised by what I saw. The thing continued to get closer, and I noticed behind it all the plants had shriveled in its path. "Ok, don't let it touch you," I commented, then proceeded to blast away at it. The first blast seemed to make a crater, but the second one knocked jello back into the area the first one hit. Only a tiny amount actually fell off. It angered the jelly though, and it sped up.

"Target practice," I said, and launched two bolts that hit the same spot, right in the center. The crater this time went halfway through it, and I saw a shimmering rock inside it. *Is it slime? Do I need to break the core? Argh, it healed already,* I thought, seeing the hole fill in quickly. I ran perpendicular to it for a bit, but it always turned to face me. *It must be sensing me somehow.* I knew that it would catch me if I kept running.

I started blasting at it, trying to get to the core, but I couldn't shoot blasts fast enough. Finally, I had an idea. I started forming a blast, but didn't release it, and instead formed the Four Twin Lightning Stabs. As I punched out at it, smaller Aether blasts came much quicker than I could normally fire. I punched as fast as I could with the technique, and managed to blast through the creature and take it down.

I cheered and then saw my hands. I had not done it properly, apparently, as all the skin on my hands was covered in blisters and open sores. "Ahhhh!" I screamed out, before trying to fix it with Aether. I didn't have enough to even start making a dent, and when a Zarorzel appeared, I was so out of Aether I didn't have the energy to even think of dodging the giant fireball that ended my second ranking challenge.

CHAPTER THIRTY-ONE

I awoke from the trance with a start, and got up to free the slot for Ming. The class was almost done, just waiting on the last ten people to finish. I looked over at the score pillar, and saw my score was updated to 6, and Jamila, Brett, Lucas, and Bridget all made it to 5 too; out of another twenty people I didn't know. I walked over to where Jamila, Brett, and Bridget were sitting with Jon and congratulated them.

After another ten minutes, everyone was done. The score pillar reformed itself, rearranging the names into ranking order. I moved from seven to five, which I felt was great. Xiao was seventh now, and Vaya had fallen to sixth, while Anberlin was fourth, Bet was third, Nicolai was second, and Ming was still first. I was shocked by Nicky's fast growth since he had been sixth last time. Also, Ming made it to level ten, which was slightly frightening. *At least he's my friend, or trying to be,* I thought.

10	Hill Lucas	Level 5
9	Hunter Brett	Level 5
8	Falconer Bridget	Level 5
7	Lo Xiao	Level 5
6	Volkov Vaya	Level 5
5	Kupiec Aiden	Level 6
4	Haodha Anberlin	Level 7
3	Volkov Bet	Level 7
2	Haodha Nicolai	Level 8
1	Lo Ming	Level 10

Crystals were handed out to everyone who passed level five. I got ten points for beating level five along with another gathering pill and a vial of healing powder. Essentially the same rewards as last week. Counselor Might then made an announcement, "Now that a sufficient number of students have reached level five, a new mode for the Training Pavilion is open to them. Once you have reached level five, you may partner with one to four others to form a group and take on a group challenge. I recommend you work with a number of different people and try out different teams. Learning to work with a number of different people will be extremely beneficial for your career and life. Good job today, there is now no one who failed to pass level one. As a reward, Physical Training class is cancelled today. Go have fun." There was a cheer from most of the class at that.

"So, who wants to team up?" I said to the group. "There are five of us here, so we could have a go at it together the first time."

"Sure," Brett said, "I wonder when we are allowed to enter again." We all shrugged, then I jogged over to Counselor Might.

"Sir, when can we enter the Pavilion as a group again?"

"If you have a team already, you could enter tomorrow evening. All the Counselors who tend the Pavilion will know that the first tiers are allowed group training now. Also, group training does not count as your individual entries per week, though you still have to wait a day if you die in the illusion."

"Thanks, sir," I said and jogged back, reporting that we could go in as early as tomorrow night. "Is tomorrow good for everyone? I usually go in for additional training in the Pavilion on Wood, Ice, and Lightning evening as well, so adding in an Earth Day should be doable." Everyone else just looked at me, then Jon and Brett looked at each other and shook their heads. "What?" I asked.

"Of course you would be training in the Pavilion as often as you physically could. Yes, I'm willing to train tomorrow, but I do not really want to train every possible day. Not everyone has your single-minded drive to get better faster," Jon admonished me, though I mostly focused on the fact that he said yes to tomorrow. Everyone else agreed to the training tomorrow. *This should be fun.*

As we left the Pavilion, we talked about what creatures we had fought and how everyone had done. When I said how I defeated the slime creature, everyone looked at me strangely again. "Yes?" I asked.

"You combined two techniques to create a stronger one, in the middle of a fight, while low on Aether? And then you did it again, with two different techniques, while running away from a creature who should have been so much stronger than you that you couldn't hurt it?"

"Uh, yeah, I guess," I said, getting embarrassed.

"You do know that we're not supposed to be able to get past level five until we reach high Haze at least? Jumping that many levels is supposed to be almost impossible. You defeated a creature that was the equivalent to a Low Smoke level gatherer as a High Mist!" Bridget finished her rant. Jon and Brett had a bemused expression while looking at Bridget.

"Too bad you still won't be able to face me," came a snide voice from behind us. *Good ol' Nicky, how I didn't miss you.* "You are falling even farther behind, and when I crush you in the tournament everyone will see how little your vaunted talent means. If you even make it there." Nicky and his group sauntered off as we stared at him puzzled.

"Well, he's got problems." I laughed off his statement. Though his words did spur my competitive streak. I wanted to win the tournament, though I doubted I would. Hard to beat Ming. I really wanted to beat Nicolai into the dirt though. "Okay, so I'm headed to the Training Field. I want to see if I can replicate the two techniques I created today. You should look at mixing techniques too, see if you can make something neat."

"Okay, but only for an hour. Then I want to go rest and gather in the Grotto," Jamila said, pulling her spear out of its bag. Everyone else just shrugged and followed us to the PT field. *Offense is better right now, let's figure out how to make this better. So I used the Four Twin Lightning Stabs to accelerate my arms and push Aether into the weapons, while I had an Aether Blast constructed at the tip. This caused the Aether pushed in to form a blast and be shot out, though with much less compression and finesse. So I need to control the Aether as it enters the weapon, to make it thinner and stronger. Also, let's not blow the skin off my hands this time. That hurt.*

For the next hour, I would send a series of Aether Blasts out using the Twin Lightning Aether Blast technique as I called it. I would then evaluate how well the Blasts formed and flew. I still wasn't happy by the time everyone else called it quits, but I decided to go gather with everyone anyway. Having more Aether and strengthening my meridians would be helpful too. Before we broke up, I shared an Enhanced Flower Gathering powder with all four of them. "Use this as thanks for joining me tomorrow. If you want, I'll make you a dose for a merit point. No more than two a day though. I don't have time to make more than that."

"Trying to make a profit off your friends," Jon teased.

"It's half what you can buy it from the store for! Win-win," I said.

"Win-win," Jamila repeated. "That's a nice saying."

Jamila and Bridget both said they wanted to buy two. Bridget handed me her crystal, and I pressed it to mine while sending in Aether. I got a little message on mine that asked how many points. I couldn't see how to input two, and when I thought that, a number 2 showed up and it asked for confirmation. "Uh, yes," I said, and it buzzed a bit and my account went up by two to 38/82. I noticed that trading with my friends increased my current amount, but not my total amount. *Hmm, I'll still have to make some to sell to the store since that does increase my total points. Total points translates to standing in our class.*

As I exchanged Jamila's points for powders, Jon and Brett asked for some too. Jon asked if he could let Lucas and Louis know, and I said sure. "I'm mostly offering this to friends in the class who don't have access to resources anyway. I'm pretty sure Ming and Bet both receive pills or resources to get them from their families, while we don't. Or at least, I

199

don't. Now, let's grow stronger and show everyone how good we can be," I said, bowing to everyone, and went to my pavilion.

To boost my gathering, I took the pill I just earned. I didn't have any powders left since I had literally just sold my last ones to Brett. *I guess I'll just make a bunch more today, and only sell back a few. I made eight points for less than three points' worth of ingredients. If I can keep that up, I'll be able to afford to take pills more often. Wow, that sounds like I'm becoming a drug addict,* I thought with a laugh. I was happy to help out my friends too, and hoped they'd grow stronger faster because of this. I focused on gathering, using the enormous boost that the pill gave to move towards the boundary of High Mist as fast as I could.

Dinner was energetic with half the class boasting about how much they improved. I received some congratulations as I sat down with Ming and Xiao. "You did well, especially for your level. How'd you make it past level five?" Ming asked. I told my story and Xiao stopped eating, staring at me. "That... is extraordinarily impressive," Ming finally said after I finished, Xiao nodding at that. I blushed at the praise.

"What level are you at?" I asked suddenly, wondering at how he had made it to level ten.

"That would be telling. Though I will say that I am not yet ready to start Compressing my Aether, though I should reach that point before the month is up."

"Uh, wow. I don't think anyone will be able to stand up to you at the tournament then."

"I won't be participating, especially if I can enter the Compression stage. So you should have a shot at winning it, if you can beat Nicolai or Bet," Ming told me, which slightly disappointed me. I wanted to face him. Though I would get beat down, I wanted to see what was possible for someone my age. *Oh well,* I thought, *maybe I can challenge him in the Pavilion some time. I just want to see how cool his techniques are.*

After dinner, I went to the alchemy lab, purchased ten points' worth of supplies, and started to make powders. I would ask Counselor Sila for a new recipe tomorrow, though I would keep making the powders for my friends. I made thirty powders in two hours, then went to the Pagoda to see my friends.

Lucas and Louis cornered me and asked for powders. Louis asked if he could do it on credit since he hadn't reached level five yet and thus didn't have any points. "Sure, no interest either. Use these to get strong enough to pass, and you can pay me back when you do," I told him, handing over two powders. Keai saw me pass them both powders and ended up buying two too. *I feel like a drug dealer.* *"Yes kids, come get your magic powder."* *Heh.* After selling twenty-eight powders to various people, I told the next person I was out, but they could buy two tomorrow first.

I didn't know half the people who purchased the powders. *Even though the class had significantly fewer than my class at the Air Force Academy, I think I've only spoken to twenty people total. I know maybe a quarter of the class's names, but that's it. Selling these worked out though. I just got twenty points and eight promised points. Hopefully by next week the promised points will become real points. Though I think I'll need to start making more doses to sell. I need to get stronger just to need less sleep, so I have time to do everything!*

After hanging out at the Pagoda for half an hour or so, I said goodbye and left. I went to my pavilion in the Grotto and took an Enhanced Flower Gathering powder dose. I had not sold two doses so I could use them, pushing myself as fast as I could. About thirty minutes into gathering, I felt a strange sense of foreboding. I continued my motions, moving through the Eight by Eight Gathering forms, but I stopped gathering. I started channeling Aether through my senses meridian and running the Iron Bones, Granite Skin technique.

A flash of motion off to my side had me diving forward, just fast enough to miss a throwing knife. The knife embedded itself in the wood of the pavilion almost to the handle. The impact was strangely muffled, like it was behind a couple walls or something. *That's what set off my danger sense, the Grotto got quieter.* I whipped my head around to the direction that the knife came from, but I didn't see anything.

I pushed more Aether into my senses, nearly overloading my ability to deal with the incoming data. The muffled sound enchantment helped. I went to draw my trisulas when I realized they were on the bench I had just dove away from. As I did, a black shadow stepped out of the forest next to the bench. *Since when are there ninjas here?* I thought, seeing my opponent was wrapped in black cloth all over.

"You have excellent reflexes. You would have been a great talent at some point. Too bad you pissed off the wrong people. Stand still and I'll make this quick."

"Screw off, assassin," I shouted back at him. I cycled both movement techniques as I had done in the Training Pavilion and charged at him. My speed must have surprised him, as I managed to get close enough to punch at him before he reacted. Punching his chest felt like hitting a wall, though it did knock him back a step.

I tried to continue the attack when he recovered and slammed his fist into my face. I staggered back, shaking my head to clear it, then jumped backwards to dodge a knife slash. The slash turned into another thrown knife, and I managed to dodge it enough to get a cut, rather than impaled. The knife barely cut into me, courtesy of my defense technique and strengthened skin. *Maybe I can win this,* I thought and charged again.

I blocked a slash with my left forearm, turning it into a grazing injury, and got inside his guard. I used the Four Twin Lightning Stabs technique with just my fists, and nailed him backward into a tree. He grunted in pain, then kicked me away from him. With my sight still enhanced with Aether, I saw him engage a technique and he blurred with speed. A blow to my gut was followed by one to the face, and I was flipping through the air.

Another thrown knife went into the meat of my left bicep, and I was down an arm. I pulled the knife out and threw it back at him, but he just laughed as he caught it. I used a small amount of Aether to stop the blood loss, but I couldn't heal the wound in any reasonable amount of time. He blurred at me again, but this time I was ready.

I pushed as much Aether as I could into my combined movement technique and into the general body enhancement technique we had learned. This combined with my senses enhancement let me keep up, ducking under an attempted throat slash. A gut punch forced him to bend as air left his lungs, and then I tried something else new.

I formed an Aether Blast on my fist, and slammed it into his head with an uppercut. A flash of light and he went flying through the air. The backlash, though, shattered most of the bones in my hand. I staggered towards where he landed, hoping to find information as to who hired him on him, when he got up. *Well, crap,* I thought. I could see his face now, he was average in almost every way. Normal, the kind of person you wouldn't look twice at. His eyes were bloodshot and his nose and lip were bleeding.

"Congratulations, I haven't been injured by a target in years. Just because of this, your death will be painful," the man said, rage evident in his voice. A blur and then a knife was sticking out of my left thigh. I collapsed to my knees, and then a backhand sent me to the ground face-up. A sadistic grin on his face as he stood over me, he lifted his knife and slowly lowered it towards me. *Well, I died once already, what's one more time?* I thought, trying to hold back the gibbering terror as he went to end me.

A look of surprise flashed over his face, then he was blown away. I picked my head up and saw a flash of orange light as he turned into a pillar of flame. The heat was enough to singe my skin, even twenty feet away. *How, what…?* I couldn't form complete thoughts until I saw the Crimson Zarorzel swoop around the flame pillar, which increased in size. I dragged myself, crawling away from the fire, when the noises of the Grotto suddenly returned. Shouting could be heard from all around, voices screaming "Fire" or "What is that?"

Not a minute later I heard a yell of "Aiden!?" followed by a rush of Aether entering me. The healing was weak, but Jamila had only just started learning. The healing cleared my head enough to think, and I had her help me to a seated position. "My bag, over there, has some healing powder in it. Can you get it please?" I asked, still woozy. She rushed over and grabbed the pack, brought it back over, and handed it to me. I gritted my teeth and pulled the knife out of my thigh before liberally sprinkling the powder over it.

"What happened?" she asked, worry streaking her voice.

"I was attacked, the Zarorzel saved me. Explain more detail later," I said, really not wanting to explain while my jaw felt shattered. More and more students arrived over the next minute, until a boom announced the arrival of the Headmaster. With a gesture, the fire pillar was dispelled.

"Aiden, what happened here?" Headmaster Glav asked, fury registering in her voice. I had just explained what happened when Counselor Stojka arrived and helped the rest of my injuries close up. The deep puncture wounds closed somewhat, but not all the way. "So you have no idea who it was or why?" the Headmaster asked when I finished.

"I have a suspicion who hired the assassin, but no proof, ma'am. And any possible evidence burned with the body. I won't complain, though, as if the Zarorzel hadn't saved me…" I trailed off. I looked up and saw the Zarorzel looking down at me. I smiled at it, and it nodded to me in a strangely human way.

"He says you give good treats and you friend. Save friend. Defend forest, defend students," Counselor Taiga said, walking up. "Good job on befriending a level five Elemental Beast. Especially a Zarorzel, they are notoriously difficult to get to trust gatherers. Not that either one of you is ready for a soul bond."

"Is he able to walk?" Headmaster Glav asked. When Counselor Stojka said yes, she helped me up. Counselor Stojka handed me a pill and told me to take it when I got back to my room. It would help numb the pain and let me sleep. The Headmaster then escorted me back to my room, dismissing all my friends and classmates. When we reached my room, I felt a pulse of Aether come from her, then a bubble was formed over the door and windows.

"I am sorry that you were attacked at my school. I will be looking into this, and whoever is responsible will pay for this insult to the school and me. You will be watched more closely from now on, to prevent a repeat of this, though you should also work on getting stronger. You won't be able to rely on external factors saving you every time you get attacked. You did well against the assassin, but if he hadn't wanted to toy with you, you would be dead. Now, take the pill and sleep." Headmaster Glav watched me until I took the pill.

She left and I got undressed, feeling extremely tired. *Wow, this stuff is better than Benadryl. There's no proof it was Nicky, but I know it was him. This place isn't the safe haven I thought it was. But I won't let him drive me out of here. This is my home now, and I will fight for it.*

END OF BOOK 1

AUTHOR'S NOTE

Thank you for joining me in following Aiden's journey. We're just at the beginning here, with many more books to come. For more news and information about the book, other books I'm working on, or just to point out all the mistakes I made, join me on my Facebook page at https://www.facebook.com/authorchrisvines/. I'd love to hear from you.

If you liked the magic system, it was based somewhat on modern Wuxia and Xianxia books. To find more novels like this, but usually better written, check out the Western Cultivation Facebook group at https://www.facebook.com/groups/WesternWuxia/, and definitely read Will Wight's Cradle series. For a more eastern flare, check out https://www.facebook.com/groups/cultivationnovels

If the application of levels to the magic system tickled your fancy, but you wish there were more hard numbers, look no further than the GameLit Society group on Facebook at https://www.facebook.com/groups/LitRPGsociety/. Especially check out Siphon by Jay Boyce, who did the portal fantasy into a magic school much better than I did.

https://www.facebook.com/groups/TheFantasyNation / is a great place to find new authors in the fantasy genre.

Thanks for sticking with me. Your support enabled me to send this book for editing, resulting in the second version. I hope you liked it, and I'll see you again when Aiden returns for Elemental Gatherers Book Two: Chaos Rising.

DRAMATIS PERSONAE

Students of Azyl Academy

Kupiec Aiden – The Main Character and Chosen of Darkness
Noptep Jonathan – Aiden's best friend
Lo Xiao – Younger son of the Lo clan Head
Lo Ming – Elder son of the Lo clan Head, heir to Lo clan
Haodha Nicolai – Only son of Haodha clan Head, extreme jerk
Haodha Anberlin – Daughter of Haodha clan elder, cousin of Nicolai
Builder Thomas – Minor noble, flunky of Nicolai
Demos Stephan – Son of a city official, flunky of Nicolai
Pederson Elric – Son of a merchant family affiliated with the
Haodha, flunky of Nicolai
Volkov Bet – Elder daughter of Volkov clan Head, heir to Volkov
clan
Volkov Vaya – younger daughter of Volkov clan Head
Naanva Jamila – daughter of a baker, very high talent
Travail Louis – son of laborer family that work for the Nopteps
Skipari Maove – daughter of merchant
Weber Lea – minor noble
Falconer Bridget – daughter of a Beast hunter clan
Pescador Philippe – son of laborer family
Hill Lucas – minor noble
Hunter Brett – son of a Beast hunter clan

Faculty of Azyl Academy

Headmaster Glav – Headmaster of Azyl Academy, strongest person
in Azyl City
Counselor Sila – teaches Gathering and Channeling, Alchemy, and
Herbology
Mentor Gutierrez – fourth tier that assists with Gathering and
Channeling
Mentor Lo – fourth tier that assists with Gathering and Channeling
Mentor Granjer – third tier that assists with Alchemy and Herbology
Mentor Bonde – fourth tier that assists with Alchemy and Herbology
Counselor Might – teaches Physical Training and Basic Combatives
Mentor Jameson – Fourth tier that assists PT, teaches dual weapon
wielding
Counselor Kowalski – Teaches Gathering and Channeling and
Blacksmithing
Mentor Kowalski – Third tier that assists with Blacksmithing,
nephew to Counselor Kowalski

Mentor Hodowca – Fourth tier that assists with Blacksmithing
Librarian Narwan – Head Librarian, extremely eccentric
Counselor Whynn – Teaches Gathering and Channeling and Inscription
Poko Karl – Servant in dining hall
Counselor Chokhmah – Teaches Martial Arts to upper tiers
Counselor Stojka – Teaches Gathering and Channeling and Healing, Head Healer
Counselor Taiga – Teaches Beasts

Civilians of Azyl City
Kupiec Jordan – Aiden's adoptive father
Kupiec Elena – Aiden's adoptive mother
Noptep Alexander – Jonathan's father
Noptep Holly – Jonathan's mother

APPENDIX

Gathering Tiers and Levels
Aether Gathering tier - Low/High Vapor, Low/High Mist, Low/High Haze, Low/High Fog, Low/High Smoke, Beyond Smoke - Can advance to Condensation from High Fog or higher, higher is better for advancing through and beyond Condensation

Aether Condensation tier - Initial, Foundation, Circulation, Threshold, Complete - Can only advance from Completion

Aether Core tier - Seed Core, Foundation Core, Constructed Core, Completed Core, Perfect Core - advancing to Perfect Core requires Tribulation

Beast Levels and Equivalent Gathering Level

Beasts:
Level 1 - Low Vapor
Level 2 - High Mist
Level 3 - High Smoke
Level 4 - Circulation Condensation
Level 5 - Complete Condensation

Elemental Beasts
Level 6 - Seed Core
Level 7 - Completed Core
Level 8 - Perfect Core
Level 9 - Beyond (More information at higher levels)

Primordial Beasts (examples instead of Gathering Level)
Level 10 - Lightning Monarch
Level 11 - The Kraken
 Level 12 - Kyubi-no Kitsune (ruler of central Great Western Forest)

Made in the USA
Columbia, SC
16 December 2020